retrOrlando

retrOrlando

a novel by
Ross Stein

iUniverse, Inc.
Bloomington

retrOrlando

iUniverse books may be ordered through booksellers or by contacting:

iUniverse
1663 Liberty Drive
Bloomington, IN 47403
www.iuniverse.com
1-800-Authors (1-800-288-4677)

ISBN: 978-1-4620-5101-4 (sc)
ISBN: 978-1-4620-5102-1 (ebk)

Printed in the United States of America

iUniverse rev. date: 09/08/2011

Special thanks to The Cure, Madness, The Smiths, The Pet Shop Boys, Sisters of Mercy, The Psychedelic Furs and countless other great bands of the 1980s whose music served as constant inspiration for this work.

Author's note

This book is a terrific work of self-aggrandizement. It is remembered fiction. All of the people and locations herein are real, only the names have been changed. What is left after that comes mostly from memory and a handful of notes scribbled on stained cocktail napkins, the insides of matchbooks, and the backs of random receipts. The rest is poetic license.

It is my wish that this book doesn't offend any of those upon whom it is based. They all hold special places in my heart, and I can only hope that I do in theirs.

I

There's something about approaching a city skyline at dusk that just gives me the feeling of an endlessness to the night. I find there are infinite possibilities in life, innumerable destinies to be searched out, found, lost, rediscovered, and lost again, all in the streets and alleyways at the feet of the great concrete and steel monoliths of our cold civilization. The height! I see the outline of those tall buildings all different shapes and sizes and I see the unknown. I see the future.

Long glowing lights climbing up the gray and blue faces of skyscrapers from the avenues below cast undershadows on the sills and overhangs, gloom like a campfire storyteller with plastic flashlight held beneath ghoulish, spooky chin. Random room lights, some on some off, leave you shivering in paranoia about being trapped in vacant hallways and isolated stairwells alone, while secret secretarial rendezvous occupy the corner office when everyone has gone home and the Mexican cleaning staff are still three floors below and it doesn't matter anyway because they can't hear a thing over the roaring of decades old Hoovers and violent floor buffers, 'so come on baby my wife won't find out. What's to worry?'

And up top on the roofs, where the cool evening breeze flows over glass pyramids and rattles red-tip flashing antennae, the multicolored signs shouting names into the night bright enough to be read from airplanes, with floodlights beaming cylinders of white lasers straight into the sky as if they were trying to get Heaven itself to notice and come down and 'Bank with Barnett.'

So there we were, Chaos and I, and Chaos at the wheel cruising across the highway night from the east at eighty-five miles an hour in his black Firebird, the windows open, T-tops dropped, and the stereo blasting the Brian Setzer Orchestra from all ten speakers of a mean, beefy Monsoon sound system (swing making a minor comeback that year, '98). *Jump, Jive, and Wail!* Prima did it better, but who cares? We're both pumped and full of juice so sing it you beautiful bastard SING IT! Horn bliss and strumming swing bass kicking us through the blackness: heartbeat, balls, and drum.

His eyes were narrowed and glued to the red tails of the traffic ahead that he deftly wove in and out of, one hand knuckling the top of the wheel, the other resting coolly on the shifter knob with his elbow bent and situated on the console, his whole body leaning into the spine of the car with that perfect amount of James Bond casualness that only the immortally cool can compose while they teeter on just this side of catastrophe. The wind cycloning through the open roof and typhooning in the back seat, ruffling not a single strand of his perfectly quaffed hair; causing not one unwanted crease in his sharpened collar, black and plasticy as the night. Even the wind, the very night itself, parting around us when we roared past.

We rode on like that, the Orlando skyline just starting to creep into view over the horizon as the Firebird crested a hump in the highway. Chaos was in his groove, the music running through his blood, his heartbeat racing to match the fierceness of the engine firing on all cylinders not two feet in front of us, a hungry shark streaming through the undercurrent, devouring the darkness.

And as he plowed us on to our destiny, I sat beside him, my eyes fixed on the lights in the distance and the infinite possibilities that lay beneath them. Years later, when all of this was behind me and I found myself rolling into bigger places like New York or Philly, and even later into Osaka and Seoul, in that dreamy purple futurenight of the city light multiverse, I still reflected on those rides into Orlando, when the long black hood of the car knelt down and the expanse of that navy inkiness exploded Big Bang from behind the trees and Lake Underhill, Eola Heights, downtown, all of it suddenly lay out before me, moving slowly across the horizon while everything else went zipping past in the blurry machinegun fire of my periphery.

We were simultaneously driving and being driven. There in the distance lay it all. At the feet of those great stone and iron monuments, beneath the lights, behind guarded doors watched over by grim faced gorillas in black shirts, black pants, arms crossed and bulging biceps in the dark corners of the city skyline night; that is where we were headed. To hear the music, to drown our brains in the warm embrace of wine and liquor, to chew our lives to the quick. And for me, to her. We zoomed on.

II

But wait, it's all too sudden: the rush of impending destiny, crashing towards me like a great wave, white caps and gaping mouth, the dripping teeth waiting to devour me whole, chew me up and drag me down to the black depths of the greatest, most wonderful misery of my life. Let me first go back to the beginning, over a year back, when it was all new and the unknown, the real personal unknown of the night still lay out there, before all the parties and drunken revelry and sex and money and endless discourse of young love and sorrow. It is deserved—indeed, it is necessary—to go back a bit and start all of this properly. All things proper in their proper time.

I fell in love with a girl once. Eden Cole, a perfect vision of purity and soft flower petal delicate innocence that stole my heart.

It had been two years since I'd come to Orlando looking for my future, trading in harsh New Jersey winters and oil-slick summers for breezy palm trees, sunshine and clean southern air. I'd sloughed off the suburban shore town of my upbringing, with its gloomy corner 7-11s, culture-killing strip malls, silvery diners of old and small-town nowhere (Billy Joel and Bruce Springsteen would sing endlessly of such places with a sort of reverence, but anyone who'd lived among them wanted nothing more than to get away, far, far away). I'd graduated high school, left old friends and haunts behind in search of new adventures at college over a thousand miles from home.

Settled in, campus life was good and steady, a regular routine of classes and study. I made new friends, enjoyed new freedoms. Six months into that first year I even took up with a girl, from New York of all places. Kessa Marek. We found a little off-campus apartment, moved in together, bought cheap furniture, and played house. Domestic bliss. It lasted more than a year, but then, as all things do, it came to an end. Since then I'd been living the bachelor life, in a small one-bedroom across the street from campus. Lonely most nights, focused on study and not much else. I took a job to help supplant the boredom. That's when she walked into my life.

Eden Cole. Days would go by when all I would do is gaze at her from across a room, watching her busy herself with the daily tedium of work or laughing and chatting up friends, or sometimes just leaning against a counter or wall, chin resting on her hands, or her hands pocketed in her jeans, lost in her own thoughts. It was those times that I liked the best, when I caught her in momentary repose, regal almost, serious eyes behind dark rimmed spectacles in the midst of some inner question or pondering, thin lips pursed in boredom or sometimes parted ever so slightly in wonder. An image of beauty that could have been captured by Rembrandt or Titian, pale smooth skin, black arched eyebrows, angular angelic stare, perfect breasts, but with a shadow of the darkness brought out by El Greco. Stormy skies over my Magdalene.

Darkness was the source of Eden's beauty, and that's how I had first found it. Maybe it was the poor lights under which I first saw her, pale yellow and cutting weird shadows around her face. She was leaning over from behind a display countertop, arms bent before her and hands clasped with interlaced fingers resting on the glass, eyes gazing off to nowhere in particular. Tired, weary, bored, but stunning in her simplicity; plain green T-shirt and faded jeans, short bleached hair layered over dark roots, gripping eyelashes and captivating in the lostness of those sepia windows to her soul. I knew the moment I saw her I would be dreaming dreams of foolish hope and vanity, endless fantasies of love, raw sex on the brain, passion in the heart. I knew from the moment I saw her I had to have her, would do anything to make her mine.

On that first day we didn't speak a word, our introduction brief. I was coming in, she was going out. Ships passing in the night. Days went by when all I could do was watch her, never speaking more than a few words of kind greeting, or maybe a simple question of procedure, but never any more than that. It was her gaze. Whenever I approached and she cast her eyes on me my heart leapt to my throat and blocked the words from coming. It was all so awkward and not the least bit embarrassing, but not for lack of trying on her part. Behind the serious face and penetrating dark eyes lay a soft creature, friend to all, a lover of animals, and a truly warm heart. Later, after a friendship blossomed and trust built between us, she would confide in me in one of our closest moments how she thought I didn't approve of her or some such nonsense, me being collegiate starched collared and pressed slacks and she wrinkled, dyed and a self-described mess. So cold I seemed to her in those early days, aloof and uninterested, but when all it was really was just idle schoolboy fright that kept me from letting her feel the warmth that was kindled in my heart.

I started writing about her almost immediately, that first night in fact, when I was back at home in the dim loneliness of my room, madly scribbling away these imaginings, these thoughts from infinity; every detail of her beauty documented first between the pale blue lines of a journal, but much later too on the backs of torn cocktail napkins or the insides of match books when late night visions of her haunted me in vulnerable moments when I longed her to be near. Poems, the first of many to her, about her, that I someday imagined I would give her when she least expected and would be grateful and read them and cry tears of first embarrassment, then love, elevating me to a status in her eyes, making me worthy to breathe her air and lay forever kisses upon her perfect lips.

The wild, crazy first days of infatuation and love. I began planning immediately.

III

Milton said Chaos was the existence of confusion and jumble and void that God separated himself from to form the universe, and it was through the realm of Chaos that the angels fell on their way to Hell. Chaos ruled Chaos and was consort with Night, and through the emptiness a bridge was built to lead Satan into Eden and cause the fall of man from grace. It all started with Chaos.

I had met Chaos at the same time I'd met Eden, and as is often the case when someone whose life is organized and planned and follows the straight and narrow collides with a shooting star, such as mine did when I met my friend, chaos indeed ensues.

And so it was with me that I was immediately drawn into the pull of this great man: smooth and debonair, square-shouldered and cut, in purple Kangol hat over wild spiked blonde hair reversed in exact hip casualness over big, intense eyes, smirking at the world going by. When Chaos walked by you could almost hear his theme music playing in the eternal soundtrack of your own mind. He was music come alive, walking amongst men, always stepping in rhythm, flowing, but with a hidden ferocity as the coming of a storm—a tumescent presence commanding a reverence reserved for greatness attained through endless trips through the void and unnatural communion with the night. Drink and rhythm and women. And in the hallowed halls of the pantheon of friends I have made over the course of my life, stored deep in the vaults of my memory, his place is held at the highest, marked by a golden shield and reached only by traversing a path of scars.

I don't know what it was that he saw in me, his almost polar opposite, that he saw fit to allow me to enter his atmosphere. Where he was the embodiment of cool, I was squareness defined: friendless, studious, and ignorant of the ways of the street. Perhaps he saw the opportunity to corrupt a fellow soul, as was his wont, drawing them from the light into the night. Or maybe it was that he just wanted a new companion to share it all with. But whatever the reason, he unfolded his wings and took me under them on those first days when I walked into the shop where he was working with Eden and the others.

The Mineshaft was a culture tourist's wet dream. Located on the first floor of a two story rotunda mall expansion attached to the old Church Street train depot in downtown Orlando, the Shaft was the largest shop in the complex, so big in fact that just after I arrived the owner bought the abandoned spot across the hall and expanded the store over there as well. It was in this smaller, more intimate setting that I would spend most of my days and nights.

The owner's daughter Jen ran the show mostly. She was a redhead and oblivious, but absent most of the time, so we were left to run things pretty much unsupervised. We sold garbage. Exotic garbage, but garbage all the same. Wooden totems from Indonesia stood in the corners, mahogany witch doctor masks from Kenya hung on the slated walls, crystal geodes from South America and stone figurines from Bali lined endless rows of shelves. And jewelry, thousands upon thousands of beaded and chip necklaces and bracelets made from every type of stone imaginable. It was the type of place that had overly expensive stone spheres and glistening amethyst geodes shining in glass display cases under sharp designer lights, and cheap silver rings ornamented with glass for three bucks a piece next to the register. There was even a large wooden table strung with little leather pouches that tourists and little kids could fill with all manner of polished rocks and rough minerals. This was a big draw, especially for the nuts, and every wannabe wizard, holistic healer whack job for fifty miles who came to us, looking for just the right piece of sodalite to cure their stomach cramps, or a chunk of malachite that they swore if they wore it around their necks would ward off the flu.

Working in the depot was like working in a fish bowl. Everywhere were walls of glass. The whole mess was set up to resemble a great turn of the century transportation hub, complete with ornate wooden columns and trim and intricate wrought iron railings painted evergreen. The floors were laid with little hexagonal tiles organized in various mosaic patterns, and at the center of the building stood a grand staircase leading to the eatery housed above. A late-century saloon, complete with waitresses dressed in period costume who poured drinks and waited tables stood near the street. All that was missing were strollers with canes and straw boaters. Ragtime was pumped in low through a sound system, all in an attempt to transport visitors back to a big city train station circa 1910, but inside our store it was all new age Enya and Gregorian Chants and Clannad. But just outside, beyond the smell of buttery popcorn and sweet funnel cakes, past the faux nostalgia, the depot sat square in the center of the club district, where the denizens of the city paraded past on their way to their merrymaking. Not the 'could you take a picture of us beside this locomotive? Wow honey, it's like I'm an old-timey engineer!' tourists, but the real day to day dwellers who saw past all of it and were bored and unimpressed.

The Mineshaft was where it had all begun for me. It's the place I'd first laid eyes on Eden, the place Chaos came storming into my life. It was home to an endlessly revolving door of humanity, some who stayed, like Deirdre Blake and The Sage, who flashed like gold in a pan and became my boon companions while others disappeared and are lost from my memory, washed away by the passing years. But it was the hub, the wheel house, the starting point of our lives together. For us, working at the Shaft would make excursions into the drink, drunk, wild night after closing time a breeze.

Chaos sensed my attraction to Eden almost immediately. We'd already begun swapping stories and pasts only a few days after we'd met. I'd told him about moving down, starting school, and the failed relationship with Kessa that had ended badly some months earlier. Chaos, in turn, kept me perpetually entertained with tales of his sexual exploits.

He caught me in a stare on more than one occasion in those early days. I'd dropped a few casual comments about her, made some random queries. I think it made him feel good, that small amount of guy trust, and he reciprocated by feeding my ego. It was he who crushed me early on, telling me that she was already spoken for. I asked for more details about her, but all he said was that she was a vegetarian, she really liked animals and volunteer causes like save the whales and stuff like that, and that her boyfriend was a real dick. I remembered then what Pushkin had

9

written how 'nothing enflames love so much as the encouraging remark of an outsider.'

"But don't let that stop you," he'd said. "The guy's a total tool. You should get in there and show her you're the better man. I would have myself but she's not my type. Too smart. I like 'em dumb. Conversation be damned! Besides, how's a girl supposed to talk anyway when I'm balls deep down her throat?"

"You're all class, you know that?"

"Hey, I'm classy. I almost always buy her a drink first."

"Your honor, I rest my case."

"Well, Eden'd probably be a three drinker. Way too much trouble. Besides, I'm all about Nikki."

Nikki Savage was Eden's close friend from high school. A near drop out, after school she bummed it around, worked, never really got an education. She was short on personality and high on vanity. From the one or two quick exchanges I was privy to, I learned she wasn't exactly on the path to becoming a Rhodes Scholar. Currently she was working (or sleeping) her way through night school. She did have one thing going for her though; Nikki was stunningly fuckable. She exuded sex, from the raunchy attitude to the porn-star looks and short attention span. She had a fantastic body, flawless skin and you knew from first glance she would be filthy in the sack. The whole package screamed 'fuck me.' She was right up Chaos' alley, but was having none of him, despite months of his trying, apparently quite unusual for him, and it drove him on all the more. Later I'll tell how it was ultimately I rather than he who did in fact wind up with Nikki's head in my lap. The only girl I ever snaked away from the great master girl-getter. The student becomes the teacher. But more on that later.

A little more about Chaos here. My friend, to whom I owe so much for opening my eyes to a new world of endless parties, music, women and disaster, was above all other things a consummate chick magnet. He was truly gifted, the Casanova of our time. When he entered a room he commanded the full attention of all present. Chaos didn't walk, he strode, always in that mystical rhythm that had drawn me in, with shoulders back and cut chest out, chin up and devious eyes scheming everything, knowing everyone. And the smile, always a grin cracking at the corner of his lips, like he was the only one in on a prank being played on the whole world. Always with a joke or jibe, he saw all of life as a great game or comic book, like he was the star of a superhero, dramatic, slapstick comedy. When serious he was Brando, Wayne, Bogart, and Grant all rolled into one. Coolness, swagger and charm. Other times he was the Joker, a wild crazy kid on the loose, the Artful Dodger, with a laugh like a hyena and flashing murderous eyes. He was impossible to read. And women just melted at his approach.

He could have any woman he wanted, anytime, anywhere, period. He was truly a man of the world; no concerns for race, creed or color; he'd fuck them all with impunity. Sex was his religion, the bedroom his temple and woman the graven image to which he ritually sacrificed an endless stream of willing participants upon the altar of their own self loathing. He was a god among men, my mentor and teacher.

But if Chaos was my Achilles, then Nikki was his heel, because no matter how much he laid it on, she sloughed it right off. It wouldn't be until much later that it became clear to me what it was that he lacked that she was so in need of.

IV

The Sage was Chaos' friend from years earlier, before I'd met either of them or come stumbling blindly into their picture. And if two is a pair, three a trio, and four a circle, then five did make a confederacy (The fifth member, Deirdre Blake, was older than us all—her thirty being senior in years but not in spirit to my mere twenty-one—but beautiful in her own way: a kind soul, as lost and misplaced as the rest of us, being introduced and accepted into the group not too much later when she joined our employ and took to smoke and drink and joy and long nights ending in sad mornings, proving herself an invaluable companion and worthy of her own place in my pantheon. A true open heart.) Five of a kind, and while Tolkien would call it a Fellowship, we would cast all titles aside and just be five lost souls.

I felt an almost immediate kinship with the Sage when we'd met, introduced by Chaos as it were, and exchanged those first primordial thoughts that would soon bubble up and frame the evolution of our friendship. There was something gravely intellectual about his ways, the manner in which he spoke and carried himself, like a distinguished pipe-smoking man of letters, a Cambridge Don among the commoners, that separated him from everyone else I'd ever known, even Chaos. Where Chaos was raw, Sage was reserved. Where Chaos was the center of attention, Sage recoiled from the spotlight. He was the man on the mountain, the guru, the bikkhu (all cause for the name of reverence I've given him here). Sage was Sydney Carton whispering his case at the foot of the gallows; he was Benjamin the old ass braying at pigs and refusing to read the writing on the wall long after the paint had dried. And he became one of my closest compatriots.

A collector of Gothic art pieces and bladed implements, many of which adorned the walls of his little rented house in Eola Park, Sage talked my ear off those first few weeks we got to know each other, mainly because I believe he sensed in me a kindred spirit: a man who desired to be a man of letters himself, questioning everything, seeking to understand all. One who both read and listened. An open well for him to pour his knowledge and thoughts into rather than bounce off of like a stone wall, as was the case with Chaos, who neither read nor was concerned with the goings on in the hearts of poets and authors, but instead sought only his next empty sexual conquest and an open ear to brag about it into (mine always being open and eager). Sage and I clicked instantly, and for many nights we sat up, usually in his living room, but sometimes in the back room of a bar, or even just out wandering the deserted side streets of his neighborhood in the middle of the night, talking existence, eschatology, the past, the future, love, anything. There was no spirituality in him though. He had no love of religion, no God to speak of. Philosophic musings and pagan midnights were where he found his pleasure. Sage would have been more at home in 15th century Gaul or Firenze than here, attending secret all-night orgies of wine and flesh, burning bibles and letting blood. But then he wouldn't have survived it long either. Soon we would all be wanted men running from the stake in the heresy of the night.

I learned too that he was engaged to be married and when I asked why, after weeks, I'd not yet met her, he would deflect. All he could say was that she wasn't the type to enjoy 'hanging out with the guys,' but he assured me she never minded when he and I would stay up all night yakking and getting drunk, making two a.m. runs for more cheap wine and smokes (it was he who'd gotten me started), she asleep, always when I came by, in the next room. Chaos told me he'd met her once or twice and that Rebecca (a name revealed) was a terribly jealous, spiteful girl who hated all of Sage's friends, even his brother, and when she eventually met me she'd hate me too. But Sage loved her deeply, dearly, and more than life itself. I never asked my friend about any of it. Instead I was content to enjoy our nights of discourse together in quietude and mutual appreciation. He even made a gift once of a pair of throwing knives he said he wanted to bestow on me after he saw how much I admired the impressive collection of iron and steel weapons hanging throughout his small rented house. In fact, when I told him how Chaos and I had taken to fighting . . . Wait, not yet. Not about that just yet. There is much time yet left to shed blood before this story is all told.

V

One Saturday night about two months into that tumultuous year, Chaos told me that he and Deirdre were talking of going out to a nearby nightclub after closing and I should come, get out once in a while, instead of my usual going straight home to studies and bed on a perfectly good weekend. I needed to start enjoying life more. This was all before I fully knew just what type of man he was and I found out just who I was and before we would become such close blood brothers and confide in each other, trust each other, and agree to stand side by side with each other and fight the Devil himself if he ever came for us (we being just work buddies up to this point, friendly, but still somewhat distanced by misunderstandings of our respective worldviews and opinions on what the meaning of our lives really was). But after that night our lives, our friendship, would be cemented and my life as I knew it would be forever changed and I would find myself walking a path completely different than the one I'd been preparing for. It would be the first time I'd ever been out to a nightclub before, my life up to that point being plain, safe and generally non-eventful, concerned only with study and the pursuit of material and monetary success.

If he's lucky, a man gets three, maybe four, defining moments in his life. I'm not speaking here of milestones like an eighteenth birthday or a twenty-first birthday, or a communion, or even his wedding day. Those are events popularized by culture, commercialized points we are all conditioned to expect, prepare for, and then reflect on in the framework of a greater socially adjusted, pre-constructed, monotone past. No, here I am speaking of those times, few as they are, when a man makes a decision that will forever alter the course of his life, his destiny. A time when he leaps before he looks, when he stands firm where he should back down, when he sacrifices everything for a single belief against the wills and wishes of everyone who holds him dear. For some these moments lead to failure, despair and regret. For others they lead to glory.

As I stood there with my friend, mulling over whether or not I was too tired or broke to go out with him, I had no idea that I was standing at the precipice of one of those defining moments of my life and that after that night was over, nothing would ever be the same again. I would be a different man, a better man.

When he told me Eden would be going too, the deal was sealed.

The Florida Room was only a few blocks away from downtown and maybe a five minute drive from work.

As closing time approached she came to me, a smile on her face. My blood raced, as it always did when she was around. I tried to be cool, but fumbled like an idiot as always.

"I hear you're coming tonight Stone." She always insisted in referring to me by my last name. It made her feel superior I think, or maybe she just liked the toughness; hardening her exterior when inside she didn't know how to talk to me, our relationship still on uneven ground. Either way, I loved it.

"I thought I might take a break from the books and join you yeah," I said.

"Good. It's good for you to get out. Can't be all serious and quiet all the time."

"I am not," I objected.

"Yes you are. Two months and you've said like three words to me. You, like, never talk to me. What's up with that?" She was drilling for fun. I could tell she enjoyed pushing. She was quick to see the little boy in me. Some women can just do that.

"Yes I do. And besides, you're not exactly a freakin' Chatty Cathy with me either," I muscled back, asserting.

"I came over here, didn't I?"

"True."

"So?"

"All right, I promise I'll talk to you tonight. How's that?" I put my hand over my heart, making a ridiculous play and evoking from her a glorious smile that practically melted my heart. "I, David Stone, promise to make extra special time this evening to talk with you, Eden Cole. But you have to promise to do the same."

"Agreed," she rolled her eyes playfully. "You know that's the most you've spoken to me at one time since you've known me."

Chaos hurried the last customer out the door, hastily counted the till and locked up. We fled outside and jumped into our cars, ready for whatever the night had to offer.

Though it was a short drive and I hadn't yet had a drink I was already dizzy with joy and anticipation. My first night out at a club, and with Eden at that, the joy of it, the anticipation of maybe finally getting closer to this woman who'd so captured my heart. We poured out of the parking lot and sped away in a great convoy, a wagon train of explorers with Chaos in the lead, followed by me, then Eden and finally Deirdre bringing up the rear. Chaos drove as he lived, fast and reckless, barreling on ahead in a ridiculously shabby wreck of a Mustang he'd dubbed Stanley, that he'd picked up for $500 a few days before (his first car, and the antithesis of cool, with a broken passenger door held fast with twine strung across the cabin and a horn that beeped whenever he turned the wheel too far left), so that my excitement about the hours to come were pricked with fear as we raced around corners and foot to the floor ran yellow lights, careening through intersections. I had to stay with him since I had no idea where I was going, he and Deirdre being the only two who knew where the place was, so I immediately felt responsible for getting Eden there since she was following me. It was the beginning feeling of honor and chivalry that I felt for her, a self-formed sense of pride I took in framing myself as somehow her protector and keeper. Deirdre had given me a CD earlier in the evening, Sisters of Mercy, and *Temple of Love*, a sound and groove new to me yet old in itself was crashing out my open windows and I was singing out loud and happy and full of life looking for the imaginary fire from the fireworks up above they sung about with one eye and watching for cops with the other as we raced on.

The Sage was absent from our revelry. When I told him where we were going and asked if he would come along, all he could say was it was a fag bar and why was I going?

I asked Chaos if it were true and yes, The Florida Room was a gay hangout, notoriously so it would turn out, but Saturday nights were special.

"Ladies night. Wall to wall lipstick lesbians," he said with glee. "Chick on chick action everywhere. It's awesome. And there's a stage show at midnight. It's cool, but I wouldn't go any other night though."

I wasn't sure how I felt about going to a gay bar and was having second thoughts. Not that I'm homophobic or anything. I was just unaccustomed to being up close and personal with the gay lifestyle, coming from a relatively sheltered suburban upbringing. In my straightness I had made certain assumptions about gays, drawn certain lines that after that night would be scuffed out and forgotten. Up to that point my life, I found, was just that; a series of lines drawn down, setting the boundaries of what was and wasn't acceptable, where to and not to go. But what are boundaries but arbitrary marks on a map? It is the essence of a line that it exists only to be crossed.

"If any dudes hit on me I'm gonna be very disappointed," I said.

"Don't worry," Chaos said. "Tell them you're with me. Call me Rock Hardon. But if anyone asks, I'm the pitcher. Gotta keep up appearances."

"And I'll be Terry Handfulls."

Hours later leaving the Sage to his own devices and my own better judgment behind, I set out to chase adventure.

We came up to the club; a low, unassuming building oddly placed in the shadow of a highway overpass in the suburban Eola Heights neighborhood, adorned with nothing outside except a small white and red neon sign over the door. And as if they were anticipating our arrival we found a little stretch of street right around the corner with space enough for the four of us to roll right up in a row, zam! Chaos took the lead and strode right up to the door all chin-high confidence and swagger, no line waiting for us at the ten o'clock opening.

Security was a joke; an old fag, narrow, with an ostrich neck and thin moustache. A Village People John Waters in navy rent-a-cop uniform, complete with leathery utility belt, stitched chest patch, and long antennae radio. Why the radio always caused me to wonder. He was the only guard in the club. If trouble broke out, who was he going to call for help?

We paid at the door and the first thing I noticed were four mean-looking women playing pool near the main bar. All short haired, except for one sporting a mullet; blue jeaned, tee shirted, no tits, man face, dirty. When one was shooting, the others were looking around aggressively, a pack of wolves staking out their territory and scouting for mates. They immediately eyed Eden as we passed. A good-looking skinny brunette was busy behind a small bar wiping it down and chatting up a couple of blondes. Chaos led us into the rooms beyond.

The DJ was cranking out Erasure and already there was a small crowd moving under the black lights on the large chessboard dance floor. Two guys leaned on a rail sipping green Midori sours in plastic cups through thin black straws and talked seriously about prejudice, or eyeliner. Behind a second bar, bigger than the first, a fat blonde momma, hog-faced and caked with makeup, stood guarding the liquor looking always at the ready with a smarmy remark and sneer, but actually quite friendly and just wanting for someone to love and understand her, "Not like my piece-o-shit ex-husband Ray." Anyone, everyone: man, woman, young, old, undecided was a honey to her and it was always "What can I getcha honey?" or "Another beer honey?" or "You're sexy aintcha honey?" but never "Whaddya want?" Sharon was her name and in time she'd come to recognize me, Chaos and the others and then every time it was a guaranteed good time when Sharon was tending bar because it meant bawdy jokes, laughs and usually a few free rounds.

We crossed the confetti carpet to get some beers and I saw the TV above the bar playing a love scene from *Bound*, no sound, and Gina Gershon is fucking Jennifer Tilly and this is further broken up and interspersed with flashes of old Betty Page fetish movie clips and I saw Eden looking too and tried to think of something humorous to say but came up flat. But she looked back at me and smiled and I probably flushed but who could tell under those lights anyway and when she looked away I caught a glimpse of myself along the mirrored wall and felt stupid for not being better prepared.

"Let's check out the deck," Chaos shouted over the thundering music, and we walked across the dance floor, four in a line, snaking around a few women dancing and went through a set of double doors that led to an open air enclosure out back. It was tiki themed out there, and there was yet another bar, a few palm trees, yucca bushes, tables and slipshod wooden boardwalk desperately in need of some care. There was no one out there. Even the bar was unmanned, so we went back inside.

Deirdre look at her watch just then and announced that we needed to, not wanted to, not thought we should, but that we *needed* to get our places for the show that was about to start in the back room. We followed her to the cavernous entrance.

The pink and green tubes of flowing neon chased each other curvy and serpentine up the side of the wall next to heavy double doors to form the outline of a leaning, coconut heavy palm tree: the two large nuts, tree trunk and splayed fronds arranged just so as to convey to anyone who entered the necessary ridiculous proportions and genital likenesses, and continued their trail up above the dark doors to spell out "Coconut Lounge" in humming, fuchsian luminescence.

I stood for a second taking a pull off my beer when Eden pushed on ahead of me. Deirdre slipped her arm under mine, smiled, and led me in.

It was a narrow room, maybe thirty by twenty feet, with a low stage running along the far wall and a ten foot long runway cutting up the center. Six tables, three on each side, that you had to step down two steps to get to framed the runway and a glittering silver and blue sequined curtain hung behind the stage. Beams from two spotlights crisscrossed themselves midway across the room and shone on the curtain's shimmering disks, reflecting colorful pale ovals of light that danced dreamily up and down the walls like bubbles in oil. A gleaming disco ball haphazardly splattered the light like confetti.

"Looks like we're early," Eden said.

The room was empty. We were the only ones in the place. I looked at my watch. A quarter to.

"It doesn't start until eleven," Deirdre said. "And then after that there a strip show. I saw it last week. Pretty wild."

Strippers? I looked to Chaos who leaned back behind the girls and flashed widened eyes and an evil Cheshire grin. I smiled in kind and we exchanged that secret knowing nod of approval that only the perpetually horny can muster on command.

"Not exactly my cup of tea," Deirdre said fluttering her eyes, affecting a blonde southern belle, which was belied by her Goth black mascara, black lipstick and auburn hair. "I much prefer my naked bodies tall, hard and with a cock thank you very much."

"You're not going to find that on anyone here," Chaos said. "At least not one that doesn't have to strap it on first. Well maybe that one back there playing pool. She's probably had that operation I've heard so much about."

"Operation?" I said.

"Yeah, a strapadicktome. All the dykes want one."

"That's something I never got," I said. "If lesbians aren't interested in sex with men, why all the rubber dicks?"

"You've been watching way too much porn," Eden said.

"It's a legitimate question."

"I never understood it either," Deirdre said. "Latex is good, but there's just no competing with the real thing."

"What's the difference?" I asked.

"Here, let me demonstrate," Chaos said unzipping his fly. "You're gonna need to stand back a little."

It was all good fun and horseplay, lewd jokes and innuendo for a while, but then more people started slowly filing in.

"Should we grab a table?" I asked.

"Not unless you've got a bunch of singles you want to part with," Deirdre said. "Besides the view's better up here anyway."

Various groups formed and more and more people were arriving; women, men, straight and gay alike, dozens of them. And before I knew it was standing room only and Eden and I were pushed shoulder to shoulder, leaning over the railing overlooking the lower floor. Front row seats. It was perfect.

Up on the stage the big white ovals of the spotlights started to snake in a figure eight and the music, which up to this point was turned low and mixed with the sound of the thumping bass coming from the main dance floor outside, suddenly blasted to life in our ears and a shiver of excitement rippled through the crowd. *It's Raining Men* and a man's voice, all effort and gusto of trying to sound as effeminate as possible while still extending over the music and crowd noise burst forth from the speakers and all attention was drawn to the glittering stage.

"Haaaaayyyy everybody! The Florida Room, Orlando's hippest, hottest, wettest spot and the place to be on Saturday night is proud to present Eleven O'clock in the Coconut Lounge."

Applause, hoots and whistles rose from the crowd. It was all getting started.

"Now show some love and help bring to the stage your host for this evening, Miss Cassandra. Give it up everybody!"

And the room suddenly erupted in cat calls and more applause as the sequined curtain parted and the spotlights centered and from the darkness behind the stage there emerged onto the runway a muscular queen; black, six foot two even without the silver pumps, could've been a power forward if only the world were a little more understanding, and flowing blonde wig with curls running down both shoulders. He, or rather I really should say she, was practically naked, clad in a tight silver and red number that was really nothing more than a few strips of lycra crissing and crossing at all the right places to conceal the necessary parts of her anatomy so as not to break any public nudity laws, but that was all. The rest was smooth dark skin, thick red lips, implants, and a wiry but taut musculature.

"Hello Loungers!" she yelled into the red dildo mic clutched in her hands; hands adorned with inch-long glittery Orient red nails. It was then that I realized that as a result of the low budget Miss Cassandra was both announcer for herself and mc of the show.

I looked over at Eden but she didn't see me. She was mesmerized by the spectacle taking place, her deep brown eyes wide behind her glasses, the profile of her cheek, chin and lips fixed in a smile as the staticy white light flying off the disco ball played across her face and Cassandra continued her introduction, sometimes evoking laughs from the crowd, and sometimes hootchi-cootchie whistles. Chaos was already making eyes and smiles with a group of three cute brunettes. He had stray-dar and could immediately spot the straights in the crowd.

Cassandra played to the audience for another minute, her words as lost on me as I was lost in Eden's eyes. But then she called the first act to the stage and the spell was broken when Eden suddenly sensed me staring and looked at me and I quickly darted my eyes away like a frightened child.

I would often look at her like that, stare really, but never leer, from the side. Her eyes, those deep beautiful windows to her heart that I would get so lost in, would be fixed on a book, or a stage, or some other source of joy, but not me. I was hidden from view, a phantom in her periphery, watching from afar, though never more than a few feet away. Her attentions directed elsewhere, but mine focused on the gentle upward curve of her eyelashes, the smooth slope of her nose, the roundness of a tender earlobe. My affections composed a portfolio of still shots to be hung on white walls in the empty gallery of my mind and forever viewed by and audience of one. Love in profile.

Years later a good friend of mine would tell me if you want something like love to work then you have to engineer it. *Engineer.* That's the word he used. Like love is some type of machine that we stand apart from and have to tend to like a custodian.

And so I found myself, the hapless Chaplin tramp, standing before a great gear works: giant greasy black cogs and huge swinging brass levers, pendulums, and a great quaking steaming boiler about to blow its top. A mad, smoking Big Ben clockwork and I, with my lone monkey wrench and tarred overalls, black soot smeared across my cheeks, running to and fro like a wind-up maniac trying to keep it all from exploding.

"Our first performer comes to us all the way from Jack-son-ville. Anyone here from Jack-son-ville tonight?" A guy raised his hand.

"That's how they say it up there, isn't it? Jack-son-ville?" she laughed, self indulgent in her own small glory, being for now the star in this way off-Broadway production. "Anyway, I want you to give it up for our first performer of the evening. Everybody give a warm Coconut Lounge welcome to Jeremy Taylor, or as we like to call her, Cruella DeVille."

Miss Cassandra fled stage left and for a second the music quieted and we all hung in drippy anticipation. But then quickly the intro picked up. *I'm a Bitch* from Meredith Brooks, and the curtain parted again and out stepped Cruella DeVille. And it really was too! And not the Cruella of the cartoon, but the Cruella of Glenn Close. A winter Cruella. It was amazing! This guy had it all; the white fur coat and half black, half white fur hat, black dress, tight red gloves and white powdered face, thin red lips and spaghetti thin arched eyebrows. A complete package. A spitting image.

She strode sharp and stilted-like to the end of the stage while the intro continued, and when the lyrics picked up started the show.

Her movements were eerie, animatronic in nature, robotic and precise. First this arm, then that one. Pointed, accusing fingers and clutched fists, popping hips and locked knees. She didn't turn; she pivoted as if her feet were nailed to the end of the runway. The wild, glaring eyes and veins protruding from the thin sheath of skin covering her neck gave her performance all the more vivacity and depth. A wax statue come to life.

The people went nuts in there. Dollar bills were flying up from all corners. One guy stood directly in front of her and stuck a fiver in her belt and she just bent a little at the waist and looked at him acknowledging his presence with a mechanical smile and crow's feet eyes so as not to betray the authenticity of her performance, and never stopped singing, always keeping her lip movements exact and in perfect time with the music. She took one long dragon finger and ran it seductively under the fella's chin while the whistles and hoots rose to a fever pitch and egged her on.

She left and next up it was Reba McIntyre's turn and up stepped a big guy in red wig, older it looked to me, but still full of life. Had blue eyes, and even Reba's wonky one that sort of crossed a bit.

"I talked to him a few weeks ago," Deirdre said. "He used to go on tour with Reba as a double. He'd distract the crowd and make them think she was in the back but then she'd appear up front. His real name is Donald."

"Are you a fag hag?" Chaos asked. "You seem to know way too much about that guy."

It all went on for an hour. We poured back out into the main club and things there were in full swing, the crowd swelled and more came in by the minute. Chaos ran to get us more beers and Eden and Deirdre left to use the ladies room and suddenly I was alone in the dark, deafened by the driving, thumping bass. I tried to find Chaos but he was lost across the packed crowd on the dance floor.

A tall cowboy-looking fag danced past behind me like an apparition riding the rhythmic techno waves that intoxicated the room and sent queen and dyke alike into a mad flurry of shaking shoulders, gyrating asses and snapping fingers. Tall, muscular, tan in a clear vinyl jacket and pants, as see through as cellophane, he was naked beneath, shaved clean of hair on his chest and legs, and wore nothing save for a shimmering silvery pair of tight briefs that hugged his junk close to his leg but saved nothing for the imagination. An equally shimmering pair of boots and imitation Stetson completed the look that brought eyes upon him wherever he roamed. Just a high plains drifter out for a good time.

"There's a new sheriff in town boys," Chaos shouted over the din as he returned with drinks and Tex disappeared into the crowded throng. "William H. Boner. A.k.a. Billy the Prick."

And it was a roiling mass he shook into, a sweating sea of bodies feeling the surging beat pulsing through their arms, up and down their legs and racing along every hair to meet in a cacophonic car crash of feeling and sex in their chests, only to drip like molasses down their bellies and literally pool in their crotches. Damp armpits and moist panties. I told Chaos how this was my first time ever going out to a club.

"Wait. It gets better."

"When?" I asked, full of both anticipation and fright.

"Just wait. Here," he said handing me two beers. "For when she gets back."

"You're a genius," I said.

"It's all in the details."

Eden and Deirdre came back and I passed Eden a bottle and she smiled and I saw that he was right, it really all was in the details. This was going to take a lot of work.

Suddenly a new show started, no intro, just the fluxomed masses pushing up and gathering round the stage to get a better view. It was five minutes to midnight and the anticipation hung all around me, thick and soupy, a gumbo of smoke, sweat and failure. What would come next?

Lori would be first, and without warning or indication that any such thing was going to start, she leapt up on the far end of the runway just before the heavy black curtain lining the far wall of the dance floor. The DJ cranked the music and the anthem blare of the anvil bass beat thumped in my chest like medieval blacksmiths making ready for war as the crowd suddenly screamed to attention and Lori strutted to the end of the stage.

Hers was a vacant expression: large hollow eyes, small mousy face, pale. But beautiful, with sharp nose and pouty parted lips, short close, almost crew-cut jet black hair. A firecracker of energy, not more than five foot two maybe, she danced a kind of wicked sexy Nuevo jitterbug that, with shimmering silver one piece with frayed hems and shoulders, evoked a 20s flapper girl high on cocaine. Everything about her was sharp, from the flicking and flailing of her wrists and arms to the scissor-like way she clipped her legs and kicked her heels. You felt like she was dangerous at any distance.

"Look at those eyes," Chaos yelled in my ear. "High as a motherfucker!"

And she was. That abandon in her eyes that kept her stare clear over the heads of all those around her and prevented it from focusing on anyone in particular was the result of nothing short of five lines of that fine white manna that finds itself dispersed not from the fingers of light from above, but rather the pockets of the dwellers of the lowest sewers of this dim, mortal world.

She danced like that for three minutes or more, jutting and juking back and forth across the runway, shaking her smooth pale hips and kicking the bills that lay at her feet this way and that way, any which way, until the DJ in his tower of power at the back of the room suddenly called out something muffled and unintelligible over the mic and the crowd roared in approval and the music switched suddenly to something Gothic, mechanical and grinding, heavy on guitar and short on kindness. Lori strutted to the center of the stage and in one flash dance animal thrash tore her dress off and flung it over our heads to reveal a tiny, taut physique barely concealed in black vinyl teddy and one fierce green dragon tattoo that snaked its way down her left side from her breasts to her navel.

Insanity reigned. In the Coconut Lounge is had been mostly men, docile in their reverie, quiet in their joy. Wild, but controlled by an unwritten sense of decorum, like they were all members of an elite club to which only they were privy to the rules and code of conduct. But out here it was the women, the more deadly of the species, who dominated the scene. And they were fierce in their admiration, frightening in their praise—a disorganized horde all pushing, shouldering, chiseling their way closer to the stage, closer to her, who drew the daggers from their eyes; a fine, violent line between hunger and awe. They surged forward scraping and shoving to get closer to her, to look at her gyrating flesh and the tiny, tight and undoubtedly divine glory hidden just beneath those inky vinyl panties; the fantasies of the damned, wet, flowing heavy and hot like rivers of molten iron. Or better than look, perhaps to touch, or best of all, to smell her.

I looked as Eden took a hesitant step forward, but the way was barred by backs and flying elbows, money in clenched fingers flailing about overhead, a heavy crew-cutted dyke with ripped jeans and untucked plaid man's shirt giving us a nasty look over a thick shoulder. She was bigger than the two of us combined. Chaos and Deirdre had already pushed up with the rest and were pinned against the stage waving money, Eden and I long forgotten. Lori was grinding like a machine against the surging bodies, stray hands tearing for breasts like wild beasts. Her hips were stuffed full of green, and more rained down from all sides.

I spotted a space toward the back and tapped Eden on the shoulder, silently pointing the way. I made a hole in the wall of bodies and she followed close behind, and then it happened. I felt it the way one feels the first warm spring breeze, the kiss of the infinite against your skin that gives pause, that stops the flow of time across the universe, and for just that instant there is only you and that eternal caress. There is perfection in this world, objective perfection that requires no thought, no examination, only pure acceptance and belief that what you are beholding is the end of nothing and the beginning of everything. I have known this perfection. It was what I felt when she laced her fingers around my wrist that first time, the first moment that she touched me burned into my memory forever, as I led her through the throng of bodies shifting and thrashing about like great trees of a storm swept mountainside forest.

I looked back over my shoulder and she was smiling, her head ducked down so as not to catch a stray blow, but she was smiling at me and not through me. Right at me, and I smiled back, my throat cold with fear and excitement, full of icy breath and the sticky, coppery taste of adrenaline, my heart swelling with triumph over this small gesture, this innocent touch. Would she have taken my arm had she known?

The frenzy whipped on, and Lori was working the crowd for all they were worth. Chaos sneaked a fiver down the back of her bra. Another guy tried to stuff a dollar under her garter, but fumbled when she turned and the money fell to the floor like a dead leaf. Women were pawing at the stage trying to get over each other for just a piece. Humanity cast off like a shawl, gay and straight alike. Monkeys all of us, make no mistake about it.

Eden waited her turn, a dollar folded in her fingers (and one in mine too). We were like two kids on the sidewalk of old eyeing a taffy puller work its magic, the candy dancing safely behind plate glass, gleaming moist and hot, our eyes bulging in anticipation. Then finally she came.

It was raw damp flesh flashing before us. Lori was almost spent, the faintest heaving in her chest, her breath and blood racing, but enough left still to impart upon us a final push. She lowered herself on hands and knees like an animal, her face mere inches from the front of Eden's jeans (the most enviable of places), and lingered there, like she were a slave girl revering a golden totem of her ancient god. Slowly, slinking serpentine she rose to full height and the roles were reversed. Now Eden eye level with the bare navel of the slave, gently slipped the dollar along the edge of her thigh and wrapped it under a tight garter. But that wasn't the end. No, it wouldn't be over with such little fanfare, for Lori knew, as I did then, that perfection does exist in the world and it demands to be recognized.

She looked into Eden's eyes. No other in the crowd, neither man nor woman received that treatment, never. There were none worthy. But here stood a girl more beautiful, more radiant than the rest. And she saw it and bent to it, lowered her face to meet the face of my angel, with sleepy bedroom eyes (which everyone saw and cat called and whistled for more), and lingered for just a second as they gazed into each other's minds, before turning and leaving the stage. I had never seen anything as sexy as that moment in all my life and would capture it, internalize it, and store it in the deep recesses of my memory to be used as the measure, the gold standard by which all others were felt for years to come.

The show continued, another girl came out and the money flowed like water. I must have burned though at least thirty bucks by the time it was all finished, and it was a great time Eden and I had standing there, side by side, watching the parade of flesh, laughing, pointing, gawking. At one point she congratulated me on picking such a prime spot to watch the action and I just thought to myself it's all in the details.

When it all wound down and the last girl had come and gone and everyone broke up and just went back to dancing and drinking the night away I needed a piss, but was terrified of leaving the relative comfort and safety of the group. And it was just professional courtesy and common sense that I not ask Chaos to accompany me. I was in uncharted waters, a straight man in a gay bar, and just standing there watching the stream of people going into the johns at the end of the hall I was even more baffled to find that they were being used interchangeably. Bullish women with broad shoulders and gender issues were strolling right into the men's room while light and airy fruits were floating into the ladies'. My social ineptitude was making its presence painfully known in my bladder and I was seriously contemplating running out onto the street to piss when Deirdre emerged from the ladies room.

"I don't know where to go," I said desperately.

"The ladies' room is much cleaner than the men's, but there's a line a mile long in there."

I settled on the men's and decided to keep my head down and focused on not getting caught staring or sending out any kind of signal. Stupid, I know, but this *was* my first time in a gay bathroom.

Inside it looked like any other dingy can, two urinals, three stalls all occupied, cracked tiles and flyers taped haphazardly about. Despite Deirdre's suggestion, there was a line of five guys standing along one wall waiting their turn, and I took up my place as last in line. Hands in pockets, eyes on the floor, we shuffled along. Four feet in one stall; that one I was definitely not using.

Suddenly there was a crack in the aether and a tall heavy-set fag tiptoed in wearing a ridiculous curly pink wig, white tank top, jean cut-offs and lacy tutu. He was older behind a set of bifocals, wore a tiara with plastic butterflies bouncing around on springy wires on his head and in one hand held a short plastic rod; glittery, a child's twirling baton I think. At the end there was a shimmery Mylar poof ball, probably a large cat toy. And with no words, but certainly to the tune of a song playing in his head that only he could hear, he systematically made his way down the row of waiting men, tapping each one of us gently on the head with the tip of his wand, blessing us silently. No one really even took notice, except me of course. Then silent as a cat fart he left. He didn't even have to piss.

My turn finally came but it was an open urinal not a stall and after that fiasco there was no way in hell I was going to open my pants in that room unless it was behind a locked door. I waved two guys past and when a stall finally opened I ducked inside, held my breath over the stinking wet bowl caked with cigarette ash and a mound of soaked paper rising off the top of the tank like a little Mt. Fuji, pissed and ran out, no flush.

The pink fairy busied himself making rounds at the pool tables as I snaked past and found Eden sitting by herself watching Chaos and Deirdre tearing up the dance floor.

"Dance?" I asked, for some reason emboldened by recent events in the men's room, and certainly not the least bit by the four beers in me. Certainly not.

"Don't be obvious about it, but ever since the show those guys at the end of the bar keep checking me out."

I spotted a group of Hispanics, all baggy jeans and gangbanger tattoos across the room. They looked over and probably talked about me, sized me up and laughed.

"They must think I'm your gay friend."

"It's really uncomfortable."

"Want me to say something?" I asked. "I'm pretty sure pinky over there's got my back. He wields a mighty big wand. We kinda made friends in the can."

She laughed and I suggested we just walk away, go outside and check out the deck, and she agreed. But I made sure to walk past Chaos and tap him on the shoulder so the thugs would know I wasn't alone, safety in numbers and all.

I bought us beers and found a couple of seats at an empty table. It was quieter outside. Music was pumped in, but it was more reggae than techno and at much lower volumes, so that you could actually have a conversation with someone and not shout at each other like idiots.

"Thanks. I hate it when a guy stares like that. I mean if you want to say something, then say something. Don't just stare."

"Did you really want one of them hitting on you?" I asked.

"God no."

"Then I'm glad I could help."

"My hero." Then giggling.

"What's so funny?"

"You. Mr. New Joisey," she said over-affecting my accent, squinting with a tilted head and shrugged shoulders, Mafioso style. "Glad I could 'elp. I made friends wit 'im in the can."

"I can't help it. It comes out more when I get, you know, agitated."

"You mean scared?"

"I didn't say that," I said, then put it on thick. "I ain't scared'a nuthin'." She laughed. I told her it was all stupid anyway and said again how I couldn't really help.

"You shouldn't. It's funny."

"I don't really sound like that, do I?"

"Sometimes. It's one thing I like about you Stone." She was toying with me again. My God she was beautiful. Maybe it was the adrenaline, or maybe the drink, but I heard myself saying it before I could think about it.

"So it's just one thing then?" I said, my turn to play. "I guess I gotta start trying harder."

It was the beginning.

VI

Eden's was a beauty of simplicity that, when I think back on it now, through the filter of my present mind's lens, was rooted in a deep belief on my part in the perfection of both her person and her soul. Hers was a beauty that lay much deeper than the superficially corporeal, that animal shell of flesh and blood and bone and sinew that we all find ourselves both confined in and attracted to at the same time. Rather it lived in the vibrations that her soul, through her eyes, sent out across the vast distances that we two occupied in the rock and dirt physical world.

Warm vibrations, cosmic in their complexity and at the same time innocent in their simplicity, with the self same deitific ability to traverse both time and space and penetrate my heart no matter where I found myself.

And like an ancient penitent, prostrate in supplication to the all powerful, all seeing, all knowing One, I worshipped her always, in darkness and in light, but especially in darkness, when I found myself sitting in the blackness of my room, alone, wondering where she was, what she was doing, looking at the phone, waiting, hoping she would call. My every movement, every thought carefully orchestrated and choreographed for her, for through those dreamy vibrations, and in the eye of my mind, I could see her seeing me, and making sure I was doing my utmost to impress her, impress upon her the importance of my love, how I would do everything I could to please her. And just like a flagellant monk in ragged torn cowl in dim, moist Dark Age Spain or England or Germania lashing himself with leather horsewhip to please his Lord, I sat clothed in darkness

31

lashing my gut with beer and cheap wine and whatever else I could get my hands on.

And I'd lay back and close my lids, eyes rolling back in my head, straining at their nerves making the blackness even blacker still, and I would see her eyes. And the vibrations would seek me out, piercing my soul, and my heart would fill with sobering warmth, arming me against the assault of another lonely night without her.

VII

Chaos kept a lizard in his apartment, a monitor about three feet long named Jasper that he kept in a thirty gallon glass aquarium on the floor of his closet. Jasper ate all sorts of things I'd come to learn, but his favorite meal was feeder mice that Chaos picked up at a pet shop around the corner from his home. A few days after our excursion to The Florida Room, when we'd both finished our shifts at the store, he asked if I wouldn't mind giving him a lift home (Stanley the Mustang having suffered a fatal engine seize a few days earlier) and stopping on the way to pick up Jasper's food.

The pet shop, a shitty little place that stunk of mold, cedar chips, and cat piss readily gave us two little innocent white mice in a brown paper bag and I felt sorry for them, their little juicy eyeballs and pink noses: cute, nuzzling, and completely unaware of their fates. The clerk, Donny, was a friend of Chaos' from someplace, probably high school, and looked terribly out of place. He wore a long flattened psychobilly mohawk that was slicked back over the top of his head while the sides were shaved razor clean. He'd adorned his face with a steel lip ring, an eyebrow ring, a nose ring, and about two pounds of silver hanging from his ears, and beneath the thin fabric of his pressed white shirt shone the outline of a wife beater and a faint assortment of tattoos. He was a punk and this was his embarrassing, time-consuming, soul-sucking, I just wanna rock day job. But he was cool and since he hated everything about working in that place he let Chaos have the mice for free.

And that's when he asked us if we'd be interested in a spider.

It needs to be said that there are only a few things in life that I am truly terrified of. When I was ten years old a small squadron of yellow jackets attacked and stung me multiple times. Since that trauma I had made some small adjustments to my lifestyle including taking all of my meals indoors and avoiding flower beds, gardens, and nature in general.

"If you don't bother them, they won't bother you," my mother used to (and still does) say whenever they come around and I have to get up and run away like a child. Bullshit. They bother me with their very existence, and if by not bother you mean fly right into your fucking face, land on your shoulder like a ninja and then follow you buzzing and swooping as you're tear assing away, then yes, they certainly don't bother me one bit. And I can hear the hippies and tree huggers, "But the bees pollinate the flowers. Without the bees nothing would grow. We'd have no food man." Fuck you. We grow all kinds of shit indoors without them. The future is hydroponics.

But I digress. Among my other lifelong fears: needles, being eaten alive by a large animal, clowns, getting a paper cut on the tip of dick (long ways), clowns (again), getting caught masturbating by my mother, and spiders. I fucking hate spiders. So suffice it to say I was none too thrilled when Chaos leapt at the chance.

It also needs to be said that while I hated arachnids of any shape, size or color, Chaos was completely enamored of them. More directly, he was a *huge* fan of Spiderman. I never knew if he truly believed that he could be bitten by one and magically adopt its powers, but I knew he'd be willing to try. Spidey was his idol.

Around the corner from the hamsters and gerbils and across the aisle from the fish tanks stood the spider wall, a veritable horror house of creepy crawly nastiness, all tucked away in individual plastic terrariums and stacked neatly next to other insectoid frights like scorpions and giant millipedes.

I stood a step back when Donny grabbed one of the boxes at random and took the lid off. He and Chaos looked in at the giant bulbous hairy body of the beast with thick black crooked legs poised in the corner. Donny took a pen from his pocket and poked gently at the thing to get it to move, but all it did was flinch and try to recoil further up the corner of the box. Not satisfied, he put it back and grabbed for another one when I turned and a particularly colorful group of fish in a nearby aquarium caught my eye. That's when I heard the scream.

"It's on me! It's on me!"

I spun around and saw Donny frozen with fear, the terrarium in one hand, the lid in the other, and a huge monster, a fucking behemoth of a spider, scurrying up the front of his shirt, obviously none too pleased with all that poking bullshit. Chaos had bolted clear across the store and I turned tail like a coward and did the exact same thing and we left Donny standing there flapping his hands and dancing like a little girl holding a live grenade. I peered around a shelf and watched him gasp in horror as the thing was almost at his neck, then with one swoop swat the bastard off his chest with the lid of the box, slap the lid back on and throw the whole deal back on the shelf. When it was all over he just stood there panting like he'd just run a marathon and we slowly came back over.

"That was so cool!" he said laughing giddily like an inmate at Bellevue. "That thing coulda killed me!"

"Man you screamed like a little bitch!" Chaos yelled. He was flushed red with laughter.

"And where the fuck were you, Spiderman?" Donny punched him in the chest.

"Hey can I see a scorpion next?"

"I'm getting the fuck outta here," I said. "You're not bringing any of those things in my car. You can fuckin' walk home."

Chaos' apartment was a wreck, which was its usual state, from the pile of unwashed dishes spilling onto the counter in the kitchen to the sheets duct taped over the windows. Broken furniture culled from curbside drive-bys or maybe from the Salvation Army was disorganized and mismatched. Spilled beer and vomit stained the already worn through carpet. There was a strong biting stench coming from an overflowing litter box in the kitchen that hadn't been changed in, ever, I think. The cat was his roommate's. I knew my friend lived in poor surroundings and that his confident air and positive whimsy belied a truth hidden in a tenement. I'd been trying to think of a way to help him out, but knew I had no money to lend. I think he sensed it and was ashamed.

We got back with just the two mice in hand, no spiders, and went to feed Jasper, but when we got to the closet we found the door open and the aquarium inside empty, the screen and wood lid laying next to it, the phonebooks that had anchored it in place cast aside.

"Shit," Chaos said. "Ok, so we should not move."

"Why?"

Monitors, for those who may not know, have a nasty set of fairly long claws as well as a fierce bite and toxic saliva so that if you do happen to get nipped by one it's surely going to require a trip to the hospital and injections and all that mess. They generally have an unpleasant disposition and a tendency to attack just about anything. I mean, it is a fucking dinosaur after all.

"He was probably just hungry. Went looking for dinner. Little fucker couldn't wait. That's the problem with lizards. No patience."

"What do we do now?" I asked stupidly. "What about Snatch?"

"Eh, it's Chris', and I never really liked cats anyway."

Chaos handed me a baseball bat from the closet and took a wire coat hanger for himself and together we began carefully poking and prodding around the piles of clothes, shoes, boxes and milk crate furniture that is the wreckage of his room. He checked the closet, probing in between heaps of unwashed laundry while I carefully punched at a box with the end of my bat. There were clothes everywhere. I don't think he ever actually washed anything. He just wore things until they got too dirty, then he went out and bought new things. Probably why he was almost always broke and spending money he didn't have. But he was always so well dressed. I'd never really realized the squalor he lived in until that afternoon.

I got on my knees to peek under the bed.

"Don't do that! He gets you with that tail and he could knock your eye out."

Clownishly he started calling out to Jasper like you would a lost kitty and giggling in his maniacal way at the absurdity of, well the absurdity of two idiots trying to catch a giant angry escaped lizard.

"He's not in here," I said. "Kitchen?"

"Not yet. We do this tactically. Kitchen is too far away to make a clear run. We'd be exposed for too long, clipped for sure." Then to his watch "Delta Tango, we're Oscar Mike. Bedroom clear. Moving to secondary bedroom, over." He was loving this. His whole life was a game.

We moved from the bedroom down the hall to his roommate's, hugging the wall with our backs. At the door he turned to me, nodded, then plunged into the room with a crash, tumbling across the floor and slapping against the far wall in a crouch. It was just as a wreck as his, with unwashed laundry strewn about, stacks of movies and CDs everywhere, a TV perched precariously on an inverted milk crate, a mattress (no box spring) on the floor and three fist size holes in the wall. But no Jasper.

From the bedroom Chaos belly crawled (I walked) with the coat hanger in his teeth to the living room, but still no luck. Snatch was watching uninterested from the top of the fridge and Chaos was pondering using him as bait of some kind when we heard it coming from the bathroom behind us. I flicked on the light and there was Jasper, all three scaly pissed off feet of him, curled up behind the toilet, hissing.

"There you are. Hiding where it's cool. Back up, I don't want him to scratch you when I come through or it'll be hospitals and vets and all kinds of terrible shit."

The lizard continued hissing and backing up as Chaos climbed into the tub trying to maneuver over him to get at it from behind. Jasper moved quickly though, whipping his tail and scrambling right at me, an awkward blur of flapping talons clinking across the smooth tile floor.

"Get him!"

"Get him?" I said and pulled the door shut, the Jersey accent Eden found so cute now coming through in spades. "Are you insane? I'll beat 'im to death wit this fuckin' bat before I 'get him.'"

I stood poised with the bat at the ready and from behind the door could hear Chaos cursing and a lot of slapping, hissing and tail whipping against the wall and then Chaos said it was ok and open the door but stand back, and when he came clamoring through he carried Jasper out in front of him like a baby with a fresh load in his pants, only this wasn't to avoid a nasty smell, but the biting sting of a whipping tail and scratching claws. He ran down the hall giggling and unloaded Jasper into the glass box in the closet, replacing the lid and weighing it down with the phone books.

"You ought to consider investing in something heavier," I said.

"He never gets out on his own. I must have forgotten to put the books back on when I took him out last."

"Wait, you take that thing out on purpose?"

The bag with the mice was sitting on top of his dresser and Chaos took one out by the tail and held it up next to the glass eagerly watching the poor little thing squirm and kick.

"Hungry?"

"Hey if you want, you can bring some of your laundry over and do it at my place. It's only a buck a load." I figured any little bit might help.

"Really? That'd be great. You sure it's no trouble?"

He lifted the lid and dropped the mouse right in front of Jasper, but he didn't even flinch at it. It immediately ran for cover, frantically looking for a way up, out, to freedom, but still Jasper remained uninterested, the fluster and excitement of his recent escape probably working the appetite out of him.

Chaos started rummaging through piles of dirty clothes and stuffing random items into an Adidas duffle bag on a folding beach chair.

"You got anything to eat at your place?" he asked slinging the bag over his shoulder.

"What about the other mouse?" I asked of the crinkling paper bag on the dresser. "You maybe want to put it someplace where it won't get away?"

"Nah, it'll be fine there. I'll give it to him later. If it gets out Snatch'll get it. Chris hardly feeds that fuckin' cat anyway."

We hit the lights and left, but not before Chaos took a crumpled handful of bills from the back pocket of a pair of jeans laying on the floor.

"My last fifty for the week," he said holding it up to his face. "For after dinner. You got any cash? I know this place. You like tits? I like tits? Who doesn't like tits? Best kinda tits? Tits in your face. Delta Tango, LZ clear, we are a go for extraction, I repeat that's a go Poppa Charlie."

Out he dashed and off we went.

VIII

There's a strip bar at the end of the night that just as well might be at the end of the world for all its dismal gloom and dank back alley stickiness. Club Risqué.

It's where Chaos and I ended up after a dinner of frozen pizza, beers, a late showing of a crappy movie (Godzilla), and more beers. Now the hands on my watch are rolling high up on midnight and we're pulling up feeling fine because last call is at least two hours away and we've still got about seventy bucks between us.

He strode with the confidence of a conquistador and threw open the tinted glass door (foreshadowing I think the innumerable tinted glass doors I would later find myself throwing open on the Hooker Hill in Seoul in the not too distant future, though with much less bravado than he was doing now, mine being slouched shoulders and hat down low over eyes, gazed fixed on my ashamed first time feet) leading us into a sort of dingy foyer marked by a long defunct, empty 80s cigarette machine on the left (the kind you'd find in a New Jersey diner perhaps? Plastic gold pull knobs and faux wood paneling. Where were Billy and Bruce?) and a funk-stained wall carpeted floor to ceiling in black on the right. It was all another first for me, but I didn't want to say anything and embarrass myself. I was just going to let things go where they may.

With chin held high as always and me following quickly behind, Chaos paid both our covers to the bearded fat roadie type guarding the door and walked into the main room, which was as sorry a sight as the foyer. Longer than it was wide, a raised black runway with two gold poles rising from it ran the length of the far wall. A hallway to the bathrooms at one end and a small bar at the other framed the stage. The wall behind it was mirrored floor to ceiling and you could only sit on one side staring at your sorry reflection staring back at you, asking how on earth you ever ended up in a place like this? A few tables stood scattershot through the whole joint and pink and red lights swirled about casting just bright enough that you could make out where you were going. But that didn't matter much because if you found yourself in that hole, there was a good chance you'd reached the end of the line and weren't going anywhere anyway. I thought of Eden and wondered what she would think of me if she knew I'd come to a place like this. Could she see it in her mind's eye? Was she even looking?

Chaos went to the bar to get us beers and I found us a table close to the stage, which wasn't that difficult, there being only four or five other guys in the whole room. Most of them wore ball caps, flannel or ripped beer-stained tees and looked like truck drivers just come in off the road. Chaos and I must have looked a sight unnerving for them, he in vinyl pants and shining silver shirt, wild hair and earrings, and I in pressed collared black shirt and freshly washed jeans.

The music was something unremarkable, David Lee Roth singing about girls or sex or booze or whatever and up on the stage was Crystal as the DJ let us know with a low growl. She was a tiny number, thin, with the face of a runaway and the eyes of a thief, but she looked much taller up there on the stage with her legs wrapped around that pole. Her outfit, if you could say that the single piece of thread she wore constituted an outfit, consisted of a pair of red pumps, two glittery red pasties, and a matching G-string that accented a small, but still shapely ass that from where I was sitting looked like it would fit perfectly in the palms of my hands.

"Nice," Chaos said nudging me as he returned with the beers. "Jessica says she's a real bitch though."

Jessica was the real reason we'd come to this dump. She was a dancer Chaos had picked up and been seeing on and off for the last three weeks, by his standards a relatively successful relationship. I'd met her only once, when I stopped by his place one Sunday morning and she was passed out on his couch. When I asked him why she'd slept there instead of the bed he just smiled that Cheshire grin.

"We started out in the bedroom, but somewhere in the night I managed to fuck her clear over to the couch!" Then he threw his head back and howled so loud I thought for sure it would wake his roommate or her at the very least, but Chris was out of town and Jessica didn't stir a muscle. I looked at her there, face down on the couch, wearing a shirt, but no pants or underwear on, her bare tanned ass staring back at me.

"You want a piece?" he asked casually lighting a morning butt. "She won't mind."

"What, now? You're not serious?"

"Of course not," he giggled. "I'd wake her up first. Fucking a sleeper? That's just rapist Dave. Perve."

But Crystal finished her set on the stage and the DJ now called up Nadia, and down stepped Crystal and up stepped Nadia. I couldn't be bothered with Nadia and as I watched Crystal sashay over to our little table I felt the grin of Chaos on my back and then thought to myself that maybe coming here wasn't such a bad idea after all.

"Who wants a dance?" she asked, her deep, raspy voice belying her small figure.

"My friend here definitely does," Chaos said, and before I could protest he slammed a twenty on the table and pushed it my way, lighting a cigarette for himself while speaking through squinted eyes and curling wisps of smoke. "And it's his first one ever, so make it a good one. Dave, pay the lady."

I took the twenty folded between my fingers and held it up for her, not knowing exactly what to do with it. She pushed my hand right back on the table, leaned in and whispered in my ear with a voice like a full bodied wine.

"Wait till I'm done. I might just make it worth more to you," she sighed and lingered there to allow a single warm breath to swirl around my ear. I felt her straight brunette hair brush against my cheek and the tops of her bare breasts resting against my chest. The whole thing gave me the sudden cold shiver of midnight in winter.

She slid both hands down to my knees and forced them apart to make room. I pulled my shirt tails down to hide the huge erection she gave me with her words, just her words.

And now it was her body that spoke to me in moist circumlocution. The music disappeared from my ears and the seedy grime and hopelessness of that end of the world bar fled my sight and there was just her. She was like a column of water freestanding right there in the middle of the room, sprung straight up out of the filthy black speckled carpet, rolling and rippling and contorting to the dirty thoughts in my mind even though hers were probably a million miles away.

"Jessica here?" I heard Chaos ask from far away.

"Not tonight baby," she replied, disinterested. "Called in sick."

"Well shit on a stick. I was looking forward to wearing her ass as a hat."

"What? I'm not good enough for ya?"

"I didn't say that. You're doing just fine. What do you think Dave? Dave?"

Everything slowed down when she moved. Time meant nothing. She was bestial, tearing at my face with her eyes, thrusting her bare hind cheeks in my groin and grinding against the pulsing hard-on raging just beneath my jeans. Her lips were before mine and she was licking them, her mouth expectant, offering, brown eyes burrowing deep through mine into the back of my head. I was fixated on her thighs. They were long and creamy, and I thought about Eden and wondered if hers were as mesmerizing.

"Mental note," I said to Chaos over the cranking music. "I have to see Eden in a G-string. If I do nothing else before I die I have to do that."

"Oh yes?" he inquired through a wisp of fresh smoke.

"Absolutely." I don't think I had been more serious about anything in my life.

"You really dig her, don't you?"

"My friend, I think of nothing else," I said turning to him, Crystal still churning between my legs. "I've thought of nothing else since the day I met her."

"Then go after her."

"I don't really know how," I said.

"I'll help."

"Seriously?"

"What are friends for?" he smiled conspiratorially.

"Good. We start tomorrow."

"So it's a mission then?" I could see the excitement growing in his eyes.

"At dawn we commence Operation G-String. You up to the challenge soldier?"

"Whatever I can do to help, General" he said suddenly giddy. "I like this plan. Let's make this thing happen." Then pointing to Crystal's crotch, "Can we borrow this when you're done?"

IX

After that night Chaos and I took to each other like two old immortal souls who'd first met centuries, maybe millennia ago, when we were just Roman peasants, or Egyptian date growers, or maybe just mute grunting cavemen painting our mutual exploits side by side in the dark caverns of Lascaux, but who'd only recently found each other again and connected seamlessly, as if we'd parted ways, or lives, only yesterday.

In those early days, the embryonic stages of the evolution of our refound friendship, but more kinship really, we were inseparable as childhood buddies on the first day of summer break. The talking was a furious whirlwind of ideas and theories that we bounced off one another in all night laugh fests that lasted long into the following morning, usually culminating in doubled over, tear streaming, rolling on the floor cackling. Sometimes our sides hurt for days and our ears felt like they'd pop any second, Chaos sucking great breaths and bellowing out his tremendous laugh; a clown's cackle that would have frightened children and set doctors to pen writing torrid notes about unstable psyches and crooked worldviews. The talk was sex mostly, girls, and Eden.

"Tonight we gotta go to The Red Room and see my friend Rob the barback over there. He knows the bouncer at The Hog so they'll let us in free and we can meet up with Gina, this sweet chick who works at my bank. I told her we'd be there around eleven and she said she'd bring her cousin, but since there'll be two of you, you and Rob will have to duke it out for the cousin, but Rob's a pussy and you can take him."

That's the way it always was with Chaos. He seemed to know everyone in town. Had a friend here, an old buddy there, knew this girl from that place, and so and so was her friend. The women were always gorgeous; it was part of his gift. We never went anywhere he didn't know someone. His entourage was citywide.

And always the liquor, lots and lots of liquor; wine by the bottle and beer by the case. We ran through it like water. Drunk at night and drunk in the day. Drunk at home and drunk at work, and if not drunk, hung over and thinking about getting drunk again. It was a rolling, roaring start of the greatest friendship of my life.

One random afternoon while we were fucking off at work, debating the greatness of Bruce Lee and what he would have done for American action cinema in the 80s had he lived, we discovered something new and wonderful about each other and that was our theretofore unknown mutual love of martial arts and our unlived childhood fantasies of being real action heroes. Many a night we'd both spent in our youths battling countless invisible foes with cardboard knives and broomstick swords, sometimes out with friends traipsing through the woods, other times alone in our bedrooms, the central figures in our imaginary one-act plays. We resolved to nurture in each other our skills and set about taking regular intervals from normal life, when we were usually inebriated and unobserved, where we would spar madly with one another, no pads or protective gear (we couldn't afford any anyway). These matches almost always started out friendly, but quickly descended into serious life on the line bouts of fights to the death. Cinematic. A real-life movie of two men in a cramped apartment or on top of an empty parking garage at midnight, or in a stark stairwell, battling it out. It always ended in bruises and blood, usually me doing most of the bleeding, he being much faster, stronger, and more agile that I, and with a few years of formal kickboxing training under his belt, but I'd studied Tae Kwon Do for a little while so I got my shots in every now and again. Once he took me, and himself I suspect, judging by the look of joy on his face after he'd done it, the look of "holy shit I can't believe I just pulled that off!", by complete surprise and swiped both legs right out from under me so that for a fleeting second I was completely airborne and hanging in the atmosphere like in a slow motion show before crashing back down to the earth and right through the cheap particle board coffee table in his ramshackle apartment. That one cost me a sprained wrist and fractured pinky.

But it was all great fun and split logs for the furnace in which we'd forged our forever friendship.

∞

Downtown. Broad daylight. 2:00 p.m.

I'm at work, but doing nothing, standing alone, watching her through the plate glass, and she's standing around too, doing nothing in particular. She's not concerned with the walkings back and forth in the hall, the roar of a bus engine pulling away from the stop just across the way, the buzz and whir of cars flying by on the street outside. A troupe of Brazilian teenagers, a tour group all dressed in uniform yellow tees and short, short, should be illegal in this country but perfectly acceptable on the beaches and back alleys of Rio, green shorts, being led by a squat, rectangular barrel of a man carrying droopy white flag emblazoned with the tour company name on flimsy plastic stick tucked into a huge backpack probably stuffed with airline stubs, maps, guide books, language books, and bottles of water and barking some sort of instruction in Portuguese as he marches them on. I look only for a second, distracted by a blur of tanned legs, Indian lips and bubbly giggles, but then turn my attention back to her. She's seen none of it.

Time is passing like a slug, and I'm alone here and she's there and it's just the two of us separated by a single sheet of glass, but it's an impassible wall, and torturous all the more because I can see straight through it, pretending as if it's not even there, but I know it is, material and hard, cold as steel and a window into a future I keep trying to get to but can never seem to reach.

I'm scribbling a poem down on the back of a discarded receipt in part because I'm hoping she'll notice and ask what I'm working on, in part because I need to do something with my hands. It usually works out this way. Anyway it's to her.

A strand of hair,
A tear filled glass,
Empty bottle
My kitchen table at midnight
Just random words on a page. 2:07 p.m.

X

A gray August morning. It's 7 a.m. and I'm driving back to work, hungover from another long night out with Chaos.

The last month has seen a switch in routine from strictly classes then study then work then home to work then Blue then home then Risqué then work then maybe I'll just skip this one class then home then The Florida Room then there'll be time to study later . . .

It's been a whirlwind of bars, clubs, music and skin, and with Chaos the party never ends. The schedule seemed almost etched in stone with us making the rounds, making appearances with the regularity of celebrities. The Florida Room on Saturday nights with Deirdre and Eden for the shows, Blue on Mondays, a laid back lounge with a smattering of booths where we'd often find the Sage ruminating over a glass of bourbon and book, The Copper Club on Tuesdays, a special place Chaos and I'd found while wandering the midnight streets one evening and heard the dreamy eclectic asymmetrical rhythms of trippy acid jazz emanating from within. We'd just gone in for a drink and stumbled right in on a regular Tuesday night institution, Funk n' Bass, with trip hop blaring from the speakers and sometimes live slam poetry being presented on stage. It was a grand joint, lit dim, crammed with people shoulder to shoulder and local artwork hanging on the bare brick walls in back, beyond the long, long, mile-long bar and crowded dance floor. We'd agreed that it was the place to be and pacted right then over clinking martinis to make it our regular Tuesday night.

So we'd closed Copper last night, for the fourth time this month, and now, as I say, I'm driving back to work with bleary eyes and cloudy mind, kicking myself for not calling in sick, but not too bothered by it all since I know Chaos is opening the store with me and so the day ahead should be as amusing as usual.

But when I arrive at the dark doors to the Shaft the place is still as quiet as we'd left it the night before. No Chaos to be seen, so I take a seat on the floor, close my eyes to block out the impending headache, and wait. Eventually approaching footsteps and the sound of clinking keys in the lock above my head awaken me and it's Sage stepping over me to get inside.

"Closed the Copper again?" he laughed, kicking me in the side as I climb to my feet.

"It was wild. Some new live band. Free CDs. You shoulda been there."

"Next time. You still coming over tonight though?" I was in no condition for sparring and forced a weak cough to emphasize the point.

"I don't know. Last night was rough. I need sleep. And I gotta put in an appearance at my Expository Writing class at some point. We'll see."

"Vigor is good for the soul," he said. "You don't practice you'll get rusty."

"I'll think about it." Then remembering our missing compatriot. "Where's Chaos?"

"He didn't call you?"

"No. Why? Should he have?" I ran through a nervous mental list of things that could have befallen him after the previous night's debauch: shot, dead in a ditch, DUI . . .

"He's gone to Jacksonville. His father died last night."

"No shit? When? We didn't leave till three."

"I don't know," he said. "Said there was a message from his mom when he got home. Called and asked me to cover for him. Told Jen he'd be gone for at least a week."

"I had no idea. Well that sucks." It was a genuine blow.

"I wouldn't mourn too much. They were never really close."

"But still," I said. "He never talks much about his family."

"I don't know much myself. Just know when we were in high school he wasn't around. It was always just his mom and brother. They'd divorced a long time ago. He was a drunk I think, or maybe drugs. He told me one time he'd gotten better. Clean, new job and all, but I don't know. But I think they were sort of reconciling, maybe? Or at least trying to?"

"I never knew," I said. "I never asked. A week?"

"At least."

"Bummer. Well, at least I'll get to catch up on school work."

"There's that."

"So why weren't you around last night?" I asked, shifting topic to something hopefully more upbeat. "Problems with the little lady?"

"Maybe," he said unexpectedly and suddenly I felt the nosy shit for asking.

"Seriously?"

"No, it wasn't anything major. Wedding stuff. Everybody has arguments, right?"

"It's coming up fast, isn't it?"

"It was, but there was a little bit of overwhelming going on there for a while. We decided to put it off till March."

"So you've still got plenty of time. No worries."

"Still, it's a bit much sometimes," he paused and drifted slightly, but then came back. "All the more reason you should come over tonight. Rebs went out to Tampa with friends for the rest of the week. Got the place to myself."

"What about Chaos? Think we should maybe do something?"

"What's to do?" he said. "He'll be fine. He's Spiderman. He always lands on his feet."

XI

Two weeks or so after his father passed away Chaos returned from his trip up north and called me as soon as he got back into town. I was out at class and was welcomed back home by a short, excited, and cryptic message on my answering machine.

"Come over," he said. "You're gonna shit yourself. Emerald Glenn off the John Young Parkway. Apartment 17B."

Confident in my continence, I changed into more comfortable pants anyway and consulted the phone book for the number to the place. The sultry sounding girl on the other end when I called spoke in hushed tones like a phone sex girl. I was half tempted to ask what she was wearing just for a laugh, but just asked for directions instead.

"3945 John Young Parkway," she oozed. "Just past the County Corrections Facility."

Just past the what?

Not knowing what to expect, but expecting it to be extraordinary nonetheless, as it was with everything Chaos did, I headed over.

The extravagant stone and bepalmed signage complete with bubbling pond and flowing waterfall indicated Emerald Glenn Apartments was off my left and when I turned in I was greeted by a guard house, gate and an overweight bespectacled security guard in powder blue shirt, bearing a clipboard and a serious "I'm practically a cop so no funny business or I'll have to call the real cops" look.

The rent-a-cop asked my business and I gave Chaos' name and apartment number. He ducked into his little guard shack fort for a second and made a phone call while I waited patiently and looked at the two large iron gates barring the road ahead. A green Jaguar driven by a leather skinned middle aged blonde with big sunglasses and incredible tan rolled quietly passed as I waited and the gates magically parted at her approach. After a few seconds the guard hung up and waved me through.

The gates parted automatically and I followed a little winding road lined with thick evergreens and clean white signage directing me to the left, then to the right and finally up to a parking spot next to a huge pool surrounded by a wrought iron fence and beautiful, bikini clad co-eds tanning behind dark glasses; faces to the sky, white sun sparkle glaring off their lenses and the shimmering of sweat glistening off their thighs. Music, The Red Hot Chili Peppers, was playing out from someone's stereo sitting next to an empty lounger. I nuzzled my little red Honda in between a spotless Mercedes and a brand new jet-black Firebird with all the trimmings. The lot was full of BMWs, Lincolns, and Lexus. High end cars for high end living. My hatchback was totally out of place.

Chaos waved me up from a second floor balcony overlooking the pool. He was practically bursting with anticipation when I asked what was up, who we were visiting at such nice digs. Neither of us knew anybody who lived in as swank a place as this.

"We do now!" he said with glee and led me back to apartment 17B. He opened the door to an immaculate one-bedroom pad, brand spanking new, fresh construction, never lived in before; huge kitchen, vaulted ceiling, a living room bigger than my bedroom and a bedroom bigger than my living room, double vanity in the bathroom with Roman tub and Jacuzzi jets. His things, mostly clothes and CDs packed in various liquor boxes, shopping bags and milk crates, were strewn about everywhere. There was fresh beer in the fridge and a half empty box of Cheerios on the counter. Mixed in with it all were bags and bags of new clothes as well, many with high end logos like Armani and Hugo Boss.

"Dig it," he announced and strode into the center of the room, arms outstretched, glorying in his magnificent step up. "Welcome to Casa de Chaos. A.k.a the Pussy Palace."

"What is all this?" I asked, not really believing it all. "How?"

"My father. He left me a boat load of money. Almost $200,000!"

"No!"

"Yep dude. I didn't believe it either," he said, his face full of joy. "But it was in his will. A payout from his life insurance."

"Cash?"

"Mostly. Got it last week."

"What are you gonna do?"

"I put most of it in the bank, but I figured I needed some new clothes, right? And I wasn't about to keep my new duds in that hole me and Chris had, so I figured I needed a new place to keep 'em in. And check this out."

"Where's Jasper?" I asked as Chaos practically sprinted past me and back out the door again.

"I let him go!" his voice echoed through the tunnel as he ran down the stairs three at a time and skidded to a stop before leaning smug and content on the hood of the smoking black Firebird parked next to me, striking a casual, arms folded "I'm the man" pose.

"Check it out my man!" he said almost exploding with joy.

"No! Holy shit!"

The car was incredible, like a huge sleek midnight torpedo glistening in the Florida sun: big wheels, shimmering chrome rims, gun metal interior, raised hood scoop, tinted T-tops and an unbelievable sound system, 12-CD changer in the trunk and audio controls on the steering wheel, all state of the art. The thing fucking screamed cool.

"I call it Kit. Dig it!"

He hopped in and told me to go to the hood. With the turn of a key a digital red light lit up in the Ram Air hood scoop and started chasing back and forth, just like in the TV show.

"How awesome is that, right?" he said jumping out and joining me at the front of the car. Together we just stared, mesmerized by the racing red light like two infants who were seeing balloons for the first time. It felt like we were standing in the shadow of greatness, living out a childhood fantasy. It was like a dream come true.

"Dude," I said. "You're the fucking Knight Rider."

"I know."

"Dude, you're my hero."

His face spread into a grin wider than ever and that welcomed all the adulation and reverence I had for him and could possibly give at that moment. He had ascended to the rank of almost a mythical being, impossibly great. First the clothes and endless supply of women. Then the incredible apartment. And now this. I was mystified by his luck and his life. Then his eyes flashed and his mind was suddenly seized by a new and fantastic idea.

"Come on. We've got lots to do. Time to take the town."

Back in the apartment I sat on the folding beach chair from the old bedroom amongst Chaos' chaos while my friend was busy in his new bathroom fixing his hair before a huge double mirror and vanity.

The living room and dining room were one large area and a half wall with granite countertop partitioned the kitchen from these. The single bedroom sat off this area near the front door and an l-shaped bathroom with two doors accessed both the bedroom and the living room. A glass door off the dining area led out to a screened in corner balcony that overlooked the back of the development where new construction was still underway. Beyond this, across a field maybe a thousand yards long, was a barbed wire chain link fence marking the outermost perimeter of the corrections facility.

"It's a little close to the jail, don't you think?" I asked.

"Yeah, but what can you do? I wanted this place the second I saw it. Besides, they're putting up more buildings. You won't be able to see it from here anyway."

"Seeing isn't exactly the thing I was concerned about," I said quietly calculating the uneasy distance in my mind. "But it's certainly an upgrade, albeit a little sparse."

"Furniture's coming tomorrow I think. Black leather everything. Gonna be awesome. Can't wait for you to see the table and chairs I got. And a huge fucking TV and surround sound."

"That should certainly bring in the ladies."

"For $1200 a month it ought to. Christ!"

I nearly swallowed my tongue. $1200 a month! I couldn't fathom having that much money at my disposal. It was incredible the amount of money he'd spent on it. But it paled in comparison when he'd told me that he'd bought the car in one lump cash payment. $40,000. In a little over two weeks with the car, clothes and deposit on the apartment he'd already blown through almost $50,000. He still had over $100,000 tied up in the bank with plans to invest, but seriously.

"Maybe you ought to think about slowing down for a second. Take stock of what you've got and what you could really do with it?"

"No time," he said emerging from the bathroom, hair a wild tussle and freshly dyed black. He wore brand new Doc Martens and black stovepipe jeans. And the shirt, a shimmering, glittering blood red vinyl number that gleamed with the collar opened two buttons to show off his tanned chest and thick silver beaded necklace. He was a man transformed. He wasn't my poor friend anymore. He'd become a rock star.

"Well then," I said, resigning myself to fate and all the possibilities that awaited us and this new, grander existence. "Your chariot awaits my Lord."

"We're off then," he said.

"Where to?"

"The future, my lad. The future."

XII

The Firebird was a ferocious ride. It hugged the ground like a go-cart and once inside you got the feeling from the enveloping seats that the thing was almost swallowing you up in a huge leather lined mouth. With the tinted windows up and t-tops on, the interior was cavernous. The massive engine slept like a lion, but when Chaos turned the key and gassed the thing it roared to life like some giant mythical sea monster arching up from out of the hoary depths to terrorize villages on a distant shore. And when he put it in gear, it didn't go. It launched.

At every red light Chaos gunned it, played with the clutch and let the car growl and buck like a stallion trying to break free its reins and when they turned green we lurched ahead of the pack of cars in a great heave that left everyone in the tire screeching dust. The Firebird was more than just a mere machine, it was an extension of Chaos' massive personality. They were symbiotic. They'd needed each other, and neither knew it. Neither had been complete until they had found the other.

Now we were cruising up Semoran Blvd. under yellowed street lamps and a gibbous moon shining bright in a clear night sky. A ten-speaker sound system was blaring White Zombie's *More Human Than Human* and it was all I could do to keep my teeth from cracking apart.

"Where we headed?" I shouted. The tops were off and the windows down and the wind was howling past as we cut the night like a knife. "Risqué? Gold Club?"

"Someplace new," he said with a smile. "I'm thinking we've been spending too much time in those holes. What I'm in the mood for is someplace more refined. A place with some class. I'm thinking Velvet."

I shrugged. It didn't matter to me where we went so long as we just kept it all going. Chaos stepped on the gas and like a shimmering black bullet we shot off into the night and the ladies that awaited us there.

We pulled into the lot at Velvet, the newer and, so I'd heard, higher class cousin of the eponymous Velvet Room. Velvet Room was located on South Orange Blossom Trail, or just OBT to the locals. OBT was not a place you wanted to be, even in the daytime. Its anagram was synonymous with drugs, disease, crime and generally individuals of low standards in every sense of the word. It was also home to most of the city's strip bars, so it will come as no surprise that I had never ventured down there. At least, that is, until I'd met Chaos.

In the weeks after that first night out at Club Risqué, there'd been a steady stream of seedy joints ventured to in the wee hours of the night. Places with ridiculous names like the Go Go House and Pink Kitty, and an all black club called Destiny's that we'd stumbled into mad drunk and gotten laughed right out of. We'd been up and down the trail at least a dozen times. I ate into my food money, and Chaos, well he always somehow managed to find a few bucks here and there. Cheap beers and cigarettes, sticky table and dirty girls.

But the worm had turned, and with newfound riches came opportunity beyond Chaos' wildest imaginings. This night his eyes were on an establishment of much higher caliber. And Velvet brought that and more. We rumbled up slow and a tuxedoed valet took the keys and a folded ten spot from Chaos' casual fingers and rolled Kit off with a low growl. Two more tuxedoed gents barred the door; one bald with a neck tattoo creeping up from under his white collar and the other with a chest like a submarine door. The music driving from inside flooded out into the parking lot.

"Can't say I've even been to a place like this before," I said marveling at its clean exterior.

"It's a sight better than most of the dumps in this town," Chaos said. "Worlds better than that hole where Jessica works at."

"Where's she been anyway?"

"I dunno. I haven't talked to her in weeks. Besides I've got the cash now and she was trash anyway." Another Chaotic relationship out the window with a disinterested shrug.

"Well there're other fish in the sea."

"You can keep the fish. I'm just out for some new pussy."

"Nothing makes you forget old pussy like new pussy," I pointed out.

"Wise. Hey, who told you that?"

"You did."

"Oh yeah, right. Ha!"

Inside the first stop was the ATM where Chaos pulled out $600.

"Here," he said, counting off two hundred and stuffing it in my shirt pocket. I wanted to protest, but he was off before I could say anything. I just followed him in.

For as high class as Velvet was advertised to be, with its clean, stuccoed exterior, besuited doormen and valet attendants, I was not that much surprised to find that it exuded just as much sleaze and prurience as all the rest of the places we'd found ourselves in, proving definitively to me once and for all that strip clubs truly rest at the bottom of the world. And it was fantastic.

The place was dark, mirror lined and reeked of cigarette smoke. Leather booths lined the walls and black table tops dotted the aisles surrounding the stage. There were two bars that I could see, each one servicing one half of the place. An awful carpet, red with a nauseating black and gold angular pattern running slant wise across it, a casino carpet, covered the floor. The stage, shaped like a penis (intentionally?) with a long shaft and bulbous rounded head stuck out into the middle of the room and was lined with a low brass railing where patrons could rest their chins and keep their hands off. Velvet, as Chaos educated me, like every other strip joint in the area, was on a strictly "no touch" policy (at least that's how it was on its public face, conforming to the ridiculous laws of Christian conservative American society). But I would find out later there are always ways around a law. And though billed as a topless bar, Velvet was in Orange County and so according to ordinance the girls had to wear pasties and thongs.

"One day we'll go out to Nep's," he said once. "That's a *real* place."

Neptune's, or Nep's for short, was a true, fully nude bar out in Tampa where the cover was pricey, the drinks pricier, and the dances well worth the extra dough. Rumor was that you could even touch the girls there.

I followed Chaos to an open table beside the stage and ordered two beers from a scantily clad waitress in black miniskirt and nylon top.

Up on the platform a leggy brunette was doing her thing. Three poles stood strategically placed along the runway and she used them all. The DJ drove her and the rest of us on with Ratt's *Round And Round* blaring from every speaker. After many more trips to many more strip bars with Chaos, some glorious, others real dives, I would formulate a theory that the standard music fare that worked best for strippers were 80's hair and heavy metal bands. How many nights I lost brain cells and myself in the legs of beautiful girls all to the lyrical stylings of Poison, Van Halen, and Motley Crue.

And surrounding us in that house of flesh sat the lecherous, the deviant, and the lonely. Fat old businessmen in cheap suits and short ties, their guts bulging over their belts, balding salesmen and off the clock security guards drinking to forget their labors and lousy home lives. There were a few groups, guys you could see were out of the office and out for a good time with each other, but for the most part, people were alone. Sad forgotten men, depleted of purpose, waiting in the endless purgatorial night for a sunrise that would never come again. Save for Chaos and me, and the girls of course, no one looked under forty in the whole place. Our beers arrived.

"I'm really sorry about your dad," I said.

"Thanks. He wasn't a particularly good father, but he wasn't a bad guy really. He was trying, toward the end there at least. My mom couldn't forgive him though, but I understand that."

"He cared enough to set you up with all this."

"That he did." He paused in brief reflection. It was one of maybe only a half dozen moments of genuine seriousness I'd ever witness him have. For just the briefest few seconds the movie stopped. "A toast!"

We raised our beers.

"To my father," he said sincerely.

"To your father," I echoed.

"And to money," he added. "And to new cars. And good friends. And new pussy."

"To new pussy!" we sung in unison and drank deeply from the bottomless bottles of good fortune.

"It doesn't get any better than this, does it?" I asked.

"I believe it does."

Around the room, interspersed with the crowd of forgotten souls of the night were the ladies of the evening. At least eight at first count, they were giving table dances for $20 a song. Some were sitting next to guys, chatting them up, listening with mock interest about their dead end jobs or their dreadful lives, all the while buttering them up with smiles and coos and emptying their pockets with every dance.

"Pick one," Chaos instructed.

Blondes, brunettes, pale, tanned to perfection. Smooth skin, long flowing hair, high heels, sequins and thongs. And breasts. Perky, full, and heaving. Velvet didn't invest much in their décor, but they certainly knew talent when they saw it. Most of them fakes to be sure, but enticing nonetheless.

"Not gonna find a set like those on Eden," he said pointing out a pair of 38DDs attached to a freckle-chested redhead sitting at the bar.

"That's fine," I said waving it off. "Hers are real. Who needs fakes? Hers are perfect."

Still, it couldn't be denied that it was hard to keep the ethereal dream of Eden's beauty fixed in my mind when there was so much bare ass around. Eden was a vision, but this was tangible.

These were the picture girls a guy like me could only look at from afar; the unattainable ones. The ones that wouldn't give me the time of day if they'd met me on the street. And here they were for the buying. There were white girls, black girls, Latin and Asian girls. A veritable smorgasbord of ass. I reasoned that these frequent journeys into the seedy night with Chaos were mere stumbling blocks along the road to paradise; hiccups, mortal failings. Tests. Tests of my morality. All journeys require trials of faith and devotion. Job had his boils. Jonah had his whale. I had silicone.

Then she caught my eye. Split impossibly high and dirty blonde. She wore a glittering baby blue slit dress with matching heels and sat cross-legged next to some loser, a short butt lazing between her long fingers.

"That one," I pointed. Chaos acknowledged my selection with cool raised eyebrows and lit a Newport with a newly purchased silver Zippo. No more plastic Bics for this man, no sir.

"And that one for me," he said eyeing a redhead with short hair slinking over to the bar.

Def Lepard started up and as Ratt faded away and I saw my blonde get up and start over toward us.

"Twenty for the dance and ten for the tip." Chaos advised. "You tip her good and she'll hang around."

Suddenly she was upon our table in all her tanned glory and stood between us gazing down with dark, heavily painted eyes.

"Hiya guys," she said, her voice as sultry as her appearance. "You look lonely. Want some company?"

"By all means," Chaos said pushing out a chair with his foot.

"What're your names?"

Chaos gave them then offered Lexi, that was her name, a cigarette.

"So what're two good looking guys like you doing in here?"

"Me thinks the lady doth flatter," I said trying to be witty.

"What?" she asked.

"What he means is, thanks for the compliment. We are two good-looking guys aren't we Dave?"

"I would say so," I said.

"We're here because it's my buddy Dave's birthday," he lied.

So far it had been my birthday seven times this month alone. At this rate I estimated I'd be dead by 2005.

"Really? Well, would the birthday boy like a dance?" Lexi purred.

"Oh I think he does. And it's on me."

Lexi stood before me smiling and with one flick of a delicate finger undid the latch behind her neck holding her dress together and it fell to the floor in a pile at my feet. She gently muscled my knees apart and with the same bewitching finger pulled the elastic of her thong over her hip and I slipped a twenty underneath. At almost the same time the redhead from the bar came over and introduced herself to Chaos. I think she said her name was Kari, but I wasn't sure. I was too busy.

Ten seconds into Lexi's gyrations and I was battling a raging hard-on. I was zoned in on her thighs, even when she was leaning over me, pendulous breasts dangling perilously close to my cheeks. Her legs were fuller, more muscular than most of the others I'd seen and it was because of Lexi that I decided, right then and there, that I was, always had been, and will forever be, a leg man. She sensed that and worked her dance anew, straddling my legs and sitting on my lap to grind her crotch into mine. I know she must have felt it through my jeans but she worked it nonetheless. With one hand around the back of my head and the other planted on her hip I saw she had deep blue eyes, and with them she looked into mine, hazel and red rimmed from smoke and drink and the evil thoughts she was stirring in my brain and sought to draw them out. That's when I figured her for an Aryan witch sent there to suck my soul away and make me like the others in that lost place. I fought her spells and incantations off until the end of the song, determined in my mind and strengthened with the knowledge that if I could defeat this temptress, and any other for that matter, that the love I felt for Eden was sound and strong and true.

A poem came to me. I scrawled it on the back of a cocktail napkin.

Old devils haunting my midnight
Dancing veils and flashing skin
Will your beauty and grace
Rescue me from this sin?

That First Fight

We opened the windows and turned up the volume on the stereo, because all endeavors of the foolish heart require themselves to be set to music, and our evenings of destruction would be no different. It was all part of a grander plan that we'd concocted for ourselves, mystical in nature, primal in act and carried out with abandon that can only be willed by men with eyes and minds with a much larger sense of consequence. What was being done had to be done. There was a force greater than both of us commanding that we bleed together to seal the bond of our friendship.

The weapons had been purchased earlier in the day; two swords fashioned of ash, painted black, and carved after the style of their samurai forbearers. A time and place had been selected, and at the appointed hour we set out.

The stars were out in all their shimmering glory, pinpoints of light arched in an endless dome overhead, not a cloud in the sky, as if they'd come out and lined up to watch, a captive audience. We'd selected the roof of the campus parking garage for our first confrontation. It was lit well enough and isolated, guaranteeing us the privacy we were seeking. We knew we'd be misunderstood, that the sight of two people willingly beating each other for mutual pleasure and whimsy would be condemned as some sort of blasphemy against the prim and proper ideals of Judeo-Christian society. "This is civilization," they'd say. "There's no place for that type of behavior here; man is not an animal, his body is a temple, not a house of pain." But they're wrong. The body is indeed a house of pain, a storehouse of lost memory and forgotten dreams. It's where we keep our deepest, innermost fears and insecurities. It's where I preserved the images of Eden, and where I retreated to every night, wondering why it was that I loved her so. But no matter how deeply I turned my thoughts inward, I could not place it. Was it her eyes? Her smile? No, these are purely physical attributes. Beauty is not concrete; it's abstraction, forever changing as the body ages and decays. We see in each other only that which we want to see, and appearance is no different. No, my love for her ran deeper than the superficial markings of eyelashes and lipstick. It was her very nature, the essence of her, her mere existence that I loved, and these are not things easily explained by reason and mortal words. And as is true with all great loves, and now, in hindsight and with the knowledge that comes only with age and time, I admit I still don't know, and probably never will.

But I only knew it was on nights like these, when I spent hours plumbing the depths of my soul for the answer as to why I loved her so much and came up empty, that the release I was looking for from the pain I brought on myself could only be remedied by breaking my skin and crushing my bones. And in Chaos, I found a companion who was happy to oblige.

If love and some disillusioned (now in hindsight of course) belief that somehow my soul and hers were connected and that on these nights when the adrenaline was coursing through me and my body stood bent and broken, she was somehow watching me, and knew I was bleeding for her, that it was bringing me closer to her was the reason I picked up a sword, then Chaos' reasons were a mystery to me.

His enjoyment seemed to come from a purely adolescent joy at living out a childhood Robin Hood or King Arthur fantasy. He was my hero, so it would only seem fitting that he fashioned himself the hero of his own world; the swashbuckling Errol Flynn fighting off the scarred Sheriff and his minions. When he picked up his sword, his eyes leveled and the now familiar grin narrowed to a smirk and he was transported out of that barren parking lot rooftop to a high mountain cliffside, or the roof of the World Trade Center, or some other grand place fit for a duel to the death. For him, like in everything else he thrust himself into it was all about the rush.

And so under the grand expanse of the sky, in the quiet solitude of the early morning hours, witnessed by none but those whom we brought into our minds, we rolled up our sleeves, cranked up the music to shatter the silence, and beat each other senseless.

That first night it was a dance: him circling me, me circling him, round and round, the wooden death sticks clutched in our hands, eyes narrowed to the task, no breeze, deathly quiet save for the hum of a streetlight burning overhead. A high noon waltz at midnight. He struck first.

The sound was deafening, a crack of wood on wood that blasted out into the darkness, chest shivering, teeth chatteringly real. The peal of a lightning strike not created by some God, but right there, by two men. We knew we'd found our true calling. It was the beginning.

XIII

It's Sunday night and we're gearing up to head downtown after starting the evening at Chaos' new apartment. Deirdre suggested we try a club called Thebes. We've never been, but she has and says that Sunday nights they play retro British synthpop and the place is full of Goths, and she really wants to go again so we agree to check it out.

Now she's telling us to put on the radio because the DJ, a friend of hers, is also the DJ at the club and he starts off playing at eight o'clock for a show called Sunday Retrorlando. Chaos emerges from his sanctuary in front of the vanity mirror temporarily and grabs the remote for the stereo and tunes it in and turns it up. It's Joy Division and Ian Curtis drones out *Love Will Tear Us Apart* with solemn grace, while the keyboards float out long heaven organ chords over his head in rhythmic waves of synthesized ecstasy. I think of her.

"He hung himself you know," Deirdre puts in while we two just sit and listen and Chaos is back at the mirror perfecting his hair.

"You know I'd heard this song before but never knew who it was," I said, not knowing then, in the days before I'd met everyone, who half the artists were that I'd heard a million times over on the radio or in the movies. After a few minutes Ian gave way to The Psychedelic Furs, then Bronski Beat and Lords of the New Church.

"What time does it open?" Chaos is calling from the bathroom. He's selecting cologne for the evening. In the weeks after getting the new pad his vanity has become a crime scene of dripping shampoo bottles, gooey mousses, shaving cream, vitamins, and multicolored vials of cologne. He finally selected a red liquid labeled "Joop."

The furniture arrived weeks ago and true to his word, it was all big black leather couches, a huge entertainment center with 50" TV, surround sound, the works. The dining room table was a glass top number with wrought iron frame and matching high back chairs in the gothic style. He got a new computer, stereo, and camcorder. The bedroom was crowned with a king sized bed complete with heavy wooden head and footboards that he'd strung chains from so the whole works looked like a medieval drawbridge. There was a $1,000 Chinese tapestry covering one wall in the dining room that he'd bought one blurry afternoon while we were Drinking Around The World at Epcot Center (wine in France, tequila in Mexico, sake in Japan, you get the picture). The Pussy Palace was nearly completed. There was a life sized cut out of Spiderman standing in the corner. The finishing touch was a screeching blue macaw he'd named Romeo perched in a man sized cage out on the balcony.

Money brought material bliss, objects to amass and surround himself with. But it brought much more than that; it brought untold adoration of the female persuasion. It always struck me as mathematically curious that Chaos' increased wealth coincided paradoxically with an increase in cheaper and cheaper women. Not that the ones he'd had before his inheritance were any of significant substance or standard, but the ones that followed certainly lowered the bar. There were buxom air-headed party girls picked up with a smile and flash of cash in bars all over the city (and a few in others). There were strippers (it is, after all in their nature to be bought), so many that I lost track of them all, sometimes two at a time, though not physically, that is to say simultaneously together, the elusive threesome still eluding even the craftiest of craftsmen. No, for Chaos it was Kelly on Fridays and Saturdays, Michelle on Wednesdays, and so on. There was a Hooters girl who didn't even know who the president was let alone that she was just being used as a sex toy, the butt of endless jokes when she wasn't around. But none of that bothered my friend, not in the least. With money came an endless stream of ass, and nobody was turning off the tap anytime soon.

"I hope you're protecting yourself," Deirdre would say all matronly, not that she cared. "Now be honest. What's with all these sluts? Tell me you're being safe?"

He would giggle and shout.

"Of course! Well if by safe you mean yanking it out and shooting all over her back, then yeah, we're safe. Oh, and I never give them my real name."

It's where he lived. Always on a knife's edge of disaster.

"You're a pig."

"Last week I told someone my name was Templeton Peck. You know, from the A-Team? Faceman?"

"Dirk Benedict," I said.

"Ohhh that's a good one too."

"No. That was his . . . never mind." She gave up. "Idiot."

"So wait, you don't use condoms?" I asked. Not that I really cared to know the answer.

"Never. I prefer the Nikon method. Point and shoot."

"That'd make a cool superhero name if it wasn't already a camera," Deirdre said.

"What exactly does 'Joop' mean?" I asked as he emerged ready for whatever. "I mean, what language is it anyway?"

"It's Spanish," he said definitively. "It means 'you'."

"What kinda bullshit is that? It doesn't mean that."

"Sure it does. I bought it last week and then picked up this Rican chick and when I tried to stick it in her ass she screamed and said 'joop etter not do dat! Ha! Good times in the poop shoot."

"You mean Joop shoot."

"You idiots finished?" Deirdre asked. "Are we gonna go or what?"

"All right, all right don't cream yourself," Chaos said. "But actually, go ahead if you want to. It's a leather couch."

"And which one of you boys is gonna help me with that?"

"Why not both," he said playfully. "I'll take the back, Dave you take the front. Finger cuffs!"

"All right, let's do this," she said.

"Oh hey, look at the time," Chaos said looking at his bare wrist. "Can we take a rain check?"

"Hey we should call Eden and see if she wants to go," I said.

"Go ahead. Sage already said he'd meet us there."

"Could you do it?" I asked Deirdre. "If I do it it'll sound all awkward and fucked up."

"Sure thing baby," she said and went to the bedroom.

"You know you're gonna have to tell Eden at some point," Chaos said after she left. "It's been months."

"I know. I'm working up to it ok? I don't want to come off like a total ass to her, you know?"

"Oh totally. Eden's a fox."

"She's perfect. But it's more than that." I confessed.

"If you want I can put in a word for you tonight. You know, talk you up and everything."

"No. Don't say anything. Wait. No."

"She'll be there later," Deirdre said emerging from the other room. "Let's blow."

In the car and we're breezing past traffic on a glistening highway. It's just finished raining and the air is thick, humid, but clean, and hangs heavy, but at eighty miles an hour shooting up the interstate we don't really notice anymore. Wisps of rising steam from the asphalt dance at the edges of the roadway and through the glass roof of the car the sky is a patchwork of purple clouds with holes punched through where faint watery stars are peeking in. Chaos and I are listening to The Smiths to keep the vinyl feel of the evening going. Deirdre brought her own car and is following behind, but falling back as Chaos puts the pedal down, but she's all right with it. One ride in the Firebird with him was all she needed to know she didn't trust him with her life.

"I mean what do you think of her?" I'm suddenly asking of Eden from out of the blue of my own revolving thoughts. Big mouth did what exactly, Mr. Morrissey?

"Who?"

"Eden?"

"I don't know. I never really looked at her like that," Chaos shrugged.

"But you said she's a fox?"

"I was just fuckin' with you. I know you're after it. I'm not really interested in her in that way. We're just friends. We went to high school together, so."

"I didn't know that."

"You didn't know?" He was genuinely surprised. No sarcasm. This changes everything.

"No." Then the thought strikes me and I practically stop breathing. "You guys never?"

"No. Never. I mean I thought about it once years ago, but we were just friends."

"And now?" I asked hesitantly.

"We're still friends."

"No, I mean now?"

"Oh, no way dude," he said with severity. "I wouldn't think of it. I know how you feel about her. I'd never do that to my best friend."

A brief silence settles on us and Morrissey fills the gap telling William how it was really nothing. That was the first time Chaos called *me* his best friend.

"It's just," I start, suddenly losing where I was going and ending abortively.

"You don't have to explain it to me," he says reassuringly. "I know."

"She's perfect, you know?" I start again, foolishly redundant. Bumbling. She does that to me. "I've never met someone as perfect as her. She's smart, funny and principled. And beautiful. I mean I look in her eyes and I just forget everything else. She's just beautiful."

"She is definitely hot," he adds supportively the only way he knows how. "And she likes you. You can tell. You could totally drill her."

"But that's just it. I don't want to 'drill her'. I want to be with her. There's a difference."

"You love her."

"I love her."

There it was, out in the open. I'm not sure I had actually said it out loud up to that point. Thought it, sure, even wrote it down, but never said the words.

"You think she's interested in me?"

"Sure. She always smiles when you come out with us. She always comes over and talks to you at work, doesn't she. I know Eden. She's shy as hell. Think she'd do all that if she wasn't interested?"

"Yeah, but I keep thinking those are just friend things."

"No way dude. Chicks don't make guy friends unless they want something more with them."

"This is true," I concurred. Chaos may have been a womanizer and a man-whore, but all those nights with random women did pay off in a wide breadth of knowledge about the female of the species. It was insight that I completely lacked, as evidenced by my past failed relationships. "But she's got that douche Jamie."

"Fuck him. You're totally the better man."

"So you say."

"I met him once. The guy's a complete ball sack, surfer jack off."

"No shit?"

I couldn't picture a girl like Eden with a surfer. My head instantly filled with images of some tanned, ripped, long-haired jock type in knee length bathing suit and shoulder blade tattoo with a diving board in his pants. I found out some time later, when we finally did meet face to face, that I wasn't all that far off.

"We all went out one time. This was before you started working at the Shaft. He spent all night drinking with two of his douche friends and Eden just wound up standing there talking to me most of the night. He didn't even care. It was like she wasn't even there. I think they were fighting or something or maybe he was just being a drunk cunt. She wanted to go like twenty minutes after we got there, but he drove so she wound up staying for like three hours. And he got drunk and loud and shit and embarrassed her. She had to drive his drunk ass home."

"Is he our age?" I asked.

"No he's older. Like twenty six or something."

"Big guy?"

"Kinda. Tall and pretty ripped. But I bet you could take him."

"I might need help."

"You know I got your back bro. Just name time and place and we'll fuck beach boy up good. OBT ghetto style."

"Think she'd ever ditch him?"

"I think she's looking for an excuse. If the right guy came along. And that guy is you, so you better get in there before some other dickhead does."

"I'm working on it."

"Tick tock my friend." We roared into the night.

XIV

If music is a religion, then Thebes was its church. A wild joint, a cathedral of synthpop that Goths and squares alike came to worship at on the evening of God's day, when all was dark and the altar was crowded sometimes three deep with drunken penitents and sticky with spilled vodka; the pulpit tended by an invisible DJ wildcat who drenched all in attendance with drippy retro grooves and nostalgia for a decade passed never to come around again. Sunday Retrorlando.

It was only fitting that *Under The Milky Way Tonight* was playing when I arrived that first night. The Church for the church. It makes me laugh now when I look back on those first visits to what was to become one of my many second homes to think that I grew up with all that fantastic music but never once heard; it forever being just background radio noise proving no distraction to other childhood concentrations like playing manhunt in the woods around my hometown on sunny Saturday afternoons or building Lego towers on the floor of my bedroom.

But from the moment I stepped into that place that first night my perceptions of the past and the future would be forever changed. It's always a gift to find music that genuinely speaks to you that you can take for your own and use as a measure of what your life means. The Church bled into Talk Talk. *It's My Life*. And I stood there near the entrance way taking it all in and listening to the keyboard strike harmonic chords like the pipes of a great old organ high above the nave and I realized I must have heard that song a thousand times in my adolescence but I never once listened. It was a great rebirth I had that night.

Thebes was just one big room, with a large dance floor centered under a roof three stories up. Iron girders and metal catwalks framed the perimeter of the second story and were always closed off Sunday nights (other nights the second floor and roof top were accessible for a reggae room and hip hop rooftop but who cares because Sunday nights was where it was at and the other six nights could go fuck themselves). A large three-faced bar sat at the front of the place when you first walked in and in the far corner of the room was a high platform, only accessible by ladder, where the DJ worked his magic. The walls were generally bare save for a few randomly splattered Egyptian markings and hieroglyphs painted in broad black strokes. One wall was colored blood red and the cracked floor was cold concrete sealed smooth and glossy.

There was a professor out on the dance floor: a young intellectual, deep, reader of Faust, reflective, self important dressed head to toe in black, with thick rimmed glasses, smooth complexion and bushy pompadour raised above his short forehead. A gothic Buddy Holly in cloggy Doc Martens and studded wrist bands, head down, arms swinging, dancing a slow rocking skank to the retro asexual bars of Robert Smith leading The Cure down another bleak, hopeless journey to the abandoned depths of the human soul.

And with him the disinterested, waifish object of his disaffected affections, a pale, vampiric shell of a girl; sad, hollow eyes behind long black waves streaked with blue, with a look that seemed to beg anyone who was caught by it to please bring an end to its misplacement and suffering in this uncaring, misunderstanding world. A spaghetti strapped scarlet dress hung loosely from her shoulders and stopped just short of being illegally high on her hips, hiding small, perky, almost adolescent breasts that she probably lamented in private. Clumsy black military boots laced tight from her ankles to her knees and adorned with all manner of safety pins and razor blades kept her feet rooted to the spot as she swayed lazy and bored.

And we danced. I don't want to at first, but Deirdre is pulling me out onto the floor and the DJ is suddenly spinning The Pet Shop Boys covering Elvis covering Willie Nelson covering Brenda Lee's *Always On My Mind* and the beat is infectious and I find myself moving, actually dancing, not caring at all what I look like or who sees me because Deirdre doesn't judge, never has. And all around, the Goths, waiting in the wings; they've moved off now, because this tune is too upbeat, to happy, and you can't cut yourself to it and who cares if the world is going to end and we're all going to die and you're never going to be understood anyway. It can't be autumn forever. Theirs is the music of fall, when the sky is gray over the hills and the leaves are orange and red and gloomy clouds float like great whales overhead and it's in the woods, with dry sticks snapping underfoot and your cold foggy breath steams out of your open mouth, shoulders hunched and neck wrapped in blood red scarf, lonely, lost in the mythical autumn forest watching for the wolves. Why is it so cold?

Now they're all huddled away for the moment, cast in the shadows, waiting for their turn to return and bring the pain back with them. But not now. Now is our time, and I look and here comes Eden dancing toward us; blue jeans and black tee and a smile. It's the first time I've ever seen her (she's a self professed non dancer, perpetual stander on the side like myself), but seeing Deirdre and I out there, caution to the wind, she gave in and gave up herself to the music, and for those four minutes the place belonged only to us. Deirdre'd requested it (she always had a soft spot for the Boys, and now, since that night, so do I, and to this day cannot hear them without thinking of that moment), and she kicked her feet out and bopped her shoulders and hips and moved to the rhythm and she was so at home with it all.

Sage arrived and Chaos just watched from the bar, talking and sipping drinks, but then Deirdre waved them over and Sage shook his head, but Chaos got the spirit and he put his drink down and sashayed out, head thrown back, eyes wild and teeth flashing in a clownish grin and everyone looking and questioning why someone who looked so together should be acting so silly, but he didn't care. He leveled his eyes at Deirdre, serious, and then broke out in a wild dance, seductive, rigid, sharp, and reached for the ceiling and pulled it back down running his hand over his chest and down his belly, snaking like a pole dancer all around her, syncing the words perfectly, and it was hilarious and we laughed like fools because who really cared. Even Sage laughed, but still from a safe distance.

The Boys bled into MCL *New York* and suddenly it was dark again and the Goths started moving back in from the wings like zombies, crowding us and the lights flashed, strobes popped and it was industrial and heavy and I thought the place went almost pitch black. Chaos was down below Deirdre, bent backwards crabwalk style flashing in the white black darkness, one hand planted on the floor, the other bent behind his head and he was thrusting his pelvis up at her in a dirty vinyl scene and she threw her head back and wailed and we laughed and I noticed a small circle opening around us of people who didn't want us there because we apparently weren't taking all the darkness and gloom seriously enough.

But it all returned and the night cranked on; The Clash, Erasure, Souxie and the Banshees, Cult, Ministry, The Cure (again), Peter Murphy and Depeche Mode. Gloom and doom. Sturm und Drang and it was all there was and we danced to it, felt it pulse through our veins, drank, and ran about, here, there, hey! Back out on the dance floor, then back to the bar for a shot and then right back out on the floor again.

I found myself dancing with just Eden once, mastered undoubtedly by Chaos, who was there one minute, gone the next and I wasn't sure what to do but she just looked at me with leveled eyes, like the eyes Chaos had flashed Deirdre and moved right at me and I got scared and stepped back, nearly tripped, but she just laughed. Flashes of flirting under pulsing strobes, and I was loving it and was sure I had her.

"You were in a dream I had the other night," she said when we were just talking beside the bar, a respite from the swaying dance floor, Tim Booth singing, but more complaining how she only comes when she's on top, and I wondered briefly if that were true.

"Oh? And do you see me in your dreams often?"

"I was in my room, only it wasn't my room, it looked different, but it was still my room, you know? Anyway, I was supposed to be studying for some sort of test or something, and I heard a noise outside and I went to the window and you were standing there with a sword in your hand."

"What kind of sword was it? Did I say anything?"

"No, you just stood there for a minute, then you said 'the pumpkins are at gas station and that you ate one' or something like that."

"What?"

"I know. It was completely off the wall."

"Did I say anything else?"

"No, after you said that you walked away into the woods and I turned around and walked out and that's when I saw it wasn't my room, but a room on a house boat, which was really weird since you'd just walked into the woods."

"That is really fucked up Cole, I just want you to know that."

"No it's not!"

"Yeah, it is. It's the sign of a sick mind. I read that once," I pushed.

"You are so full of shit."

"And pumpkin apparently. And you never told me what kind of sword it was."

"I don't know, just a sword."

"Well was it straight or curved? What color was it? What was I wearing? What were you wearing? I need details woman."

"You're the expert. Use your imagination."

I wanted to say if I'd used my imagination then she would have been naked in that dream, but I restrained myself. I reached to put my beer down and my sleeve rode up my arm and that's when she saw the enormous bruise I'd been trying to hide all night.

"Oh my God, what happened to you?" she said and grabbed at my wrist to get a better look.

"Like it?" I winced. "I'm thinking of getting a matching one on the other arm. Nature abhors asymmetry you know."

"Seriously, did you get into a fight?"

I told her about how Chaos and I had taken to pummeling each other as of late in the middle of the night and told her she should come out one night and watch us fight. This, of course, would be in direct violation of our unwritten rule about witnesses, but I was confident he would let this one slide. I told her all about the late nights, the wooden swords we'd gotten, bleeding in the rain, the music, all of it. She just listened wide eyed, like I was some sort of lunatic, but it was easy to see she was more intrigued than disgusted.

"Why would you do that to each other?" she asked with mock (or was it genuine?) horror.

"Why not?"

"Well, broken bones for one, moron."

"Bones heal. Cuts heal," I was trying to sound tough. It was stupid. "It's fun. A great release. Almost as good as sex."

"Maybe for someone who isn't getting any."

"Seriously, you should come with us one time," I said. "I think you'd like it."

"I'm not going to sit there and watch him beat the crap out of you."

"I win sometimes," I said defensively. "Just not last night. It's fun, I'm telling you. Besides, it's healing. It's already turned colors once." I showed her, poking at the discolored mass and she cringed. "See, it's getting better."

"You're such a boy Stone."

"But I'm trying real hard to become a man though."

74

Chaos came by just then and Eden grabbed him by the arm.

"What did you do to him?" she shouted over the music like a mother scolding a child with scraped knees and a rip in a new pair of pants.

"Him who? Who's there? What the hell's going on here? Where am I? Who am I?"

"Freud would say you're just a version of the incestuous relationship between your id and your ego," I said. "Basically they fuck while your superego sits and watches and jerks off."

"You know Dave, I think your problem is you jerk off too much," he said.

"Actually I think my problem is that I don't do it enough."

"This," Eden said grabbing my arm and showing him the bruise. "Did you break my David."

"He had it coming," he said. "He wouldn't stroke my parrot." We both laughed.

"Listen. Stop breaking my David."

"*Your* David?" he said. "He was my David first. If you want him you're going to have to share custody. Talk to my attorney. He's from the firm of Gaag and Baalz. Heh . . . heh . . . firm."

"If I may," I interjected. "Chaos, I like you. But if she wants full custody, it would be best if I just went with her. I'd really rather be hers anyway." Then to Eden, "My lower half works fine, really. No bruises or anything."

"I'm going to get a drink," she said. "You two idiots want anything?"

"I'll take a beer," I said.

"I'll take a Purple Hooter and slice of cheese cake," he said.

"Cheese cake is good," I concurred.

"Cheese cake is da bomb."

Eden just shook her head at us two fools and left us babbling on about cheesecake and acting goofy and being children.

"You heard it," I said proudly. "She said 'her Dave'. There's no mistaking that."

"You're wearin' her down," he said. "You're in like Flynn."

I watched her at the bar and wanted her more than ever, but knew it wasn't going to be then. That if I truly deserved her, I was just going to have to wait a little longer. Chaos sensed this.

"You feelin' it tonight?" he asked. "I picked up a spare sword to keep in the trunk with your name on it."

XV

I lay in awake in bed, staring at the slated parallel lines of alternating light and dark cutting long ways across the ceiling of my room from the ill placed street lamp in the parking lot, trying to collect my thoughts around her so that I might, maybe this night, have her visit me in my sleeping dreams and not just my waking ones like she usually did.

It was quiet save for the low distant rumble of thunder lumbering its way across the peninsula from the warm Gulf waters, riding on the back of teary clouds circling ominously overhead, looking for a good place to release the burden of their pent up deluge. The phone rang, shattering the silence. It was the Sage.

"You awake?" was all he said, his voice low, grim, like calling from a distant grave. I looked at the clock. Just past midnight. I could hear the drunk in his voice. He was the only one who called at this hour.

He'd quit the Shaft weeks ago, no reason. Just disappeared. I hadn't seen him in days. Something was amiss, had been for a while, but he'd kept it to himself, withdrawn, turned in. He'd stopped coming to Thebes, and became more difficult to reach. The mood was his own, distant and gloomy, but nothing too out of the ordinary. He was always the brooding one. I never asked. It was who he was, who I was. It was in our nature.

"Come over and have a drink," he said.

"I guess."

"Bring your stick."

He hung up abruptly and I knew then he was finally ready to talk.

I threw back the sheet and pulled on my jeans, then thinking better of it and the coming rain, grabbed an old cruddy ink stained pair from the bowels of my closet and put them on instead. There would probably be blood, and mud, and what all else would come, and I had absolutely no money for new clothes but still had to look approachable and respectable for work and class. My "stick" as he liked to call it, stood in the corner, blade down, with the tip standing in my empty boot and two leather gloves wrapped around the handle waiting to be filled.

Outside the puffy aubergine ceiling was low, moving fast from west to east, and thick humid air was moist with the anticipation of rain. The musty smell of moss and sadness. I threw my sword in the trunk, popped in a CD, and raced across the city to a heady, driving metal beat to get my blood up and steel my nerves, the headlights pointed for downtown and the unknown fate that there awaited me once again.

Twenty minutes later I rolled the car up the dirt and gravel driveway of the little two bedroom house Sage and Rebecca rented in Eola Park. It was a quaint ranch-style home, built in the 60s probably, with no front yard, but a reasonable space out back, surrounded by an old gray and broken stockade fence on three sides, crawling with overgrown brush and vines, broad palm leaves lolling over the top from the trees beyond. There was a disused aluminum garden shed rusting in the far corner. It was perfectly secluded from the street, but that didn't stop his neighbor Ronnie from calling the police on us the first night we fought there (him hearing the smacking of our blades in the wee hours of the morning and convinced of our sole purpose to keep him awake). The Sage was already sitting outside, legs hanging loosely from the open bed of his black pick up. He averted his eyes from my headlights and I could see the half empty fifth of Jack beside him and a waiting glass.

The Sage was shirtless, his pale chest curved in slightly, and the early inklings of a paunch that would probably haunt him later in life hiding behind a thin layer of blondish hair. His head was shaved, accenting Aryan eyes, sharp chin, and the twelve silver rings that decorated either ear. Around his neck he wore a chain of large wooden prayer balls that hung nearly to his navel, but while seated nearly touched his knees. A deception. He was no man of God. His lower half was clad in a pair of green cargo pants cut off just below the knees, ripped threads dangling over boney shins, his feet bare and caked with the black earth.

"Drink," he said more than asked as he poured a finger of the rotgut into a glass and thrust it at me, spilling some over his fingers, before taking a slug from the bottle himself. A rumble of thunder chased across the sky and I could already hear the faint *tick plip plup* of the first drops of rain falling on the leaves. He wore a determined, intent stare, and had I not already seen it once or twice before it would have made me think he'd invited me there to murder me. But fear of death and lonesomeness and the emptiness of an unknown world beyond this one was what held us together in the here and now. It was a welcome apprehension that clothed me and him in its cold embrace, one that enveloped and penetrated us, chasing down the burning liquid numbness required to help pass nights such as these, when thoughts of her and the distance between us swirled in my unsettled mind.

So under bleak skies, awash in near pitch darkness and the steady unforgiving cold rain, we raged against each other; he shirtless and streaked with mud, and I bleeding from a rip in the skin of my forearm and with what was almost certainly a fractured ring finger. At one point while temporarily distracted and in the process of getting back to my feet after being knocked down for now a third time, I lost complete sight of the Sage and found myself standing alone amidst the driving downpour. We'd been at it for nearly two hours and I, exhausted and still bleeding, stood panting, the fire in my finger racing up the back of my hand into my arm, looking about through the thick sheets of grey rain for him. But like a mist, or a single tear in the rain, he'd disappeared into the night, and it was at that moment that I felt the fear grip me tightest of all.

I steadied my feet and raised my weapon before me, circling slowly in place trying to spy him, there behind the shed, now there maybe, beside the tree. Faint was creeping up on me, from the sides of my eyes. A rising in my gut was forced back down with repeated swallows. My shoulders ached. I was done for.

A scream. Like Johnny Reb charging up Little Round Top for one last go at glory, he came flying at me from a corner shadow. Now flashing flesh, first low, then high, he bobbed and leapt into the air. His sword, high over his head and the beads around his neck floating aqua in the morning air, came crashing down on top of me ready to split my skull. I raised my stick to counter and we met in the middle, he forcing me to one knee as the reverberating shock of our two swords meeting rippled through my arms and chest, penetrating the night like a bullet. I tried to force him back, but in a swift move he shifted his weight and his blade swept down the length of mine to the guard before thrusting straight at me, the tip just catching me in the crook of the eye where it meets the nose. There was a flash of white followed by incredible pain and I rolled back into the wet gravel and dirt of the driveway, utterly defeated.

Over me the Sage, triumphant, panting open mouthed, sweat lost in the incessant rain drenching us both, muscles taut and eyes flashing fire, unrestrained energy and power. He extended a hand to help me back to my feet and I gladly took it. It was over. Quietly, solemnly, he led me inside and welcomed me once again into his home and I, with reverence, followed.

The Sage's living room was cavernous and museum-like, just like an old Cambridge professor's would be, dimly lit, with old, cracked hardwood floors that creaked when you set foot on them and stacks of old books, magazines and knick knacks piled practically floor to ceiling. Several of his own paintings adorned the vacant spaces of white walls, one of which consisted of a foggy, purple canvas with lines of his poetry scrawled in thin white paint. The hallway was dark and the bedroom door shut tight.

There was an easel standing on a white canvas tarp in the corner with his currently unfinished work. It was a grim sight of a man with tussled hair and dark eyes screaming, naked. His hands tore at his chest and split it wide open down to his groin like a book, revealing his bowels, which were spilling grey and purple onto the floor before him.

"I've seen this before," I said. "Inferno. The Malebolge."

"It's my interpretation. You've read?"

"Not really," I admitted. "I've just skimmed. I always have a problem with poetry, especially epics. This is good though. I mean you've really captured something here. Why this?"

The Sage fell into the puffy arms of his second-hand cracked leather couch with duct tape holding one of the arms together and reached for a glass, a solitary table lamp beside him bleaching his already pale skin, giving him a more distinguished air. His were features wizened by alcohol and late nights. The melancholy that filled him most in the wee hours of the morning was creeping in, inviting me to stay and commune with his old soul found trapped in his still youthful body.

"Sit. Drink."

I eased myself into an armchair across from him, our persons separated by a low, bare coffee table and dead fireplace. I looked around for a glass, and not seeing one just took a shallow slug off the bottle.

We sat like that for several minutes, clothed in near darkness. He turned to the lamp, staring at the brown liquid in his glass, examining it, studying it in the light while I prodded around the tender orbit of my eye. There was almost certainly a nice shiner forming, but I couldn't be bothered with getting up and looking. I could see, that was all that was important. The cut on my arm had stopped bleeding. Things were looking up.

"Sorry about the eye," he said absently.

I glanced around and decided to break the silence, and started off asking if Rebecca was home.

"Sleeping again," he said, still far away, annoyed, like 3 a.m. was meant for things other than rest. I was glad for it. Chaos told me once she was almost certainly cheating on him, but he could never prove it, so he thought it best to keep his ideas to himself. Looking back, it wouldn't have surprised me in the least if it was he she had cheated on him with.

Sitting there, watching Sage shirtless and reflective, I feel now, as I did then, an extreme feeling of respect for him. He was truly an old soul. Wise beyond his years, silent, monkish, a misplaced figure from Renaissance Europe; artist, poet, diviner of great secrets and small truths, his ice blue eyes evoked memories of the cold stare of Marx or Napoleon captured in photo or canvas. Mesmerized now by the stirrings in his glass as he rotated it slowly beneath the light—first this way, then that—you got the feeling he could see time, actually *see* time. And it bored him immensely.

"What do you know of love, Dave?" he suddenly asked quietly, his eyes still focused on the glass.

"I know I've never been in it. Really in it. At least not until now. Until Eden. I thought I was once, but," I stopped, not knowing where to go with my thoughts.

"Have you ever felt love?" he continued, apropos of my answer. "And I don't mean familial love, or anything like that. A priori notions of nurture and nature. Meaningless. I mean love from a woman."

"I think I have."

"What did it feel like?" he said, now turning to me, half his face bathed in the light of the lamp, the other half cast in shadows.

"It was terrible."

"How so?"

"Well, don't get me wrong," I started. "In the beginning it was great."

"Kessa?"

"Yes."

"And then?"

"In the end it just hurt. And the worst part was I didn't know just how much it could until it was over. Then I realized how much it hurt her. I never thought it . . . what I mean to say is I thought that's what she wanted. To be apart, I mean."

"But she didn't?"

"In the end I think she did. I just believe that she didn't want to hurt me, but she couldn't bring herself to break it off. So she made it harder and harder until it was me who had to be the bad guy and call it all off. Blame transference I guess."

"And now?" he said leaning in. "How do you feel now?"

"Well that was almost a year ago. I've all but forgotten it."

He seemed satisfied with this answer and leaned back into the couch reflecting. The silence returned. I broke it again.

"Love is a funny thing I guess."

"No," he said almost angry. I was sorry I'd said it. "It's a most serious thing. It leads men to do all sorts of things, terrible and heroic."

Then he gazed off into the non-existent fire not burning in the fireplace, but one that I think maybe was burning so terribly bright in his own mind, and began reciting from the catalogue of his memory.

"There is no greater sorrow than to recall happiness in times of misery."

The hour had grown late. Sage and I sat in silence in his room for some time, sipping whiskey first, then wine, and now the bottles were nearly empty. He'd gone to the mantle and lit a couple of thick red candles then put out the lamp so now we reclined in the enveloping darkness and just found ourselves getting lost in the flicker of yellow flames casting strange shadows on the pale walls and our pale faces. Outside the rain was still falling, though lighter now, no longer the thick *thump athump* against the roof, but now just a swishing swog of background noise and rivers running down dark rippley windowpanes looking out on a deserted street at 4 a.m.

For a time our souls wandered in that dank purgatory, and that's what it really was. Purgatory. I looked at the painting of the ripped man on the easel and thought of Dante ascending the mountain, first with Virgil, then Statius. I was trying to guess which one my friend was when he cracked the quiet of our little journey with a question.

"How much longer do you think you can keep it up?"

"Keep what up?" I asked.

"Life."

"Stop talking nonsense."

"I'm serious. What's it all for? What are you living for right now Dave? What is your purpose?"

I thought a moment about school, my family, the future. But only one answer seemed to fit for me.

"Eden. My purpose is Eden. She's my sole reason for being."

"Love is neither reason nor purpose. It's not a means to an end."

"Not true," I protested. "I go to sleep thinking about her so she'll invade my dreams and make them sweet. I get out of bed in the morning hoping I'll see her so she can make the day better. No one else does that for me. I'd cross rivers of fire to be with her, I know I would. That's not just fluff talk. I'd fight off a thousand armies and a thousand more to protect her. She means that much to me. You can't say that's not love."

"I'm not saying it isn't," he said trying to assuage me. "What you feel about her is love, no doubt." Then he turned more grim. "But is that enough to sustain you? What if she were gone? Could you live without her?"

"Why are you asking me this?"

"I don't know. I've been thinking a lot lately about this kind of thing."

I thought about his question. What if she were gone?

"I don't know what I'd do," I said finally. "I'd leave I suppose. I'm here because she's here. I mean I have you and Chaos and Deirdre, but I don't know that's enough. Without her my purpose would be gone. There'd be no more reason to stay. I suppose I'd move on."

"I agree," he said solemnly. "There'd be no more reason for anything."

PART II

I

Getting closer now and the lights of the city night are looming large and larger still. Trees swoosh by in a blur, and up ahead our exit races toward us. Chaos grips the top of the wheel and rolls his knuckles like a race car driver pulling three g's in turn four on the final lap, and Brian Setzer is still wailing away with no indication of stopping. No signal, music banging and engine roaring, we cut across three lanes of traffic, slicing between cars like a bolt of lightning splitting the sky. This is Chaos' favorite part. We'd done it a thousand times before, and maybe will a thousand times more before we die. Striped white lines hugging the left tires, solid yellow on the right. Beside him the open highway and beside me a concrete sound barrier swoops in, but then backs off as we careen down the ramp at nearly eighty miles an hour. Then up ahead the curve.

If he's timed it right, green light, no cars, and nothing but open stretch of road to coast into town on. But if he's wrong, I shudder to think.

But around the curve we're alone and lo, the light is green. In fact all the lights are green, like a welcome runway, like they knew we were coming all along. Now Chaos returns the car to a more reasonable speed in these closed streets and we just cruise. The quiet lanes of South Street are mostly deserted tonight, as they always seemed to be when we come off the great 408 highway before we come downtown. The real action is still up ahead.

Crossing Orange Avenue I look up the spine of the city and see the throngs of people, the neon lights and the cruisers rolling off into infinity, and swinging the car into the big garage at the foot of the SunTrust Tower we punch the ticket and Chaos brings us through the gate, engine purring in low gear, not the least bit tired from the long run from the other side of town where he'd come to pick me up at my lonely apartment in the distant east. He lived for nights like these, when he'd come out to get me from all the way down south at his palatial pad only to fly us downtown and then back out east again sometimes to drop me off, or sometimes just back to his place to crash, ladies in tow (his apartment being only ten miles away instead of my *Dakar* twenty). It was a fiery triangle he blazed across the map, and a mission he was fulfilling, a role he played. Han Solo to my Luke Skywalker. "This was the car that made the 408 run in under twenty minutes."

Chaos bowls us up to the top of the garage, under peering stars, streetlamps and those impending towers that got my heart racing and my blood up and runs us quick into a spot in the far corner, away from the other cars.

"Security over efficiency," he says hopping out. "Don't want some no good motherfucker denting my baby." Then into his watch, "Kit, full security scan. Shields up!" The movie always goes on.

At the door to The Copper Club, the music is already pounding through the walls and glass, spilling out onto the street; syrupy nu acid jazz, smooth trip grooves, flute and bass oozing through the cracks. St. Germain and Herbie Mann blasting his flute. There are a few people ahead of us in line, but Chaos is undeterred, fingering his ID anxiously in one hand and looking out over the heads for anyone he might know.

"I don't see her," I say looking through the tinted windows trying to spot Eden, but it's no good. "She said she was coming."

"She'll be here," he says, and then Deirdre, black hair and long black fingernails is coming up the street and sneaks into line with us. "But if not, so what? Look at all the trim. There's plenty to go around. Doesn't necessarily have to be hers does it?"

"Yes it does," I say in all seriousness. "And it's not about laying her."

"Don't worry baby, she'll be here, I'm sure," Deirdre says.

But there's no use in explaining now, here in line on the street. The feelings I need to express are far greater than either of them could possibly understand. Suddenly it doesn't matter since we're up at the door and some huge Neanderthal is shining a pen light on my ID and giving me the once over before taping a paper strip around my wrist. It's a white and orange diamond pattern and totally clashes with my new red shirt.

Chaos makes a b-line for the first open space at the bar and Deirdre and I are trying to muscle our way around the dance floor to the far end, near the back, where it opens up a little and there's more space. Doing the non-intrusive shoulder tap with my left hand and trying to keep tabs on my wallet with my right, it's a full minute before I can get back there.

In the back corner, lounging in a high backed booth upholstered with blood-red velvet, stained in various places with spilt beer and whiskey and God knows what else, making it look like a piebald cow hide, is Sage. He's wearing an open necked collared shirt, blood red, with the top two buttons undone and two silver chains around his neck. The pendant dangling between the folds of the shirt is a crooked silver forefinger with a long sharp nail, a witch's finger. He is motionless, stoic, lost in tragic thought or grinding the gears of his drunken mind around some random phrase he read one time in Wilde or Byron, hidden behind black sunglasses, his legs loose before him, both arms draped at either side, one hand gripping a near empty glass of bourbon, the other a bent butt with ash an inch long depending. You'd have thought the life had left him right then and there if it weren't for the occasional effort he made to take a drag from his cig. He was like an old vampire sitting there, watching all the rest of us dancing and jumping, not caring about any of it because his immortal soul had seen it all before a thousand times over. He'd given up the simple, primal pursuit of women and the drama of friendship, settled down with a woman, and was now devoting himself to more universal thought. He sat beneath his own art hanging hook and nail on the old brick wall behind the booth; a fairly large canvas, maybe three foot by four, depicting a cacophony of thick grays and soupy reds crashing into one another at unsettling angles that practically shouted to its viewer to look away. He brightens somewhat at our approach, tilts his head up.

"Where's Chaos?" he asks.

"Getting drinks," Deirdre says. "Need another?"

Time slows down as a gorgeous brunette with unbelievably round shoulders and slinky wrists slithers by, almost gliding, disappearing into the bathroom.

"I hate to see that," he says.

"What's that?" I ask.

"A beautiful thing like that going into the can."

"Why?"

"Because if she's in there for a minute or two, then you know she's just adjusting makeup or taking a piss. But any more than five and she's droppin' a deuce and that just kills it for me."

"Jesus dude."

"You know we have to crap too," Deirdre says defensively.

Chaos comes through the crowd a moment later holding three beers. He and Sage welcome each other with a knowing nod.

"I got next," I shout over the music, but he doesn't hear me. We stand like that for only a few minutes, quietly surveying the scene. The brunette breezes past and the Sage lifts his eyebrows over his dark sunglasses and taps the glass of his watch. I shrug. Chaos misses it completely.

"I wouldn't kick her out of bed," I say.

"Not unless she didn't wipe really well," Chaos suddenly says. "But then again if there's enough Klingons hovering around Uranus there to give her the Dirty Sanchez, I say what the hell!" His cackle soars over the music. He's missed nothing. Typical. We move on.

More people are squeezing in across the room and the DJ is pushing everyone on the lower floor with Nightmares on Wax while Sage and I repose on the rail and Chaos is next to us making eyes with everything on two legs and dancing mutely with himself, one hand gripping a bottle, the other anxiously drumming against his thigh, pacing, stalking, waiting to make his move.

I head to the bar for another round. It's shoulder to shoulder, face to face, two deep at the near end, but I can see fewer people over by the front, so I snake up there in between muscley meatheads and their high-heeled skank dates. Being short does have its advantages, and I keep my 5' 7" low and soon I'm under an elbow and ponied up front row, creased twenty between my fingers trying to draw some attention from the lovely svelte bartenderess when a heavy body presses up against my back and some huge, bulging douche is trying to get in over me. I push back a little and square my shoulders, asserting by best Beta male and he does give a little, but not without a look down his long nose. Should have brought more game. When she does finally come down our way she's drawn more to my Jackson than his Hamilton. Bartenders are just like politicians. Presidents over secretaries any day of the week.

I'm ordering a beer when a voice shouts out from over my shoulder.

"And a vodka tonic!" I turn around and it's Eden trying to get closer but blocked by Hamilton's handler. She's trying to pass me a five but I wave it off casually and order her drink as well. Hamilton's pissed he's been seconded and even more so when he sees me walking off with Eden after getting her drink and tipping a fiver. Hottest girl in the bar and she's walking off with me. Stick that in your loin cloth and sit on it Crug!

"I'm glad you came," I said as Eden and I find a corner to stand in. It's quieter here because we're slightly behind the speakers. Loud talking instead of flat-out shouting. I see she's not dressed or made up for a long night out. She looks tired.

"I can't stay too long," she said over the din. "But I thought I'd come by and say hi. Thanks for the drink."

"Why not?" I asked, disappointed.

"I'm going to Chicago in the morning."

"Chicago? For how long?" A tinge of panic rose in my chest. Was she leaving for good?

"Just until Sunday," she said, much to my relief. "Visiting my sister. Need to get away for a few days."

"Things that bad that you need to tear yourself away from all this?" A girl tried to pass between us, head ducked, drink raised swishing inches from our noses.

"It's hard I admit, but . . ."

"Your sarcasm is noted, Cole. It's going in the book as soon as I get home."

"You're keeping a record?" she laughed.

"Absolutely. Every hint of sarcasm, every snide little remark."

"What?"

"Oh, you bet. It's all being catalogued for use at a later date."

"Interesting? You keep tabs on everything everyone ever says?"

"Nope, just you."

"I see. And that's not the least bit unusual." I licked the tip of my finger and ticked off a notch in the air.

"One more," I said. "It's exhausting really. I have men watching you twenty-four seven. The expense is enormous. And that's not even accounting for the psychological toll it's taking on some of them."

"Really?"

"Yes. It's tragic. Just last week Higgins, our top man in your closet, committed suicide. He'd been there for three months without so much as a bathroom break. I've been scrambling to find a substitute, but Higgins was a good agent, not easily replaced."

"I can see you've really thought this out Stone. Silly."

"Hey, you're the one who says I'm always being too serious. Besides, it's what I do. Or rather, I should say, it's what *we* do. But enough about my business. What's this about Chicago? I didn't know you had a sister there. Come to think of it, I didn't know you had a sister? I've really got to reprimand Johnson when I get back to the office."

"Let's keep Johnson out of this," she said.

"Oh he's not so bad," I said. "After a while he can start to grow on you."

"Yech," she groaned. "That was so lame."

"Hey, they can't all be gems."

"I expect nothing less than perfection from you, Stone."

"We'll get right on it. Now where were we? Oh yes, you were telling me how dreadfully much you're going to miss all this, especially me, while you're away." I was beginning to enjoy myself too much. Where was the edge of that pesky envelope anyway?

"I just don't know what I'll do in the mean time," she said.

"Count the minutes until we're reunited?"

"Maybe enjoy the city instead. I'm sleeping on her couch. She said she knows a couple of good bars to hang at. And she mentioned this one vegan place she always goes to she wants me to see."

"You should have a good time then."

"Hopefully. I've only been there once before, years ago. But it's a cool town. I thought about moving there last year. Laura said I could crash with her until I got on my feet."

"I hear it gets mighty cold there."

"Small price to pay to get out of O-Town."

"Is it really so bad?" I asked. "I've only been here a few years and I love it."

"It's easier for you. I've lived here all my life. I'm kind of over it."

"That's a shame. And Chicago is better?"

"I don't know. It was just a thought. I could go anywhere at this point."

"That could be trying on the men," I said. "You're going to have to give us advanced notice of any sudden relocation so we can get the proper surveillance equipment in place."

"Will do," she said giving me a two fingered salute. "And by the way, I never said you were too serious. You're too scary to say that to."

"Me scary? That's preposterous." Where was that coming from?

"See, that's what I mean. Throwing out big words like 'preposterous' and being all quiet all the time. You keep it all to yourself."

"We're talking now aren't we? And I think I'm getting much better about letting 'it' out, whatever 'it' is."

"And look how long that took," she laughed. "I swear when we first met I thought you were such an asshole."

"What? Why?"

"Why? You didn't even say hello to me for like two weeks."

"And look at us now, making merry," I pointed out. "You should be proud. You're the one who brought 'it' out of me. Congratulations."

"And now I can't get 'it' back in again."

"It doesn't want to go back in," I said. "It likes it here. It's thinking it's been wasting a lot of its time. And it's thinking it wants another beer."

"Would it be kind enough to get me another as well?" she leveled her eyes.

"It might be persuaded."

"You can't just be kind?"

"Of course I can. Don't you know me yet? For you my dear, I'll be anything."

I went to the bar and she headed for the restroom. When I got back Sage was leaning against the rail watching the crowd and fingering his lighter. He'd been standing behind me the whole time and heard everything.

She was just in T-shirt and blue jeans, but she was the prettiest girl in the whole damn place. He sipped a refreshed Jack and lit a fresh Marlboro.

"So," he said half expectantly, half already knowing the answer.

"I know. I'm working on it."

"You keep saying that. How long has it been? Time is not on your side."

"Why? What do you know?" I asked worriedly.

"Nothing. All this talk of wanting to leave. I just know that no woman waits forever. You need to act if you hope to make it."

"Patience is a virtue."

"I much prefer vice," he said, taking a drag. "I just don't want to see you get flattened by this."

"Whatever doesn't kill me . . ."

"Sometimes it's better to be dead my friend."

II

Wednesday is a day off for me and I spend it in typical fashion, driving out toward the center of town and visiting a bookstore or two. The solitude found in between the stacks is a soothing way to pass an afternoon, especially when the ringing in your ears is still as loud as the bells of Notre Dame. Chaos and I closed Copper after Eden left (Sage and Deirdre ducked out early too) and then we wandered up Orange Avenue for a little while, too antsy to sleep but too drunk to drive anywhere. He wanted to move on to Cloud Nine, an all night place where he knew the manager, but I talked him into just finding a quiet place to rest, and soon we found ourselves sitting on a low wall at the corner of Washington and Orange just watching people go by. Drunks, socialites and club-goers filing themselves back to their cars or up the street to the open sandwich carts for a late night bite, and sometimes bike cops circling around ominously. A paranoia had settled on me, as it often did when I drank, and I was scouting the passersby for signs of Eden, who'd maybe just made up that whole story about going to Chicago and had instead ditched me to go hang out with more interesting people. But the feeling passed quickly and replaced itself with a noxious, mind-spinning nausea, and in that state Chaos and I stumbled back to the garage, determined to get home anyway. I have no memory of getting up on the roof or of the ride back to my pad. Somewhere along the way I had thrown up. There was still evidence of it in the pocket of my shirt crumpled up in the closet.

But sleep, or the bleak abyss of unconsciousness, you decide what the difference is, was welcome and when I finally emerged, the hands on my watch nearing eleven thirty, I felt strangely satisfied with myself from the previous evening. I had accomplished what I set out to do and spent another evening with Eden. Her talk of wanting to leave still disturbed me, and I knew Sage was right and I would have to formulate some sort of new plan.

A shower and meager lunch of saltines and tuna fish and now it was coming up on one and I'm walking up the aisles of a mega bookstore looking for the next read when who do I see hovering around the sex and relationship shelves, the only publicly acceptable place to view porn in America, but Deirdre. She's gotten a haircut and dye this morning, and now it's in a bob style and it's gone from black to dark auburn. The curves frame her face perfectly and really is an improvement from the longer locks she'd been sporting as of late. As usual, she's in black, low neckline blouse accentuating large ivory breasts, knee-length skirt and sheer black stockings.

She's standing next to some bookish nerd in khakis who's perusing the titles and you can tell he's itching to say something to her, fidgeting first with his glasses, then his collar, trying to muster the courage to pick her up in this neutral, nonaggressive setting, with head down, eyes darting from books to breasts to books again. I hide away for a minute more watching it unfold, chuckling as khaki hesitantly moves ever closer to her, hiding his advance under the guise of selecting a book that's just in front of her. He smiles and excuses himself then lingers there a few seconds waiting for her to say something, but she doesn't, so he turns away shyly and opens the book. She's loving the torture, and that's when I make my move.

Standing at the end of the aisle I start to make obscene gestures with my fingers and pelvis, probably looking like a fornicating monkey, until she finally notices. She lights up at my presence and starts returning gestures in kind; sticking her tongue out seductively right next to khaki so that he has to turn to notice and thinks she's making eyes at him, but then he sees me, and flushed red he hurriedly lays the book back on the wrong shelf and scoots off.

"Aww, you scared him off," she says. "I was just about to jump him."

"And he was just your type too. Breathing."

"Will I never meet a nice boy like you?"

"It's for the best my dear," I said affecting my best British snoot. "You would have surely broken him. And I've really no time to help you bury another body."

We play like that, she the innocent girl and me the hoity aristocrat. It's our mutual escape. But soon it's down to serious business and in a flash we're sitting cross-legged in the aisle pulling book after book off the shelves to look at the pseudo porn and laugh at the ridiculous positions.

"Oh," she says eyeing a particularly tantalizing spine. "Herotica IV."

"I heard that wasn't as good as Herotica III. Very anticlimactic ending."

"There's a story in here titled Roman Holiday."

"I saw a movie of that once. Starred an Italian chick Vulvus Maximus."

"And who was the leading man?"

"Cocksus Hammersmith I believe."

"Cock sucks? Sounds like my kind of movie."

"Well, you know what they say. When in Bone . . ."

And it goes on like that between the two of us for another half an hour. We're like two big kids sneaking secret looks at our dad's porn stash in the basement. We laugh, draw looks of disdain from people who want to get down the aisle but can't seeing as how we've completely blocked the way and annexed this little corner of Barnes and Noble for our own dirty little party. No one objects, at least not openly, because prudish nature would never allow them to admit that all they really wanted to do was join in the fun.

"Who reads this stuff anyway? Seriously."

"Everything I know I learned from watching or reading porn," I said. "Proper technique is key."

"I could give a shit about technique. At this point all I'm looking for is a *key* to this rusty old lock," and she points to her crotch unladylike and I can hear the truth in her sarcasm.

Deirdre is in the middle of a dry spell. A three year dry spell. For some reason men, at least the kind she would want, don't seem to gravitate to her. It's most likely her size, and her age, which is sad because she's a great girl. Deirdre is the oldest of our little group, nearly twenty-eight, and hanging around with a bunch of drunken kids probably doesn't afford her many opportunities to meet nice guys in more peaceful settings. And in a world where appearance means so much and personality not so much, guys can't seem to look past her being a little on the heavy side. It's an issue that's plagued her since childhood, and in her late teens she turned to Goth to hide her embarrassment and anger. Ten years on she's still hiding there, behind black mascara and dark lipstick, nose rings and combat boots. She's killer funny and has a great mind, and in another life we two outsiders might have ended up together, but in this one we were destined to be good friends, nothing more.

Deirdre'd had it pretty hard. Her father left when she was very young and her mother was less than perfect. There was no abuse to speak of, but no real motivation or support either, which can be equally damning. Their relationship was less mother daughter and more woman child, but despite any shortfall of what most normal people would call love, she survived and persevered.

When she was twelve, Deirdre and her mother were in a car wreck that nearly killed the both of them. They were on their way home from dinner when their car was T-boned at an intersection and rolled end over end down an embankment before coming to rest beside a small creek. Deirdre was belted in but suffered several broken bones and major internal injuries that left her scarred all along her arms and abdomen. She lost a kidney and a chunk of her intestine. Her mother was thrown clear of the wreck, but not before losing an arm. This led to a deep seated depression that followed her the rest of her life. She developed multiple health problems and died young a few years later.

Since her mother's death, Deirdre's health had always been an issue for her. She'd needed multiple surgeries since the accident, and even now in her late twenties she's still having near recurring pain.

We sat on the floor there talking and joking for a long time and before either of us knew it the time had flown by and the sun was starting to cast that late afternoon pinkish orange tinge over everything. I suggested we ditch the bookstore and go get something to eat and maybe catch a movie. I was famished and my stomach was gurgling with that post-drinking, no food in hours, hollow-chested emptiness.

"Let's go down to Disney," she said. "Del Rios makes a really good lemon martini."

I offered to drive and soon we were off. The tenplex was showing *X-Men* and even though we'd both seen it already a few weeks before we decided to come back for the late showing. Deirdre was gushing about the dude they'd gotten to play Wolverine all the way to the door of the restaurant where a small crowd already stood waiting.

I gave my name as Baals to the hostess with as straight a face as I could muster, secretly hoping they'd call us as a party of two, while Deirdre giggled like a school girl behind my back. Sadly, they offered to seat us right away and she led us to a booth in the back where we indulged in the aforementioned lemon martinis (as good as she promised) and ate better than either of us had in a while, me grilled pork chops over cannellini and she shrimp and tortellini. There was bread and laughter and I talked of Eden, as usual, and Deirdre listened intently, at times offering womanly advice about my obsession, and at others pointing a critical finger at Chaos.

"What he does isn't love. It's not even close," she said.

"Well I know that," I said. "That's not the issue. What he does is his business. He's enjoying himself. Let him."

"It's offensive."

"Not really. I'll admit at times he can be a little over the top, but . . ."

"You can't see it because you're his friend."

"You are too," I said, trying to take the offensive.

"I know. But it's different with me. For one thing, I'm a woman."

"Deirdre, I'm shocked. Why haven't you told me this before?"

"I'm being serious."

"I know. I'm sorry."

"I'll forgive you this time," she smirked. "But see, that's what I mean. You do it too sometimes. The blow off. The mocking. It's rubbing off on you, and not in a good way. It's not you."

"I disagree," I protested. "I think this is me. I think it always has been. The humor I mean. The blasé. Not the other things. I couldn't do what he does, even if I had the opportunity."

"You're saying if you had women throwing themselves at you like he does every night you wouldn't take advantage of that?"

"I don't think so. There's something, I don't know. All the sex, it's just . . ."

"Empty," she stated matter of factly.

"I dunno. Maybe. I wouldn't call it that."

"I would. And it'll get him nothing but trouble and loneliness in the end. You're better than that. You recognize the things missing from all that. And that's something that makes you different."

"There are lots of people who think like that. It's not unique."

"Yeah, but you'd be surprised how hard it is to find them. That's why you need to talk to Eden. To show her what she's missing."

"Easier said than done," I said poking at a cream colored bean with the end of my fork.

"You need to get her alone," she said. "That's the problem. It's always a bunch of people. We're always together. You can't talk to her like that. You need to ask her out, just the two of you."

"Again, not so easy."

"Again, you'd be surprised. It's probably all she's wanting. One good guy. It's all any of us really want. Someone to share something with."

"I turn into an idiot around her," I admitted. "You've seen. All this time and you'd think I could figure it out. She doesn't want that."

"How do you know what she wants? She has to know you feel for her. She'd have to be blind not to."

"But there's Jamie."

"So what? You don't know what's going on there. She may be just waiting for you to finally say something, do something, come to her. You remember what you told me about you and Kessa? How do you know she's not going through the same thing with him right now?"

"I know," I sighed. "I want to say I'm the better man."

"Then just say it. You are. There. Done. Now you just have to show her."

By the time the bill came we were so full of pasta and chop and vodka that neither of us realized or cared how much it had all come to, we were having such a good time. We left the restaurant still talking love and sex all the way over to the theatre to buy two tickets for the nine o'clock show then walked to a Latin-themed restaurant across the way to get beers and kill a half hour before the movie. We drank Dos Equis and spoke in Spanish accents like fools and I yelled "Deirdre joo got some splainin' to do," and she took to calling me Raoul the Love Bunny for the remainder of the night.

We ran back across and got two prime seats (back row center, my favorite) for the movie and giggled in the darkness ignoring the over the shoulder, between the cracks in the seats looks and whispers from the people shot from below.

"I come a little every time those claws come out," she said when a shirtless Wolverine was flexing his might.

"That Rogue's a dirty little whore," I said and someone shushed us from up front because we were too drunk and giddy to realize how loud we were talking and I thought the manager would come and toss us out any minute.

But the high eventually wore off and we came down as the film ended so that by the time it was over and we'd staggered outside we were both pretty exhausted and Deirdre's gut began to hurt and she took to limping.

"Look, a wheelchair," I said as I spotted an unattended, unreturned rental wheelchair standing in an open parking space. It was in pretty decent shape and had working foot rests and a Mickey Mouse face printed on the back of the seat so I ran and got it and Deirdre sat down.

Halfway across the parking lot we were pretty alone and suddenly the evening fireworks display (a nightly ritual at Disney) started going off right over our heads. There were a bunch of spot lights swirling in the clouds from the roofs of the nightclubs nearby and whole thing looked like it was made for us. A couple of tourists walked toward us looking for their car and I ran around in front of Deirdre and starting shouting at her to get up.

"Rise! Rise my child and use those legs again. The Lord commandeth you. I say to the evil inside of you get out and let this child of the Lord walk again!" I was like a mad Pentecostal, flailing around spitting ice and monsters. "The demons will suffer you no more!" and all sorts of nonsense. Deirdre played along and shaking and struggling got up and started dancing around, praising God and miracles and the tourists just hurried by not wanting any trouble from two drunk crazies in a parking lot revival under fiery skies and smoke. The high returned and we danced like that, like two idiots with the spirit, all the way back to the car, her pain temporarily staved off by an injection of sudden lunacy. We were drunk on booze and life that night and for a while I forgot all about Eden and she lost the loneliness.

For some reason when we got to the car we took the wheelchair with us.

III

Weeks later. We were alone. We were talking. It was one of the moments I lived for.

"I just want to do something else with my life," she said fumbling with the words. "Go new places, see new things, meet new people."

She'd been troubled as of late, at least that's what I gathered. Concern and contemplation had furrowed her brow more and more. Thoughts of the future, clouded as they were, filled her nights, and more and more she'd been moving closer to me, questioning, seeking advice. I didn't know why she chose me, but I didn't care, if it meant I could participate in her life, even if the parts I played were sporadic and minor.

"There's nothing wrong with that," I said.

"I'm not saying there is. I'm just telling you what I want."

"See, I told you I'd get it out of you sooner or later. Only took months."

"I'm being serious," she said and looked at me with a glance that told me she most certainly was. Not angry, just determined.

"So? Go get it," I said.

"Yeah, because it's just that easy, right?"

"It is."

"Maybe for you. You've already done it."

"What's that?"

"Moved away from home. Lived away from home. I've never really been anywhere else but this town. Grew up here. Went to high school right down the street. And then Valencia. You, you're a thousand miles from home."

"And what meaningful thing does that tell you?" I said, seeing no real meaning in it myself. "I've not accomplished anything great."

"It says you're not afraid to go it alone. And you're getting a degree. That's an accomplishment."

"Says you. Besides, you've got yours too."

"Yeah, an associates. Big whoop. Great. I'm all set for a career in liberal arts, whatever the hell that means."

"It's nothing to turn your nose up at. Most people never even get that far. Besides, you can always go back for more." She threw her arms weakly out at her sides in a sign of resignation and desperation.

"That's just it. I don't want to go to school anymore. I want to get out of this place. I have to get out, you know? There's nothing keeping me here. I mean, I have my parents and all, but it's not like we've ever been really close. And this crummy job, and a useless A.A. It's all worthless. I feel like I've wasted my life."

"That's ridiculous," I looked for reassuring words. "You're only twenty-one, you've got brains, looks. You're smart and funny and that counts for something."

"Not much."

"Not so. A laugh and a smile will get you just about anywhere. The rest will take care of itself."

"I just want to travel," she said whimsically, fingering a soapstone figurine along a shelf. "Get out, see the world."

"Where would you go?"

"Anywhere. Like India. I've never been to India, and I've always wanted to see the Taj Mahal."

"Me too," I joined in.

"And Panama. And Africa. Everywhere. Anywhere! I don't know."

"So like I said. Go."

"How?"

"Save a little cash, buy a plane ticket, pack a bag, and go."

"And my car? My student loan? Credit cards?" she said.

"What about them? Sell the car, defer the loan."

"I can't just leave those things."

"Who says?"

"Um, real life? You can't just abandon everything in your life and start new someplace else, Dave."

"Sure you can. I did."

"You had help. Me? I don't. I couldn't go away alone. Not now. I mean, what about Jamie?"

"What about him?" The mention of his name hit the pit of my stomach like a shot putt.

"He loves it here. He wants us to get a place together."

"And I take it you don't want that?" I said hopefully.

"I would love to get out of my parent's house."

"But you don't want to move in with him?"

"No. And that's the problem."

"Does he know your feelings about it?"

"I've been avoiding the issue," she said.

"What about you wanting to travel? Is he into it?"

"I don't know."

"You should find out. It's a pretty big thing when you and the person you're with want different things." I knew now was the time to get a dig in. "Most things you can compromise on, but some things you can't, you know? If he wants to stay, but you want to go . . ."

"I know."

"Don't get stuck if you don't want to is all I'm saying. You have to follow your own path and dreams. If they take you away from here, then you have to go. You guys should talk about it."

"I know," she said, resigned. It was too much for her to contemplate all at once. "All right. I've done enough complaining. Probably driving you crazy."

I tipped the brim of an imaginary cap down and put on my best Bogart, sneering out the corner of my mouth.

"You can drive me crazy anytime doll face."

Eden clicked her tongue, winked and shot me a finger as she turned to go. I kept the Spade going.

"And if that Jamie fella doesn't want to go 'round the world with you, just give me a call sometime. I'll fly you to the moon, kid."

IV

The Dam was a little hole in the wall bar at the dead end of Wall Street just off Orange in the heart of the steamy night, humid downtown Orlando club scene. Normally it was cozy in an old basement Parisian jazz joint sort of way: high ceiling, blood-red walls hung with large canvases of reclining nudes in the Rubenesque style, two dirty beat up pool tables on one side, small bar manned by a ticked off brunette sucking a long, thin cig through tight disdainful lips on the other. In the back, a narrow doorway led to a secluded area with a few booths and the chipped black doors of the bathrooms beyond. Burgundy carpets stained with years of spilt beer were sticky underfoot and the paint on the walls bubbled and peeled. There were never more than maybe twenty people in the whole place on any given night. But this night was different. Deirdre had been talking about it for weeks.

"They're having a fetish show on Saturday," she'd told us one night at Chaos' apartment. "Whips, chains and leather. The works."

"Toys?" I asked.

"Probably."

"I'm in," Chaos said. "I'll be a vampire. We get to dress up, right? Check out these new fangs I just got." They fit over his eye teeth and looked the genuine article, slightly yellowed and not too obvious. "I'm getting new contacts too. Glow in the dark. Gonna be awesome. I'm gonna be one bad muthafuckin' vampire."

It would just be the three of us. Sage was incognito, had been for weeks. And Eden was with Nikki, a birthday party or some such, but I resolved to try not to let it get me down and to go and have a good time anyway, though I would have killed to see what type of outfit she'd have worn. To this day I still reflect on that lost opportunity.

So there we were, walking down the narrow alley of Wall and seeing a line of people waiting to get in dressed in all manner of wild get up; vinyl vampires and bestudded toe suckers. Goth girls with painted faces, thick mascara and fingerless velvet gloves up to their elbows. Shirtless guys, ripped and tanned, and one guy with tattoos on every inch of skin, from his bald head down to the small of his back. Pierced noses and eyebrows and ears and I'm sure more than a few labia.

"Haven't seen this many fishnets since me days at sea," Chaos announced and we shuffled our way along with the throngs of thongs, boots and studs. Deirdre fit right in. Even Chaos looked the part. He'd spiked his hair, dyed it electric blue for the occasion and went shirtless, swapping out his steel nipple bars for two glow in the dark rings. His contact eyes shone pale purple and the two fangs poked out from under his lips, like he'd just stepped out of an anime. Decked out in my usual Saturday night garb, plain jeans and collared brown shirt, I was the only one who looked like he didn't belong. And I told this to Chaos and he only looked at me and said not to worry, waving off my concern and making eyes with a cute Goth in pink bob wig standing a few bodies behind. I felt Deirdre slink her arm under mine and pull me toward her. She was already a little drunk and spoke heavy into my ear, her breath as warm as the night air.

"Don't worry, I'll protect you in there. Just don't show your neck to anyone. Or if you want I can bite you now and mark you for my own, then no one will bother you." I played along, admitting I was a little out of my element and letting her get close to me. She knew how I felt about Eden but she didn't care. I knew she wanted both of us, Chaos and I, and she didn't care which one it was or if it was both of us together, she was that hard up for it. The thought had crossed my mind more than once, just a fuck and nothing more, but I knew in the end it would destroy our friendship. She saw me torturing myself daily trying to make it with Eden and saw herself as my savior. Distance was necessary.

We flashed our IDs at the big gorilla at the door and he waved us in and immediately I knew I was definitely not in my element.

It seemed like there were a thousand people packed into that little joint, Paris now gone and annexed into a post modern German nightmare, and the sweat and pungent smell of PVC was overwhelming as we tried to muscle our way to the bar. Nine Inch Nails screamed from the speakers and we bobbed to the beat, a ridiculous three car train pushing through: Chaos with his blue spikes and glowing eyes and nipples like two great headlights in the lead, me ducked right behind him, and Deirdre with her hands on my shoulders bringing up the caboose. We passed an old couple, probably in their sixties going the other way; a leather-clad grandma leading her wrinkly, shirtless, grey husband by the neck with a chrome chain and silver-studded dog collar. There was a vinyl nurse in white with huge breasts administering shots of tequila to a couple of fags by the bar. A guy wearing what looked like a wetsuit and gas mask was casually standing in the corner. The pool tables had been covered and pushed to either side of the room and in between a low stage had been erected for a show. It was made up to look like an operating room, complete with curtains and bright white overhead lights. A surgeon in mask, gown, and leather apron was standing over the table while a little nurse, also in shiny vinyl, waited at the ready with a power drill. The patient was a buxom blonde in red fishnets, heels and short, short miniskirt. She was loosely tied to the table at the corners and writhed in mock terror, her luscious thighs covered in gooseflesh as the surgeon administered the treatment in the form of a six foot long Burmese python that slithered across her tanned body.

"This is great!" Deirdre shouted and squeezed my shoulders. Chaos edged his way to the bar and ordered three beers for us.

"Check out the wetsuit!" he smiled and caught the eye of the same cute Goth from the line. She smiled back and he tweaked one of his nipple rings and flicked his tongue over his fangs at her.

"I think she's diggin' on my digger."

"That's nothing," Deirdre said. "You should see his. Go on, show him."

I rolled my jaw and flopped my tongue out as far as I could, just to the point of my chin and curled it up. I'd always taken pride in its unnatural length and I would be remiss if I didn't say it had served me well in past relationships. I just wanted to show Eden.

"Jesus man!" Chaos shouted. "You should watch out or a Chinaman is gonna lop that thing off, wrap it in plastic, and sell it for five dolla a pound! I get six dolla American for tongue like that in Beijing. Feed whole family for month!" and Deirdre let fly with a wild cry over the music. She was at that place she loved best, surrounded by people just like her: misunderstood, misplaced, shunned. Now I understood why she loved Thebes so much. It was where she was home, a native in her own country.

"Now if I could only get a man with a thing like that to lick me all over I'd be happy for the rest of my life."

I stuck it out again and flicked it at her playfully and Chaos joined in kind. She mock blushed and turned away, then made a ravenous bite for it. We drank and laughed and the party went on and on and I wanted it to go on forever. It was a great time all around and as the night wore on I felt more and more settled in with those people. I felt like I could be one of them too, that my conventions had been all wrong all this time, and that I wasn't supposed to be the person that I had been becoming all these years. Chaos and Deirdre and Sage and Eden helped me realize that. Here were people who didn't care what anyone thought about them, the way they dressed or acted. They were surrounded on all sides by a like-minded crowd. There was no judgment or disdain or disgust in that room, only love of life and body and sex. No need for impressions, just open expressions. It was a change from the regular places we'd always been going too, even far removed from The Florida Room, and it was something I thought I could get used to.

At around one Deirdre left, complaining she had to be back to work at eight, but promising as always to meet us at Thebes the next night. I walked with her to the door to say good night and when I returned Chaos was maneuvering and chatting up a steamy blonde with blue eyes and tight red miniskirt. She was running her finger up the center of his bare six pack abs and he called me over to make a grandiose introduction.

"Liz, this is my best friend in the whole wide world David. Dave, this is Liz. She's a Pisces and enjoys long walks in the park, the color green, and dick."

"You're terrible!" she said and slapped him playfully on the chest. I knew immediately from the hazy look in her eyes she was pissed out of her tree. She could barely keep them open and made a horrible job of slurring her speech.

"I've been watching your friend here all night," she said to me through lidded eyes then whispered. "He thinks he's a vampire."

"That happens a lot," I said. "It's the earrings."

"Are you a vampire too?"

"Me?" I said, uninterested. "I'm a werewolf." I never liked talking to drunk women, especially stupid ones.

"We've got a place not too far," Chaos said winking at me behind her back. "You want to get out of here?"

I sensed where he was leading the train next, and knew it'd be time to get off soon.

A zooming car ride later and we're back at Chaos' apartment and there are five of us now. We stumbled in, the three of us, Chaos, Liz and I. I collapsed into the inviting folds of the big leather couch while Liz stretched out on the floor at my feet and Chaos went to the kitchen to fetch more beers.

"I'm hungry," Liz whines. She's been complaining ever since we left the club. In the car. In the parking lot. In the hallway. "Let's get a pizza." It was dreadfully unattractive, all that whining, and only added to the reality that Liz, for all her blonde beauty in the dim lights of The Dam, was actually not as beautiful in the bleak buggy white light of the parking lot. With a tight body and long legs she was not unattractive, but rather flawed in the natural way most people are and try desperately to hide. The skin of her forehead was oily, and the pores on her nose were probably bigger than they needed to be. And she was older than either of us had figured, thirty-five or thirty-six. In short, a skank.

"It's two a.m. babe," Chaos said handing me a bottle.

"So," she said with drunken petulance. "I'm hungry."

"We should have left her in the parking lot," I mumbled.

"I think there're some sunflower seeds still in Romeo's dish," he said. "You might have to fight him for them though."

"Where is he?" she said, completely out of it. Chaos was getting off on it.

"I don't know," he said. "You're pretty drunk and Romeo can be a tough motherfucker. Damn near pecked my balls off once when I tried to get him to perch on my cock! Where is that son of a bitch anyway?"

He went off to the balcony to bring the bird in, completely forgetting for the moment the drunken slut on the verge of a tizzy on his living room floor. It was typical Chaos flitting like a butterfly from one flower to another, one amusement to the next. A minute later he was back in from the veranda with the huge bird flapping its wings wildly in his hands.

"See, what'd I tell you," he shouted over the squawking and writhing. "This fucker's pissed."

There was a knock at the door then and Chaos tossed the bird on the armchair. Before he could get to it the door flew open and two guys strode in, all bravado and presence like my bird handling friend. They locked hands and pulled each other chest to chest in a ghetto greeting so ridiculously out of place in this suburban whiteness that all I could do was chuckle and tug at my beer. I think I felt Liz toying with my shoe laces like a little kitten at my feet and all I felt like doing was kicking her in the face.

Chaos set about organizing the introductions, which were interspersed with him shooting to the kitchen to grab more beers in between laughs and Romeo's hellish squawking. I got two names out of it, Jeff and Russell, and that they were neighbors from down the hall that Chaos had recently befriended. It was all perfect for him, as all three seemed to be cut from the same shiny vinyl yard.

Jeff was a short crew cut, but muscular: a solid Napoleon with a nose just slightly too long for his face, and big ears, but probably unnoticeable in bar light. Russell had a runner's physique: tall and thin, with a deep voice and sharp jaw line. He was also holding the squashed remains of a pizza box that, we soon smelled, contained the last remnants of their now several hours old bachelor's Saturday night pre-clubbing dinner, which endeared him to Liz almost immediately.

"Does that have banana peppers on it?" she asked springing to her feet and greedily snatching the box from Russ. "I'm so hungry."

The four of us watched as Liz, long Liz, lithe Liz, unzipped her red miniskirt and let it drop to the floor, and time stopped, revealing a simple pair of white panties coalescing at the little hump in the crook of her thighs. She absently kicked the rumpled skirt aside and folded her legs Indian style in the armchair, content to balance the box on her knees, bottomless, while she quietly, nonchalantly, devoured a floppy, greasy slice.

"Party's always at Chaos'," Jeff commented.

I was enthralled, like a buffalo had just inexplicably wandered in from the patio and sat down at the computer and began plunking away at the keys with big muddy hooves looking for a good place to get Vietnamese. Chaos just grinned. This was nothing out of the ordinary for him. Could it really be that easy?

More beer flowed and soon the last of the pizza was history. An hour later the box was now an open repository for empty bottles and Liz, back on the floor, still with only her blouse on, was back to slurring her words, laughing at nothing and telling us how "this was her shit" when Jeff popped in Eminem's new CD. She just started bopping foolishly from a half seated position at our feet. I was drunk on it all and content to just sit and watch, teetering precariously on the edge of a blackout when Liz exclaimed "it's too hot" and cast off her blouse and unsnapped her bra. Two good sized, but slightly pointed white breasts flopped out as it fell and suddenly things turned from seriously absurd to absurdly serious.

"Hey now," Chaos said from the couch. "That's not fair! You're almost completely nude and here I am with all my clothes still on."

"Then you should get naked too," she said playfully.

"I can't," he said, then looking to all of us for an audience, nudging me in the ribs with his elbow. "I've got this damned beer in my hand and no where to put it down."

"Here then," Liz said knee walking over to him and deftly undoing his fly. I watched, eyes hazy as she reached into his pants, pulled his cock out (Chaos often went commando he once told me) and began slobbering on it.

"Jesus," he cackled as we all looked on and she giggled, his head deep in the back of her throat. "About 102. Yep, she's definitely got a fever boys. Hey how about my friend here?"

Liz reached over to grab at my jeans but I stopped her.

"I'm fine," I said, but the sudden rush of adrenaline showered my brain with a hailstorm of pins and flashing purple and green blotches flooded into view from the edges of my sight as the room began to spin and a bell rung in my ears and everything just faded away.

I came to I don't know how much later. The CD was off. Romeo was gone. Chaos had moved to the loveseat and Liz was still on her knees sucking away at his dick. Jeff was shirtless behind her, on his knees, with his pants around his ankles, pounding away furiously at her cunt with what can only be described as a huge pecker. It was quite a moose cock he graced our presence with. Really impressive. And Liz was coming like wildfire, moaning and humming with delight and her lips wrapped around Chaos. Russell was sitting nearby getting a handy from one of Liz's free ones while she came again and he waited his turn, which wasn't far off, because Jeff was turning red from head to foot and soon let loose a roar as he pulled out and shot a massive load all over her bare ass and the floor. Liz hummed delightfully while Russell got up and took Jeff's place behind her, but instead of taking sloppy seconds he slipped on a rubber and aimed it straight for her asshole, which made her jump and pop the dick out of her mouth.

"No, no," she said halfheartedly.

"Yes, yes," they all said and Chaos put his hand on the back of her head and slipped his dick back in her mouth as Russell slid up her ass, and she just let him, consensual moans letting them know that's what she'd been wanting all along.

It was a mad orgy of the night, Dionysian in scope that dragged us all down into the sewer. I was disgusted with them all, and myself, but still sat and watched from the sides, never participating, like forcing myself to look on was a punishment I inflicted on myself. The repulsiveness of their insistence, and the vileness of her subjugation to them, three strangers, sickened me and I felt that I had to get out of there, but a weight sat in my belly and held me fast, not allowing me to leave, nor to look away.

Soon Russell was ready to explode and he gripped Liz's hips with white tipped fingers and dug his nails in as he shot up into her ass and collapsed to the rug behind her, arms outstretched like he were crucified, palms up, his face pointed to the fan blowing coolly the sex funk that hung in the air. It smelled of burning rubber, pizza and shit. I don't think she came again. She just sat panting, her head resting against the couch, her body quivering.

Chaos stayed on the couch a few minutes longer before silently getting to his feet. It wasn't the usual wide grin and fiery eyes he wore, but stoic lips and eyes half asleep. Bored, he surveyed the scene and retired to the bedroom, killing the stereo on the way. Jeff and Russell silently pulled on their pants and left. Romeo had made his way back to his perch. It was all ending. Liz sat on the floor and rubbed her eyes for a minute before getting up and following Chaos into the bedroom. She shut the door and I was all alone, the sole witness to the sexual mayhem that had taken place, and would not be spoken of between any of them again. In the morning Liz would leave quietly and never come back. We'd never see her again.

I felt surprisingly sober at that moment, clearheaded and wide eyed. It was four a.m. Quiet like the night, I got up and drove myself home.

∞

Trying real hard not to think about thinking. A rising retch in my stomach. Visceral. Sticky. Fingers gripping the top of the wheel, lights pointed east into the graying asphalt and the faint, faint, almost whisper of blue dawn on the horizon chasing the charcoal sky further into retreat. Four a.m. and no sun up yet, but still I can sense the coming rise of the sun again, almost feel its warm rays bathing my face, drying the tears creasing down my cheeks as I retreat, like the night, back to my hole.

The orgy made me ill and I vomited up like a waterfall, a virtual Angel Falls of sticky bilious filth on the side of the road a few miles back, and now I'm empty, much like Chaos.

I saw the hollowness of him, that empty meaninglessness that Deirdre tried to tell me about in my darkest moments of doubt, when I exalt him the most. The blank expression, joyless in the heat of it, when he's got a submissive cradled in the palm of his hand, bending to his every will and whim, devout even, just like all the rest. But he doesn't care, never has, never will. His heart is made of rocks, his liver black.

And what of Liz? What meaning is there in her existence? What purpose does such a woman serve? A common whore. Begging for it. Sex for her is just as empty, valueless enough that she would follow three complete strangers to the brink of humanity, trade it in for a collar, and put herself on display like an animal for a slice of pizza.

It's the publicness of it that turns my stomach. The seeing it. And now I'm a culpable witness in the destruction of a soul. Years from now, will she look back on this night and regret? Will she even remember the brief glance, the fleeting moment when our eyes met as I sat on the couch, drunk, helpless, paralyzed with fear and remorse and watched them defile her and she gasped with pleasure, almost enjoying it more because I was there, watching it all? Did she realize too late that she was in over her head? Did she even care she was dying, that we were literally killing her with our eyes?

Chaos didn't care, and that made him a murderer. My friend, the lady-killer.

V

And then one random Saturday night, Eden brought Jamie to The Florida Room.

He was tall, maybe not quite six foot, but taller than me at least, and that's all I needed to know. He was built too: thin frame under simple gray tee shirt, but clearly muscular, cut in the arms and neck, broad flat chest, with a mop top tussle of brown hair that hung over his ears and gray eyes, and a scruffy shag dog beard creeping up his neck and cheeks. He wore old faded jeans, frayed at the cuffs, and casual, dragging white threads of torn denim. Hippie pants that on anyone else would look degenerate and lazy, but on him said how much he didn't care about his appearance, he wasn't out to impress anyone, but didn't he just look the right amount of anti-establishment cool? Cool without trying. Aloof. Beach bum hip, surfer, drinker of Mexican beer (though we're a million miles from Mexico), listener of Zeppelin and Jim Morrison, reader of nothing more substantial than a picture book or maybe *Zen and the Art of Motorcycle Maintenance* (to him *The Three Musketeers* would be nothing more than a candy bar and *David Copperfield* just an overpaid magician), yet possessor of the one thing in the world I wanted more than anything else. The keeper of the key to the gates of paradise, and poster child for everything that I was not.

In short, the Zod to my Superman.

He stood mostly apart from the rest of us, Chaos, Deirdre and I, didn't speak to us either, and it all made me wonder why he'd even come. Eden seemed almost distracted by his presence. She hadn't invited him, that much I learned later. No, he'd come because he wanted to, knew she was coming and maybe got tired of not seeing her; her Saturday nights almost always taken up by coming out with us. Six weekends in a row, we were on a marathon run. When she danced or talked to me, he just hung back, an ever looming presence over her shoulder, taking the occasional swing of beer, eyes casually crossing the room and back again, indifferent, bored. He just swayed slightly with the music when the feeling struck him, but mainly he played it cool by the rail, hands in pockets or resting dully as he leaned over the dance floor, content to just watch it all in silence. Chaos tried to strike up with him, but the answers he got were short and depthless. It just wasn't his scene, and Jamie remembered him from the last time, that uncomfortable evening I'd been told about those many months ago, and wanted nothing to do with my friend. They were from different worlds. Dark, cavernous gaiety and late night cajoling with societal deviants was not his thing. But that wasn't his reason for being there anyway.

He was there to scope out the competition. He was there to see me. He'd had enough of sitting around his weekend nights, his girl out with her new crowd to all hours, the influence they seemed to have over her. He saw no threat in Chaos, handsome and charming as he was, too busy with flirtatious games and not caring or concerned with serious relationships. Sage was mostly a non-entity, not even present most nights and engaged to be married anyway. And certainly not any of the other men who frequented this haven of debauchery, by definition a population who wasn't playing for the home team. But me, I was different. The single one in the group, ever present, playing the waiting game. I was the friend with the waiting shoulder to cry on, the ever ready ear to be vented into: the sounding board, the comedian, voice of reason, giver of advice. I was the one she turned to when she couldn't turn to him. The one she'd mentioned to him in some random, off moment. The guy who said something that made her laugh, or the smart one who told her about such and such, something she'd always been interested in but never knew anyone else who was. The one who made her day just a little bit better by telling a funny story or regaling her with midnight exploits of getting beaten up with a wooden sword. In short, I was *that* guy.

All men know *that* guy. All men fear *that* guy. It's innate in us all, it's instinctual, an evolutionary holdover from a time before we came down from the trees, to recognize *that* guy. *That* guy is a thief, a table turner, a game changer, a sneaky son-of-a-bitch, who has nothing but time on his hands, pride on his side, an ego as big as Yankee Stadium, and usually, as was the case with me, an army of conspirators at the ready disposal to help depose the throne and crown a new king. *That* guy has power and is always a force to be reckoned with.

So we watched each other in some deathly serious high noon gloom. I went to the can; he tracked me out of the corner of his eye, nonchalant. He stepped up, whispered something to Eden, I scanned the room, my eye catching his as they moved. I offered to get her a beer when I went for one myself, he lit her cigarette. A simple game of chess. Move, counter move. It went on for hours. In the end it was a draw.

At one point the two of them disappeared. I looked all around, searched inside and out, casually though, uncaring, (I couldn't let him see the least bit of fear) as if my mind were on other things like getting more drinks, but I could not find her. Then as suddenly as she had vanished she reappeared, but only to tell me they were leaving.

"But it's early yet," I protested. "The show hasn't even started. Stay."

"This really isn't Jamie's thing. He's bored and wants to leave."

"So let him," Chaos piped up. My First Lieutenant. Old Reliable.

"I should really go with him."

"You should really stay here with us," I said.

"I drove us here."

"He can walk." Chaos again. "Or maybe he can surf home." Congratulations on your promotion, Major Chaos.

She waved goodbye and I could see she'd had enough and that our protesting was falling on deaf ears. She wanted to stay, but had to go. It was the power he had over her, or the weakness she grew within herself to bend her wants to his wishes. Had she stayed I could have declared victory, but in the end it wasn't a draw after all. The battle lost, the war still raged.

"Well this sucks," I said knowing I had finally seen my enemy and been bested. Chaos sensed it too. "Let's get out of here."

"Velvet?" he asked.

"Anywhere."

We left our undrunk beers on the rail and went out, leaving Deirdre behind.

∞

Valentine's Day. I'm at home alone, sitting on stuffy couch in quiet and lights out darkness, only rays coming in crooked and slant ways through the blinds like ripples of dune sands across the wall and part of ceiling from piss yellow streetlight outside.

There's an open pint of Jim Beam on the table, no glass, that I picked up on my way home from work. There I asked what she was doing for the occasion, and all she said was plans with him. Driving up to Daytona, dinner probably, bar afterwards maybe, and what was I doing? Nothing. Deirdre out of town and Chaos spending the night with his latest conquest. No Thebes, I'll probably just go home and relax. And home I did go.

But relaxation, calm of mind, eludes me in this empty room, Zen-like as I try to sit and forget. Time on the VCR just after midnight. She's bound to be there, wherever there is, with him by now. Does she want to be there? Is she thinking that it was a mistake? Is she thinking of me? Will she sleep with him tonight? Probably. The thought crushes me and I take a drink, a dribble of the brown liquid escaping my lips and dripping down my chin. I wipe it away with the back of my sticky wrist. I can feel a tear start to well up but I don't know if it's from the sadness or the burning in my chest. I know I won't sleep a wink tonight.

How can you relax when the woman you love is across town blowing her boyfriend?

VI

The morning after Valentine's, I ran into my ex Kessa at the grocery store shopping with her new boyfriend, my replacement, Stennis, whatever the fuck kind of name that is. I hadn't seen either of them for almost a year, not since the time I found out they'd been fucking in the apartment she and I were still sharing after we'd broken up and I threatened to throw him out the goddamn window if I ever found him in there again. Not two weeks officially not together and she's screwing this douche while I'm out at class. Probably a revenge fuck for something I did, but it's the principle goddamnit!

And there they were strolling arm and arm like the good happy couple discussing playfully the merits of chunky over creamy peanut butter when I tried to duck away before they noticed me, but Kessa saw and called me over. Stennis stood his ground next to her, standing taller than me, thinner and more intellectual looking with glasses and a fresh hair cut, whereas I, who'd been up most of the night drinking alone in the dark and sobbing, must have looked like death warmed over under the stark, unforgiving fluorescent lights in a sweat stained ball cap and third wear jeans. He asserted his dominance as best he could, inching ever slightly closer to her, and I took the hint and kept my distance when all I really wanted to do was grab a pickle jar, smash it against his skull, take a shard of the broken glass and carve out his fucking Adam's apple to make a present for her.

We exchanged the normal pleasantries, or at least as pleasantly awkward pleasantries as a situation like running into you ex and her new better man will allow. She started talking about graduating in a few months and told me how they were going to get a condo and stay near Orlando so Stennis could attend grad school and become a doctor or an astrophysicist or whatever someone named Stennis becomes. I wasn't listening. It was like she'd just forgotten how much she hurt me and wrenched my guts out, driving our relationship into the ground with her incessant depressive moods and turning me into some sort of villain of blame. I told her how Chaos and I had been getting a different girl practically every night, most of them strippers, and that I couldn't be happier having wild orgies and all night drinking binges and having sex with women who really knew what to do in bed. Actually I said none of those things, but just nodded quietly and said everything was fine with me.

There was another awkward moment of silence and a brief, halting discussion about the coming of midterms followed swiftly by an awkward goodbye as they turned their cart around to do more shopping and Stennis put his arm around her and I waited till they rounded the corner before storming out of the store having bought nothing.

In the car on the way back to my apartment I stopped at a traffic light, rolled up the windows and screamed at the top of my lungs so long and loud that I burned out my voice for the rest of the day.

VII

A month later. It's me, the Sage, Deirdre and some new blonde Chaos was screwing named Christy, lounging on the sofas and floor of Chaos' apartment while he's in the kitchen rifling around for something to eat, but there's nothing doing so he and I leave to go make a liquor and food run while the others try to console the Sage, who's sitting on the loveseat with dark sunglasses on not speaking.

Rebecca had left him. He'd come home from work a few days before and she was packing. There was a fight, screaming, broken glass, tears. She'd had enough of the starving artist and his troupe of useless juveniles. She wanted more, and told him she'd already found as much. He broke. And though in my head, and in Deirdre and Chaos' too, I know the secret tune of "ding dong the witch is dead" is playing, the Sage himself is crumbling. It's hard to see it through the cool, composed exterior, the normal self projected, but I could see it, and his call to us for *another* fifth of Jack as we walked out the door was an early indication of how the rest of the night was sure to go. He was already hammered when he'd arrived and there was no sign of stopping him. But who would? And by what right? We did the only thing friends could do at that moment. We obliged him.

The Sage had been there for me on countless nights when I was lonely and teary, cursing life and crying whys to the heavens, why wasn't it happening (Eden and me), where I was failing. Many times he sat quiet, Buddha-like, and almost Freudian even, listening intently to my ranting and trying to pick out a key thought or idea, usually about love or some abstract notion of destiny, nurturing it with me until it blossomed from just a random feeling into a meaningful epiphany that, sadly, never fully materialized. Other times he took up arms against me and we beat each other senseless venting mad caveman aggression and frustrated passion, ending those alcohol-fueled nights bloody, exhausted and somehow healed.

Now it was my turn to be the buddy to lean on and I started by refusing to let Chaos pay for the whiskey with money the Sage had thrown at him earlier. If my best friend was going to drown his sorrows it was going to be on my dime. I bought the Jack and Chaos picked up three bottles of cheap red wine.

Back at the apartment I gave the Sage his medicine and he took it with a subdued nod of thanks behind his coal black lenses. He unscrewed the top and pulled straight from the warm bottle, no glass. Deirdre just shook her head and sipped her wine pained, but silent.

It's later now and the night is wearing on all of us. Deirdre left, angry, frustrated and helplessly tired of watching the Sage rot his guts from the inside out drinking great huge gulps of that brown poison. Three bottles of wine are empty and the four of us left are drunk and tired. It's only one a.m., early by any measure, but I'm thinking I need to be going home.

The Sage wants none of what any of us were trying to give him: help, comfort, companionship. Chaos and Christy gave up hours ago, deciding instead they would just play music, joke about and be their usual selves. They were attempting to keep it normal and safe, a good play, but not working in the least and although Sage went along with it for a little while, even coming out of his shell for a bit, cracking wise like he usually does and even laughing at some of Chaos' antics, it was all forced and paper thin. Always the drink clutched in his fist and the glasses on and a biting edge to his speech and you could see he was using every ounce of will left in him to keep from breaking down before us. Deirdre just couldn't take it anymore.

But it's quieter now and we're all just sitting in the living room and the music is low and most of the lights are out when Chaos gets up bleary eyed from the couch, tells us we can crash there if we want, and turns off the lights in the kitchen before disappearing into the bedroom, Christy in tow. They shut the door behind, leaving me alone with the Sage.

The last song on the stereo is played and there is only the dull sound of our breath passing in and out. We're sitting on opposite ends of the couch, the empty space between us reserved for the ghost of his sadness. The lights in the parking lot throw an obtuse rhomboid of white against half the kitchen wall cut by the slats of the blinds that sway slowly in the night air. He turns his head in the semidarkness, his body an immovable anchor, heavy with liquor and immeasurable grief, and thanks me again for buying him whiskey, but this time with words, and I realize this is what he'd wanted all along, to be alone, the two of us, where we lost souls could just reflect and lament like exiled monks or sad poets. A kinship in our misery. Two pale figures poised in failure. A study in loneliness.

"I don't know where I went wrong?" he says suddenly, more of a question to himself rather than a statement to me, but almost laughing. I don't know how to respond. He goes on.

"She didn't say anything."

"Take a drink," I finally say, but it's too late. The bottle is empty. There's no more booze in the house.

"I think I'm going to go home," he says and slowly stands up. "I need a piss."

The light in the bathroom is off but there's the glow from outside and that's enough to get him to the toilet. That's when I hear them.

The bedroom door was shut, but the other one, the one leading to the bathroom was wide open and while he stood there Sage had a front row view of Chaos fucking Christy against the edge of the bed. They'd been trying to keep quiet but it's much too late for that and she suddenly lets loose a low moaning grunt that shatters the darkness and it's all too much for him and just as suddenly, unexpectedly, ridiculously, Sage starts to sing.

It's crazy. My friend, standing in the darkness, pissing loudly into a toilet and probably on the floor too, singing at the top of his lungs while Chaos and his slut grunt like pigs not five feet away. It's Dean Martin *That's Amore*. Wild! I almost have to laugh at the insanity of it all but the singing doesn't stop them, rather eggs them on and now it's gone from them trying to keep quiet to them trying to outdo him, drown out his singing with the sounds of their fucking. It's mad. Moaning and singing and panting and more singing, louder still, and then the trickle of urine against the bowl, the floor, and now Chaos is laughing his Joker's guffaw and even Christy is giggling and humping, getting into the act.

Hilarious. Soon I can't contain myself and I break out laughing and I hear the Sage start to cackle too and I think everything is all right, that it's just a ludicrous scene we've found ourselves in, that everything is going to be all right, and tomorrow is another day. Life for the Sage will go on. He will persevere. His mountain was shook by the great quake, but still he sits atop, above us all, looking on. Safe. Reliable. The tension of the night is finally broken with the sounds of his laughter and we leave together with me asking him to come with me to grab a bite. He kindly refuses, assures me he just needs some sleep.

We part ways in the parking lot with a promise to get together on the coming weekend.

VIII

I was dead asleep when I got the call. Deirdre was solemn, but frantic, speaking in sporadic bursts. Sage was in the hospital. He'd tried to kill himself. I needed to come down. Chaos was on his way.

I rolled over and looked at the clock. 10:30. We'd only just parted company a few hours before and everything seemed all right. Sure he was saddened by the break up, crushed even, but there was no indication that this was the direction his mind was going. He wasn't the type. Philosophical yes, dramatic, most certainly, but never a loss of control. Sage was cool as ice, it was his way. He was supposed to be the rock. If he crumbled, what hope would there be for any of us? She told me the room number. I said I'd be over soon.

"His family just flew in. It's not . . ." she stopped. "Just come."

At the hospital I found them sitting in a small waiting room, the TV on and tuned to one of those feel good New York in the morning shows where they all sit around jiving and the weather man is out in the street talking nonsense to the crowd and a stage is set up so some aged rocker can do a worthless acoustic version of a song he used to perform thirty years ago and that was never any good in the first place. The smell of sterility fills the room. Deirdre is watching the door across the hall from behind the wall of glass. Chaos is on the floor playing with a red wood block car, pushing it around the carpet and making a "brrrpppp" noise with his lips, much to the amusement of a little boy looking on. He's holding a blue block pickup truck with oversized wood wheels painted black. The boy's blonde mother is looking on smiling. She's mildly attractive and is thinking Chaos is very much so. Chaos is rolling the car off the cliff of the chair arm, tumbling it end over end and whisper yelling "aarrrgh" as it crashes to the floor in slow motion ending in a fiery explosion. He'll make a great father one day I'm thinking. No one is watching the TV. This is how the time is passed. Across the hall, our friend is tied to the bed.

"What's going on?" I asked. "What happened?"

"Pumped himself full of pills," Chaos said. "His neighbor said he emptied the medicine cabinet. Aspirins, cold meds, allergy stuff."

"How much?"

"All of it. Took everything."

"And washed it down with Jack," Deirdre said. "I mean he had that whole bottle at your place."

"Two," Chaos corrected.

"He was fine when we left," I said. "It was like he hadn't had a sip. You know him. He's like a bottomless well."

They could just stand silent. Out in the hall a janitor noisily pushed a rattle-wheeled garbage can across the linoleum. The smiling child at our feet was recreating Chaos' spectacular crash with the blue truck completely unaware of any of the tragedies of humanity.

"Can we go in there?" I asked.

"His family's with him," Deirdre said. "We saw him before. They didn't look too happy to see either of us. We only had a few minutes."

"Well I want to see him. You coming?"

Deirdre said she couldn't. She didn't like seeing him the way he was. "It's too hard," she'd said.

Chaos handed the red car to the kid and we went over.

I pushed the door to his room open slowly, trying to be discreet. Inside was quiet and bright, the curtains pushed aside letting the strong late morning sun shine through the large fourth floor window. Outside on the street below, life was going on as usual; commuters shuttling to and fro, just another Thursday morning. Sage's sister Jodi stood by the bedside. She'd driven down from Jacksonville when the call came in. His mother sat, her eyes red from wiping away endless tears, while his father just stood by her side, his hands resting on the back of her chair. Their faces were worn, drawn from the exhaustion of a frantic early morning call from their daughter and the first flight out of St. Louis. It was the first time I'd seen any of them. There was no resemblance. I took Chaos' arm and pulled him to the corner.

"What the hell happened?" I whispered.

"It was pretty wild man," he said. "You know Ronnie, the guy living next door? Said he woke up at like three and heard him screaming in his room. Sage left the front door open and when he went in the bedroom door was locked and he was screaming like hell and shit was crashing and breaking on the other side so Ronnie kicked in the door in. He thought someone had broken in through the window or something."

Over Chaos' shoulder Sage lay strapped to the bed, his blackened mouth and jaw slack, hanging dully open, his eyes vacant and glossy, his head lolling slowly back and forth in sedated wonderment.

"What'd they give him?" I asked.

"Dunno. Ronnie said he was," and Chaos tried to stifle a little giggle, "buck ass naked, standing on the bed swinging a battle ax around over his head."

"Fuck."

"Yeah," he continued. "He smashed almost everything in the room in like no time at all. The TV, all his books and paintings, even the fish tank. Poor little bastards."

The Sage farted under the covers.

"There was a pile of papers on fire in the trash can. Ronnie didn't even try to get close. He just ran to the kitchen and called the cops. It took three guys to calm him down enough to drop the ax. They were gonna shoot him. Then they wrestled him down and had him brought here."

I just cursed silently to myself. All I could do was look back over his shoulder at our friend, doped and miserable, tied down like some sort of animal, his sister and parents holding vigil at his bedside, his mother gently trying to pat some of the charcoal residue from his cheeks and chest with the corner of a damp towel. It was my fault. I had failed him.

"Are they going to arrest him?"

"I don't think so," he said. "I mean he wasn't trying to hurt anyone and I don't think he put up much of a fight with the cops."

I walked over and stood at the bedside. The Sage rolled his head at me and tried fix his eyes on my figure, but his huge black pupils couldn't focus and his gaze was more of one looking through rather than at. His moustache and beard were caked thick with the remnants of the sooty charcoal they'd forced fed him to purge whatever it all was he had taken. It covered most of his face, chest and shoulders. There was half of a handprint, someone's right, on his left shoulder where they'd held him down.

"It's Dave," I said. "You all right buddy?"

"Dave?" he responded in a hush. His voice, once so deep and wise in my eager ears was small, broken and distant, a mere whisper of its former self. His hands tried to reach for me, but the restraints held him fast and the bedrails clanked and rattled loudly as he tried to pull at them. His autonomous legs were restless beneath the sheets, moving of a will all their own, uncontrolled by his unfocused mind. After a few seconds his muscles relaxed and he rolled his head back toward the windows.

"Is there anything we can do?" I asked of his mother.

"You can go," she said flatly. "He needs us now, not any of you. You've done enough."

We paid heed and left.

IX

Three days passed. They locked Sage up, temporarily restricting him to the psychiatric ward of the hospital. No visitors allowed except immediate family. They put him on a suicide watch. He'd be kept there, observed, questioned, and medicated for an indeterminate amount of time. I was outraged that I couldn't get in to see him. Stopped at the reception desk and told to go home, that everything would be all right, he was being well taken care of. I had nightmares; visions of lobotomies, of drooling lips, of a great mind sucked away and medicated into oblivion. I feared that when he was released (if?), he'd not be the same, that our midnight communions would be lost forever. Deirdre cried the first day. We consoled each other, and found solace by occupying ourselves with work and the tedium of life. Chaos sought refuge as he usually did, between the sheets. After a while it was life as usual. All we could do was wait.

Sunday came and we took to Thebes as we always did, to drink and dance, and now to reflect on ourselves. It was necessary to get our lives back to normal, even in his absence. I reasoned, as most people would, that it's what he would want us to do. Then I kicked myself for talking like he was already dead or something. Chaos was convinced he'd be back to his old self in no time, back hanging with the gang, talking Kant and Dumas, and smoking those god awful Marlboro Reds. I took comfort in his optimism.

Eden and Nikki had been to a wedding earlier in the day and had come to the club straight from there. It was also a belated happy 21st for Nikki, and Chaos was excited, hoping that this would be the night of nights when she'd be drunk enough and he'd be smooth enough and it would finally happen; a fantastic sweaty sex crash back at his place, one for the ages, after which he could brag to Sage when he got out and die a truly happy man. For my part I just wanted to forget. I intended to lose myself in the music and the drink, and her. Sage's collapse emboldened me, made me realize the fleeting nature of love, and in a way edged me closer to my own vision of perfection and destiny with her, that sad sweet dream of tears and joy and soft lips and sunshine rain, her body pressed against mine forever. I was determined to not end up like him.

She came in, and I was standing in our usual spot, around the side of the bar, hugging the wall with elbow resting on rail with precise casualness and air of I don't care, I'm just here to watch life and live, and she came around the corner and I saw them for the first time ever: her legs.

She wore what most women call the "little black dress" but what most men would call heaven. Black brings out the beauty of a woman like nothing else can. Coco Chanel knew this better than anyone. I'd never seen anything like it and I doubted that I ever would again, Eden in a skirt, feet laced in stringy high heels and ankles round, curving up to smooth tense tanned calves rolling into the valleys behind her knees (how I longed to plant a single kiss at the foot of that valley and feel the tingling of her skin). And higher up the start of a taut, flawless thigh, tender and fleshy and further still (but wait! A vision stopped dead by a hem of demarcation, a corporeal 38th parallel, an inky line drawn across her legs that said this far but no farther, see no more but dream on still if you would dare to imagine what further glory resides under this chaste fabric!)

Many a night I had imagined that glory, the soft unfurled petals of a rose between my fingertips or like trying to grasp a single crystal of falling snow: delicate, fragile, requiring slow gentleness and attention to every detail so as not to ruin the perfection of the form. Would those petals give under the caress of careful fingers or the crystal melt at the warm breath of a soft kiss?

"Well look at you all fancified," Chaos said starting off every encounter he'd ever had with Nikki, juvenile and demeaning. It was the little boy on the playground tack. All that was missing was him punching her in the arm and calling her a dorkface. "I know it's your birthday and all but you ladies didn't have to get all dressed up on my account. Nikki, I see you shaved for the occasion."

"Fuck you," Nikki quipped.

"You look really nice," I said to Eden.

"These shoes are killing my feet," she said.

"I need a drink," Nikki said looking at the throng at the bar.

"First rounds on me," Chaos said, leaving to get the drinks with Nikki in tow, the prospect of someone buying her a drink, even if that someone was Chaos, luring her away.

"Have you heard anything?" Eden asked after Sage.

"Nothing really," I said. "He's under observation. That's about it."

"It's unbelievable."

"He's a good man. It's not fair."

"How are you? I mean, are you all right? I know you guys are kinda close. I would have come but I didn't know . . ."

"I'm fine," I semi-lied. "You?"

"I'm OK. I mean, it's harder on you I'm sure. We're not really all that close. I mean he's a friend and all, but not like you two. You know him better."

"Apparently not enough though. I should have paid more attention."

"Maybe we all could have," she said.

We stood quiet, reflecting on the state of our friend, when she suddenly changed the subject, brightening the somber mood.

"Well it's not going to get any better standing here moping about it. I could use a drink. You?"

I told Eden to stay put, that I would get it so she didn't have to walk. She told me they had already had a few at the wedding, open bar, and she'd let me get the first, but to absolutely not let her get drunk.

"We came in my car," she said taking my arm and speaking into my ear. She was already buzzed and heading for a high. "And don't let me spend all my money either."

"Put it away," I said. "I got you tonight. And if you need I can drive you both home."

"Thanks," she said. "And thanks for saying I look nice before. Sorry I missed that. I'm all bitching about the shoes. I hate dressing like this."

"Why? You obviously wear it well." I was trying so hard to be smooth.

"It's not me. I'm jeans and sneakers, not high heels and frills. You know me."

"I wonder sometimes," I said.

"I look stupid."

"Are you kidding? You're the prettiest girl in here. Look around. They're all looking at you."

"Yeah, and laughing."

"You know, enjoy it for one night," I said with all sincerity. "They're looking at you because you look incredible in that dress, better than everyone else that's walked through the door. You can go back to your old self tomorrow. But I got news for you," I leaned in secretively. "They're going to look anyway. They always do."

She smirked.

"Think what you want, I see it all the time."

Chaos and Nikki returned with drinks and the somberness of before passed and we were all laughing and dancing, the pain in Eden's feet fading as the music picked up and the liquor started to flow again. Things got easier. We all began to forget and lose ourselves in the thrill that we were alive and well, and at least for the moment, all was right with us. It was a celebration for a friend, one of those conditioned, commercialized rites of passage, and we weren't about to let it pass unnoticed.

The music was wild and musing and running all together in retro gloom and purple darkness of the cowering gothic soul; questioning everything, believing nothing, denying all, even itself. The pop never ate itself, it spewed its own guts all over and we bathed ourselves in it ritually on the evening of God's day. It was fornication, and abomination, and abortion and a contortion of the gospel of the night; live free, love all, drink deep from the wine of lostness, wander the deserted streets in search of the next messiah spouting tunes from his great round tablet tables that gave us the Law governing all. Bear witness to the revelry, shame, joy, punishment and harmony of it and come out on the other side clean. Step into the light of a new morning. But so often we forget that morning begins in darkness and the light only the white dots like pin pricks in the heavy black cloak of the sky or the pale pools of cadmium yellow light from the streetlamps lining the lonely windblown lanes.

Deirdre showed up and with her came two friends, Terry and Patrick, and I learned they were brother and sister and Patrick was so gay you could smell it on him, but it was fine because he was on fire and brought to the party that eccentric flamboyancy that only the terminally gay can bring and made us all laugh and at one point had us all in such stitches I thought beer was going to shoot out our noses when he started dirty pole dancing under the stairs and mock humping Deirdre and getting all after it. He looked like George Michael on crack, thin as a pencil, walking on pool cue legs in tight jeans and a long sleeved tee hanging loose like a smock hiding his rickety frame. But his energy was boundless and whatever it was, that spark of life, that zest that made him leave all his inhibitions behind, he had it. It went on for hours and still we forgot. They left at one.

There came a point when I found myself alone with Eden, outside in the hall. We'd crossed paths near the restrooms, me going in, she coming out. The crowd was thinning, it was getting on closing, but still the gothic horror and morose chimings of Depeche Mode and Ministry and Real Life and Concrete Blonde filled the halls, but the music didn't matter because I knew my angel had already been sent. She looked bleary eyed and I asked if she just wanted to stop, take a little walk down the hall. She agreed and we strode silently side by side, my mind stealing side long glances and more snapshots for the endless gallery.

"You," she said pointing a drowsy, accusatory finger my way. "You let me drink too much."

"I tried to stop you twice," I protested weakly. "Who am I to deny you what you want?"

"You gotta try harder, Stone."

"You have no idea how hard I try," I mumbled under my breath.

"What's that?"

"Nothing dear. Just the wind."

"Yeah sure. You're a strange one Stone, but I like you. You're OK in my book."

"Well I got that going for me."

We came to the end of the hall and I looked at her, standing there in the blanching light of a street lamp, and I realized we were alone in the quiet, the thumping of the music just on the other side of the wall but now so silent and far away. I thought this was the moment, the time and place right to say something, anything to her, tell her how I felt, take her in my arms and kiss her. But my stomach sunk and all I could muster was an abortive semi-cough.

Suddenly Nikki called sharply from down the other end shattering the moment like crystal. "There you are. We going or what?"

Well at least I wasn't the only one who'd struck out. Chaos had given up and taken off, no doubt nonplussed by yet another failed attempt to bed Nikki, but only on the inside. Outwardly it was all blue skies (even in the dead of night) for him and he was probably already onto his next conquest.

We went out the side door into the cool deserted street and I walked them back to the parking lot.

Eden was very drunk, way too drunk to drive, and so was Nikki. They said they were going to just sit in the car for a while and try to sober up. I was worried. Two pretty girls, drunk, in a near empty parking lot at two a.m. It was a bad scene and she knew it. Before she could ask I offered to stay, let them sleep it off in my car. It was the right thing to do, the chivalrous thing, and I've always fancied myself the knight in shining armor, even if my armor was just a ball cap and my steed a little red hatchback.

Eden climbed in and immediately collapsed across the back seat and Nikki got up front next to me and pushed the seat all the way back with a thunk. She bounced hard against the headrest, groaned, moaned and closed her eyes tight. I turned the radio on low for some background noise and just leaned back.

"That was the worst *wedding* ever," Eden said, her face smushed in the seat. She was slurring her speech terribly in that drunken halting cadence that accents all the wrong words.

"Who got married?"

"My sister," Nikki said, her eyes still closed, the car spinning wildly around her. She was breathing through her mouth, always a bad sign. "And the food was awful."

"There was like nothing to eat."

"What'd you have?" I asked.

"All they had was chicken or some kind of meat dish," Eden said.

"Don't talk about food," Nikki protested.

"Nothing vegan. All I ate were some mushrooms and a little pasta."

"That's all?" I said.

"There was broccoli too."

"And sprouts," Nikki put in.

"When was that?"

"I dunno. Six? Seven? We came straight here from there."

I was starting to regret having bought them so many drinks. Birthday or not, this was heading in the wrong direction fast.

"We should get you something to eat," I said. "Let's go to Subway. I think they're still open. Some bread'll help."

"No," Eden said quickly but then drifting off. "Please don't move. I don't think . . . laying down . . ."

I knew it was coming. It was only a matter of time, time spiraling toward a wet, bilious singularity. It was Nikki who gave up the ghost first.

Although I've never been a Boy Scout and am, quite frankly, a little put off by the homoerotic nature of grown men choosing to hang around small boys in the woods, I've always been a fan of their motto: Be Prepared. Careful preparation is always the key to a successful outcome. I'd already thought of a contingency of this type and was ready with a pack of Rolaids in the glove box and a stash of plastic grocery bags tucked in the pocket behind the passenger seat. What I hadn't prepared for was how to get to them if the seat were suddenly, and fully, reclined.

"Oh God!" someone said. It might have even been me.

"Wait!" I cried.

I reached across and fumbled for the door release just as Nikki sat bolt upright with teary, panic-stricken eyes staring right at me and the pall of death across her ever expanding cheeks, her eyebrows arched in horror. She leaned out the open door almost in the nick of time. It was then that I learned something new about Eden: She's what we in the industry term a sympathetic puker.

Maybe it was the horrible wet splash. Maybe it was the wretched smell. But whatever it was it arrived with a vengeance.

"Use the bags!" I called as I got out and raced around the other side of the car to help Nikki, who looked like she was about to fall face first out onto the pavement. It's a tricky business, juggling two drunken women, and I suddenly remembered Chaplin. I have no idea how Chaos does it. It's hard to feel chivalrous when you're holding someone's hair as they vomit up a wave of mushrooms (creamed no less) and broccoli between your newly polished shoes. Eden had found the stash and I watched through the back window a vision of the girl of my dreams, the perfect vision of love and beauty, face deep in a Food Lion bag, shoulders convulsing like a dog, coughing up a disgusting mess of rum and half digested bean sprouts. I just held my breath and swallowed hard and bore it all till it was over and the last sprout had sprung.

The tempest passed and the bags discarded behind the tires of some unsuspecting soul's car (ha!) I helped Nikki back up and gave them both some napkins from the glove compartment (also part of the contingency plan). Eden apologized profusely from behind closed eyes and rocking brain and I told her it was all right and to just sleep it off, I'd stay and keep watch over them. From knight to nurse in a heartbeat, but there's still honor in that, isn't there?

"I think I got some on your door," Nikki said absently, sliding further into blissful post puke unconsciousness, no apology.

"Don't worry about it," I said and opened the windows to let a breeze in. It was cool and welcoming and blew the smell away nicely. I'd wanted to, but they begged me not to move the car.

"Don't leave, OK?" Eden said.

"I'm not going anywhere. Just sleep now."

"You're the best Dave," she said as she slid away.

"Not the best," I said, mostly to myself now, into the mirror. "Just a good guy."

A few minutes later, after they were both dead to the world, Nikki shifted, rolled, came up for a second and wound up with her head resting in my lap, a tussle of blond hair and drippy mascara. I gently ran my fingers through her hair humming happy birthday and she sighed and fell back in again.

"I've always wanted this girl's head in my lap," I said to my reflection. "I just never really pictured it like this."

X

We didn't see each other for several days after that night. Around sunrise Eden had woken and together we helped Nikki back into her car. They remained there for another hour or so before driving home. I stayed nearby, keeping my sentry until they left, before wearily driving myself home in the bleak Monday morning dawn, a lone salmon swimming upstream east against the current of sober, well-rested commuters heading west into town.

My final set of midterms was coming and I had arranged with my boss to take a few days off to focus on studying. I heard nothing from any of them, nor anything about Sage. The solitude was welcome, albeit lonely, and when I finally did get back to the Shaft, for a closing shift on a Thursday, Eden was there, on her way out.

She came over, hat in hand so to speak, chewing her lips and apologizing excessively for everything that had happened.

"It's no problem really," I tried to reassure her. "Nothing a little baking soda and a good car wash couldn't fix. Car smells better than the day I drove it off the lot."

"Let me at least give you a couple of bucks for the cleaning."

"Nonsense. Forget it."

"Well I have to pay you back somehow."

"No you don't," I shrugged. "I wasn't about to let the two of you stay there by yourselves all night whether you wanted me to or not anyway, so it doesn't matter. I wanted to. It was my choice. There's nothing to pay back."

"You have to let me do this. I *want* to."

"Nope. Sorry. You're out of luck."

"Come on."

I stood my ground. She was smiling in frustration. I was loving it. A magical smile. Magical eyes.

"I'm getting my reward just sitting here watching you squirm, kiddo."

"You bastard!" she laughed and left. Outside I watched her on the other side of the glass wall shouting through and drawing attention from the passing tourists. She looked back but I just stood there smug, shaking my head and smiling.

"You're never going to let me live this down, are you?" she shouted.

"What's that?" I shouted back pointing a finger at my ear. "I can't hear you."

"You're a bastard Stone!"

"And you love it," I said. I knew *I* did.

I'm thinking of the sublimity of it all then, watching her walk out of my view. The sadness of her going away, but also the heart racing glee of seeing her reappear suddenly, surprisingly, and giving me one last look at that smile when I least expect it. She's come back! *I* brought her back! She can't leave without seeing *me* again! I raised an eyebrow and she slapped a ten dollar bill against the glass and pointed menacingly at me, miming how she was going to cram it down my throat and I quickly grabbed a plastic bag and mock vomited in it and she laughed wildly and her face ran pink with blush.

She left a second time and I watched the glass for minutes more but then I knew it was for the last time and I just stood there with my eyes closed, imagining again the vision of that beautiful pink blush and wondering how far it went down her body.

Later, when Chaos showed up, I told him all about it.

"Sounds like you're earning points like mad on the good guy scale my friend."

"I should hope so."

"She totally wants you guy."

"I dunno." Then thinking more about it and realizing he was right. The time to make a real move was coming up fast. It was do or die time.

"Do you think she blushes like that when she comes?" he asked loudly, apropos of the customers walking in.

XI

What happened next I'm not particularly proud of. Suddenly, or rather haplessly would be a better term to describe it, as the entire thing was ill conceived, unplanned, inappropriate, and all manner of undesirable, I began sleeping with Megan Chance, a girl from my Humanities class. Began sleeping is the best way to put it, since what I believed would be only a onetime thing, fulfilling a deep-seated need on my part to get one off with someone besides myself (my own dry spell of nearly a year since Kessa and I split beginning to rival Deirdre's) wound up dragging out for over a considerably longer period of time.

Megan. A simple girl with a simple name. Mousy, shy, cute, but plain really, and what Chaos would call hopelessly vanilla. She was innocent enough, book smart, but terminally naïve in the common sense department; knew nothing of the night. She rarely drank. She liked dolphins and movies with Robin Williams. She'd lived in Florida her whole life, never once left the state. She'd never heard of The Cure. When she was eighteen her father, a retired Navy man, bought her a brand new Buick. He'd insisted big cars, especially iron wrought, made in the good ole U.S. of A. were safer, more reliable than those piddley little rice burners. While other girls were tooling around town in VWs and cute little Toyotas, Megan, all 5' 2" of her, peered over the wheel of a Sherman Tank. She looked ridiculous in it. Little girl, big fucking car.

But she was likable and had a nice smile, laughed when I'd crack wise in the back of class and sort of attached herself to me. I liked it. Soon we were going out for bites to eat after class. I took her to Copper (not on a Tuesday night of course, for those are exclusively reserved for revelry with my good and trusted friend of the night Chaos my dear, and I simply cannot allow our weekly tradition to be broken). She understood. Thought it was funny. We went on a Thursday. The crowd was mellow, the music pop-ish. Then it happened.

It wasn't planned, these things rarely are. We were at the bar, then we were in the car. Then we were in my apartment, then we were in bed. A simple girl, simple sex.

When it was over she hugged me. I knew then what a mistake I had made. I thought of Chaos. Fling sex wasn't supposed to end in hugs. Fling sex was supposed to end in laughter. It was supposed to end in a short nap and someone getting dressed and leaving. It wasn't supposed to last until morning. But instead we both just drifted off to sleep.

Talking to Chaos at work later, he was all smiles that my streak was broken.

"Use it for all you can," he said. "Get it whenever she wants to give it."

"I didn't really want it in the first place," I said. "At least not from her."

"So what, dude? Pussy is pussy. Fuck her a few times, get yours. Not everything has to be a relationship."

"I know, but that's the hard part. I've never been able to separate the two. I don't do the 'casual' thing. You know me."

"Listen man, this is a gift," he said. "I mean, she's not ugly is she?"

"No. She's no Eden obviously," I said. "But she's not bad looking. She's plain. Average."

"Whatever. So you've got a not ugly girl who wants to sleep with you and you don't want to get emotionally attached. It's perfect."

"In what world is that perfect?"

"It means you've got some on tap whenever you want. That's what I mean man. It's a gift. This Megan is the girl you call when you got the itch, maybe take her out first, but in the end you get yours. You said yourself she's kinda stupid about this type of thing. If you play it right you can get ass at least a half dozen more times before she figures anything out. Meanwhile, you just keep it on the DL. Don't let Eden get wind of it." Then suddenly spawning a new plan. "Wait, better yet, she *should* find out."

"No. Absolutely not. She cannot hear of this."

"But she has to, don't you see?" Chaos said. I could see the gears of his machinations grinding away in his mind. My modern day Machiavelli.

"How do you figure?"

"Jealousy. Eden sees you've got something else going on besides her, she'll come around quick. Drop hints that you're seeing someone, little things, nothing major. Keep it vague. Just let her peer in around the sides. If she asks you where you're going, tell her you're meeting someone. Don't give names. Let her stew. She'll get curious. If she asks to actually meet Megan, you know you've got her."

"I don't know," I said uneasily. "I feel bad enough about doing this to Megan as is. I was just going to tell her it was wrong and we shouldn't do it again. You're talking about using."

"I'm talking about the ends justifying the means. It was fun, right?"

"Well, yeah."

"So why deny yourself a little amusement. She's a grown woman. She can make her own decisions. You play it distant. Don't call her. Wait for her to call you. Then play cool, let her know you're doing other things and you'll see her 'sometime soon.' Use 'sometime soon.' Always works for me. In the mean time, keep at it with Eden. Then in a couple of weeks, hit it again. If Eden comes around, great. If she doesn't, you still get to dip your stick."

I mulled it over. What he said, in a perverse way, did make perfect sense.

"See, and you said she was kinda plain. So, you can, you know, show her new things. If she's as into you as you think, she'll probably be willing to try just about anything. She's not a virgin, right?"

"No, thank Christ. That woulda been fucking awful."

"So," Chaos said resolutely. "She's been around this once before. No harm, no foul. And if you can get her to bend over a few times, then hey."

XII

A few days later Eden invited me to come with her to see a new foreign film; an Indian flick playing at the Enzian Theatre. I'd never been, and really wasn't one for foreign cinema, but that didn't matter since it was her and I jumped at the chance, even offering to drive. She said she'd buy the tickets, on the pretext that it was her way of paying me back for the disastrous Thebes back seat after party.

The Enzian was an artsy movie house, usually showing independent foreign films, and was set up with a restaurant feel; tables all through the lower auditorium where you could sit in a comfortable chair and eat and drink while watching the show. Only real drawback was the constant clinking and clanking of silverware while you were trying to listen. We'd all gone there as a troupe once before; me, Chaos, Sage, everyone, when Spike and Mike's Sick and Twisted Film Festival came to town and we all got drunk watching some really incredible claymation shorts and hilarious and sometimes even quite disturbing cartoons. That was also the first, and only night I saw Sage's fiancée Rebecca, a pale, waifish redhead with dark eyes and an unpleasant demeanor. She'd hated Chaos for a long time, well over a year, and seemed to have nothing but contempt for the rest of us, even me, whom she knew next to nothing about. But I was friends with Chaos and I guess that was all she needed to know. She was a categorizer by nature and had pegged us all as no good, and especially no good for Sage, and whom I quickly ascertained, was the main reason we rarely ever got him to come out with us when we'd have our mad nights downtown.

But it was just Eden and I this night and there was booze, so when we arrived and got seated we decided to forgo the rather overpriced fare and just ordered a couple of drinks and settled into a comfortable table.

Bollywood this was not. The film, *Fire*, is the story of a young married woman who falls in love with the wife of her husband's older brother and they carry on a lesbian affair in secret that is only discovered at the end when the older brother finds them in bed together, after which they fight, and she winds up getting immolated, hence the title.

It was pretty intense at times, and at one point I could see Eden's shining eyes glistening with tears, and I was moved by her being moved and for some reason, watching her tear up, I felt my heart warm that she was letting herself get emotional in front of me like that and that I was there to see it. She caught me looking and laughed a little and wiped her eyes, like a woman embarrassed she'd suddenly become a child again. I felt like I needed to protect her then and a swelling of pride rose in my chest at this princess laid bare. Her eyes were shining now at me and her cheeks filled with a rosy blush and I remembered what Chaos had said, but I shook it off and just focused on the moment. I wanted to do something, to kiss her, to reach out and take her hand and whisk her out of there, take her someplace safe and warm, away from all the troubles of the fire we were enduring every single day, but I was powerless to move, and I think she was grateful that I was. We both turned back to the screen.

When it was over we'd laughed a little and she'd shed more tears, particularly at the ending when the flames died down and the two lovers are reunited, albeit in dire straits, to start their new life together. In the parking lot Eden said it was one of the best movies she'd ever seen, and I in my uninventiveness and stammer could only say that I liked it for its visual qualities, even though I didn't "get" most of it. In retrospect, I should have paid closer attention, learned more from it. There is always a shred of truth in art. Sage taught me that.

XIII

A week later they let the Sage out of the hospital. I wasn't there. None of us were. His family picked him up and took him home. It was all really very quiet and private. His parents stayed around for a few days, helped clean up the house, did the shopping for him (with him really, taking him everywhere, not letting him out of their sight for a moment, even checking with a gentle knock when he'd gone to the bathroom). Very undignified, despite his reassurances that all was well again and that he was no longer in danger. It wasn't for another week that I saw him again. By then mother and father had returned to Missouri and his sister left for Jacksonville with the promise of coming back and checking in on him in a few days.

In the interim he was alone in the house. Ronnie came by for a brief visit, but then left for a week in LA. I came to visit my friend after Ronnie left, knowing that it was only when he and I were alone that we could really talk and be ourselves again.

Sage met me on the porch in characteristic Saturday evening fashion, shirtless in torn jeans and barefoot on the dusty wooden boards. He smiled at my approach and welcomed me into the living room with a bottle of wine.

"One for you and one for me," he sang and plucked a second bottle from the floor behind the sofa. I laughed at his seemingly good mood and we toasted first to misery, then to good company, and finally to recovery and life anew. I could see the spark had returned to his pale blue eyes. Things were returning to normal.

"How are you feeling?"

"Dry," he said taking a swig of wine from the bottle. "Very dry. Almost three weeks without a single drop."

"So what now?'

"Now, nothing," he said with a heavy sigh as he settled into the couch. "I'm out. Things are getting back to normal. I have to go to these meetings every week, but it's not too bad. I'm supposed to stop this too," he raised the bottle. "But that ain't happenin'. Let me tell you, there are some fucked up people in the world. I thought my shit was rough, man you have no idea what some people are walking around with."

I told him it was good to see him back on his feet again.

"Jerry said I could come back to work next week. He's been pretty cool about the whole thing."

"Deirdre said she'd be coming by later," I said.

"I know. She called earlier. Looks like I raised quite a ruckus. I can tell you there's no way in hell I'm trying that again."

"Are they going to prosecute?"

"No," he said. "Dodged a bullet there. My mom and dad were really great about that, talking to the cops and all. And the doctors at the hospital were pretty cool about the whole thing. Confused, that's what they said I was. They let me off on the condition that I start going to alcohol counseling."

I looked around the room and noticed that much of his artwork was gone from the walls. The easel was collapsed and standing in the corner, the canvas drop draped over top making it a sort of sad, abandoned teepee.

"I've packed it up for a while," he said thoughtfully. "Never was any good anyway."

"That's not true," I protested. "You've got real talent."

"Nah. No need to flatter. It's ok. The last two weeks have helped me put things in perspective. I think I need to take a break from the gloom and sorrow for a while."

"What'll you do instead?"

"Nothing I think. I've been playing with a little poetry. Nothing major. Just tinkering with some notes I made a while ago. I'm thinking of trying to put together a little book of it."

"And I'll buy the first copy when it's printed."

"You'll buy the only copy then."

"I want to hear some."

"Maybe later," he said, wizening his ice blue eyes and pointing an accusing finger my way. "Right now you and I have some unfinished business in the yard I think."

"Well if it's going to be that kind of night I need a piss first."

Sage collected both bottles and vaulted over the couch like Douglas Fairbanks and headed for the back door while I went down the hall to the john. Along the way I passed the bedroom. It was a room changed at a fundamental level. All of the paintings, his paintings, had been taken down and the walls stood mostly bare. All of his weapons were gone too. A cracked wooden frame with a few bits of broken mirror tucked in the sides stood on the floor leaning in the corner. One closet, hers, was completely empty and the door hung wide open. There was a fist sized hole in the wall above the bureau at the foot of the bed and on the floor the ghostly black circle of where the trash can fire had burned an indelible image into the hardwood. In the center of the room the double bed with its tossed, sweat stained sheets and its solitary pillow. The wood of the doorframe was split and splintered where Ronnie had kicked it in. A piece of plywood was nailed into the window where he'd broken out a pane with the ax. The hallway that had once been lined with framed black and white pictures of the two lovers was now just a barren tunnel leading to a grimy bathroom devoid of any feminine touch. I used it quickly and went out the back door.

Sage was already limbering up, swinging his stick in large loops around his body, centering it, then breaking out into swinging loops again. He twirled a figure eight and the wind whistled around the ash blade, his eyes fixed on a sapling near the edge of the driveway. In a fierce strike coming across his body he split the trunk, sending a smack pulsing across the air that must have echoed for blocks. The end of his blade snapped at the midpoint, ricocheted off the pavement and crashed into the old wooden fence, disappearing into the thick brush. We both stood for a moment, me in the doorway and he holding the snapped end loosely in his fingers. All he could do was laugh, turning to me with bright eyes and a giggle.

"Did you see that? Cheap piece of shit."

"You could cut that down and carve a new one," I said of the sapling. "Obviously better wood." He cast the remnants of his broken blade aside.

"There's probably something poetic in that."

"An omen maybe?" I said. "Now what?"

"Now comrade," he said with renewed vigor and affecting the accent of old Russian aristocracy, patting me on the shoulder and leading me back into the house. "*Vee* drink."

Two hours and another bottle of wine later I'm feeling warm and really good lying on the floor of the living room while Sage is reclined on the chair beside the window reading aloud from Tolstoy. The dull pall of twilight is creeping in and a Bauhaus CD one of us put in, which one I can't remember (either the album or who put it in) is playing low from the stereo on the mantle and I'm thinking yes, Bella Lugosi is, in fact, dead. So much for no more gloom and doom.

"So how go things on the Eden front?" he asks out of the blue, setting the text aside. "All quiet?"

"Nothing new I guess," I say, wanting to steer clear of women and relationship talk. "Nothing to report anyway."

"I'm disappointed in you Dave. Three weeks I'm gone and yet no progress."

"Well, not nothing," I told him about Thebes and Nikki and the movie and he listened and laughed at the ridiculous Buster Keaton business of me running around with the girls puking all over the place and I laughed too because it was pretty damn absurd. Then I told him about Megan.

"Well you've got something to show for it anyway," he said and drank again. "It's progress, and progress is always good. I myself am back to square one."

"Not a bad place to be," I said.

"How's that?"

"It's where everything starts new again. A fresh start, clean slate. All that."

"Wise Dave. Very wise."

"I learned from the best. Now how about some of that poetry?"

"You don't really want to hear that, do you?"

There was a knock at the screen door out on the porch and Sage rose to let Deirdre in. She'd come straight over when her shift ended.

They embraced warmly, then she asked after him.

"I'm fine, really. A temporary lapse in judgment. Nothing more."

"If you ever try that again, I'll kill you," she said, then noticing the three empty bottles on the floor. "Looks like I've missed most of the party."

"Nonsense!" Sage cried. "The sun is barely down. It's just getting started. We were just on our way to get some more, were we not Dave?"

"Are you sure you should be drinking so much?" she asked.

"Absolutely. Doctor's orders."

"I can vouch for that," I said. "I saw the prescription. And I think the proper question isn't should we be drinking *so* much, rather should we be drinking *as* much."

"How are you feeling," she said, ignoring me and addressing Sage, looking into his eyes searchingly, trying to find the shadow of the real self inside the shell. There was deep concern in her. Doubt. He saw it and gave her sobering reassurance and a smile.

"I tell you I'm fine. I promise. I was just confused, nothing more. But now I can see clearly again. And now I want to get back to my life, so if you'd like to accompany us up the street we were about to make a run." He held the rickety screen door open for her and followed her out.

"And then he's going to read us poetry!" I shouted and stumbled after them.

XIV

The party lasted for hours. As promised, after the sun had fully gone down and the wine and cigarettes had been replenished, Sage read aloud from one of his notebooks while Deirdre and I sat the captive audience. He paced the room shirtless and read two of his poems, *The Light of the Watch*, and *Dead City* the latter of which contained a definite tinge of the darkness of Poe and Blake. He spoke of a walled cemetery and thrashing sea spray, abandoned hope and unending night, but also of a distant sunrise and the birth of new shores.

I left them at midnight.

The next morning Deirdre called and invited me to lunch, and when I arrived at her apartment she was in good spirits, giddy almost, and seemed barely able to contain a rising excitement. She was practically itching to let it out.

"Where should we go?" I asked, thinking only of food.

"Someplace to celebrate," she said.

"Celebration? And what's the cause for the occasion?" She flashed a conspiratorial grin.

"The spell has been broken!"

"No! Really? When? Last night?"

"Unhuh."

"How?"

"What do you mean how? It just happened."

"Things like this don't just happen." A completely stupid sentiment on my part. Things like that happen all the time. See Megan.

"Well, this one did. I hung around for a little while after you left, but when I went to go he just asked if I wanted to stay."

"Just like that?"

"Just like that," she said with a tinge of glee. "Out of the blue."

"He's been doing that a lot lately. Wow."

I could see my friend glowing. She was excited, but reserved; Deirdre often preserved a degree of reserve. But I knew she was exploding fireworks of joy on the inside and somewhere a band was playing and troops were firing off salutes.

"I can't tell you how long it's been," she said.

"But you have. Three years wasn't it?"

"Two," she said quickly correcting me, but I knew it was more like two and three quarters. "Not that it matters."

"So what now? What's next? Was this just a onetime thing or what?"

"I don't know." She seemed genuinely concerned about this point.

"Did he say anything?"

"Not really. It was pretty quiet after you took off. We just sat around, listened to some music, and then he just asked if I wanted to stay. I said yes. He really didn't talk much."

"What about after?"

"We just fell asleep. I woke up at like five, got dressed, and left. He was still sleeping."

"Ah, the walk of shame," I teased.

"Shut up."

"Well, was it good? Was it everything you hoped it would be?"

"I wasn't *hoping* for anything. And yes, as a matter of fact, it was pretty good. He was very gentle."

"He strikes me as the type I guess. You should give him a call."

"And say what?" she asked.

"I don't know. Hey, had fun last night. Let's do it again sometime? Is now good for you? Have you seen my left sock?"

"You're an idiot."

"You know everyone keeps saying that. I prefer to call it genius."

"Be serious."

"OK. Do you want me to say something to him? Maybe get a feeler? Oh wait, you got one of those already. Ha!"

"Dick," she said rolling her eyes in disgust.

"You got that too!"

"I know! And it was fantastic! I just want to dance."

"It's a dick dance!" I said. "Shall we?"

And I took her by the hand and she spun a waltz on her heels as I sang.

"When you've just got the cock, and now you can't find your sock, it's the Dick Dance. When he's fucked you dumb, and you're so full of come, it's the Dick Dance!"

"This calls for something special," I said. "We should do something grand to mark this occasion."

"What did you have in mind?"

"Love is in the air. Well, sex mostly, but you get the picture. We should keep the mood going; go someplace where we can immerse ourselves in it. Maybe it'll bring us both some luck. Well some for me and more for you."

"Ok, so where?" she asked.

"Intersexions?"

"Oh, I like that."

"I'll call Chaos. We'll make it a group outing."

"OK, but don't tell him about this."

"Mum's the word my dear. On one condition." I smiled.

"Sure thing baby. I'll call her now."

The sex shop Mecca that was Intersexions, two floors of videos, magazines, toys, outfits and torture implements, was located on north OBT, where all things illegal and perverse met in a cosmic big bang smash up singularity of filth, and was the perfect place for a celebration. The Orlando location was just one of two serving the Central Florida area, the other being out at Vero Beach, and tailored to all needs big or small, short or long, loose or tight, thin or thick. The place was even handicap friendly.

Its exterior was white-washed brick and cinder block, spotted and stained with foot scuffs of midnight loiterers and kicked up road dust. Most of the parking was around the back down a narrow alley with a rickety chain link fence overgrown with weeds on one side and the rough unpainted red brick side of the building on the other. A jump alley. A rapist alley. We found a spot in front and pulled right up to the tinted black double doors and waited for the others to arrive.

It wasn't five minutes before Chaos rolled up thumping in the Firebird and leapt out giddy as a horny little puppy all excited and bubbling with anticipation about the dirty little goings on within. He ran up to Deirdre's window before we could even get out and pressed his crotch against the glass and began humping the car, slapping the windshield like an ass cheek and grunting an orgasm.

"Get your cock off my car!" she screamed.

"You know I don't think insurance covers this," I said.

"Is he like this when I'm not around?"

"Always."

"We goin' in or what?" he shouted through the glass.

"We're waiting for Eden," I said.

"She knows where it is. Come on I want to see if they have the latest issue of my favorite magazine."

Deirdre looked to me and I consented with a shrug.

"All right, back that thing up."

"License and registration ma'am," he said as she got out. "Insurance please? I see you don't have cock and collision on this vehicle, I'm afraid I'm going to have to pound it." And like a dog he went back to humping the car, a huge grin across his face as he bounced it back and forth, eyes wild with perverse joy, tongue waggling loosely.

"But officer isn't there anything I can do to make you maybe forget about that?" Deirdre said and got behind him, screwing him as he screwed the car. I jumped in behind her and brought up the rear.

"Nope. Sorry ma'am, it's my job," he panted. "I'll only be another minute."

"Only a minute?" Eden said suddenly appearing behind me. She'd parked around back and come up the alley. "What the hell are you doing?"

"Hang on a sec," he said and then stiffening smacked the windshield a final time, threw his head back and yelled, "RIIICOLLAA!"

"You people are idiots," Eden said as we broke up the orgy train and went inside, spent and panting. "Is this what you do when I leave you alone?"

"Pretty much," I said.

The inside of Intersexions was a veritable public library of pornography: ramshackle bookshelves organized into aisles stacked six feet high and packed with video and DVD titles all arranged by category and identified at the end of each row with handwritten signs. The sections were endless: straight, gay, fetish, BDSM, orgy, one girl two guys, two girls one guy, black, white, interracial, granny, preggo, gay, midget, gay midget, about a dozen kinds of international, chicks with dicks, chicks with two dicks, lesbian, lesbian orgy, amputee (fucking amputee!), blowjobs, handjobs, footjobs, titjobs. It was all too much. And just like a library the place was deathly quiet save for Chaos' incessant giggling coming from in between the stacks. The only thing missing was a card catalogue.

Next to the checkout counter at the front was a cork board adorned with about two dozen Polaroids of various and sundry scowl faced and sorry looking individuals, men and women, trash mostly. Beneath each were handwritten notes like "this lousy fucker is going to jail for trying to lift a deck of nudie cards", or "bitch who thought she could walk out with a nine inch dildo shoved in her boot", and above it all tacked to the wall a string of shiny multi-colored party letters reminding patrons that "CAMERAS ARE EVERYWHERE".

We perused the aisles cracking wise at some of the more creative titles like *An Officer and a Genital* and *Pounder of the Bride* when Deirdre broke off with Eden to somewhere more secluded, I knew to tell her about the night before. I stayed with Chaos.

"Oh. Asian Ass Parade 13," he said examining the back of a box.

"I don't see 1-12," I said. "Well, there's five and nine anyway."

"Hey, you out last night? I called," he asked.

"Yeah. With Sage and Deirdre. Just hanging."

"You know he doinked her, right?"

"How'd you know?"

"He called me this morning. Hey check this one out. *The Hunt for Miss October's Cunt.*"

"Well she told me not to tell you, so if she finds out you know, you didn't hear it from me."

"Not a word my friend. Her secret's safe with no one."

"It's good to see him getting back on the horse," I said, then suddenly realizing my mistake. "Not that Deirdre's a horse or anything. You know what I mean?"

"And they're off," he laughed, pinching his nose. "And around the first turn it's Deirdre's Ass followed closely by Sage's Prick. She's kicking up some real mud there folks, and Sage's Prick is looking a little sluggish around turn three. Here they come down the home stretch. It's Deirdre's Ass and Sage's Prick, Sage's Prick and Deirdre's Ass, and, but wait, what's this, here comes Nikki's Lips. Nikki's Lips are making a go for Sage's Prick, but he's got his nose right on Deirdre's Ass."

Upstairs Intersexions was stocked with all manner of toy, outfit and accessory for the deviant in us all. The first thing we encountered walking up the steps was a great wall of dildos, a virtual shrine of fake dicks of various color and size, all wrapped in plastic and plastered with crazy names like *Intimidator, Mr. Softee, Analator* and *Purplesauraus Rex* (my personal fav) and hanging from hooks or standing on shelves. There were whips and cat-o-nine tails slung from a metal display tree and black leather masks with zippers across the mouth and eye holes draped over foam heads. There was a faceless white mannequin standing off to the side with a nine-inch black strap-on dick drooping limply from its crotch, the dummy's hands out at the wrists, palms down and taking a step as if it were trying to sneak up on you. Around to the left a nylon chain swing and stirrups hung from the rafters with a hand written price tag of $179 in red ink standing in the seat as it swayed ever so slightly under the breeze from an overhead fan.

"Good Lord," Eden remarked of a particularly huge double-headed job, maybe two feet in length and looking like a shimmering raspberry Jell-O mold, resting on a glass shelf, like it was some sort of centerpiece.

"That's like something out of Revelations," I said. "And I looked, and the Angel blew the fourth trumpet and lo a great two-headed penis rose from the sea and smote the land."

"You could beat someone to death with it," she said.

"I think that's the idea. You want it? I have some extra cash."

"No, really, that's ok. I'd have no place to put it."

"I can think of somewhere."

"You're a perve Stone."

"I was referring to your closet."

"If you're so hot for it why don't you buy it for yourself?"

"I would, but then really what would I do with my other one. And you know what they say, two heads are better than one, but four is . . . well . . ."

The banter was broken suddenly when Chaos swooped in like Kirk Douglas, brandishing an enormous rubber dick like a Roman gladius, whispering 'hya! hya!' as he lightly jabbed the tip between Eden's shoulders and she just rolled her eyes.

"Freak."

"We really have to stop bringing the kids here," I said.

"This one might be a little too much for you," Chaos said.

"It's more the size I'm looking for," Deirdre chimed in.

"What do you need it for? I heard you already got yours."

"You told him?" she said shooting me a look of betrayal and disappointment.

"Relax. It's not like we don't all know about it. And no, Dave didn't say anything."

"Great, so *he* told you," she said, referencing Sage. "I guess it wasn't that important then if he's already bragging about it to you."

"He wasn't bragging. He called to ask me what to do."

"About what?"

"About you. This. All of it."

"And what'd you tell him."

"I didn't say anything."

"Well what *did* he say?" Eden said.

"Not much. He just said you two hooked it up. I asked if everything was cool and he said it was. That's about it."

"You're a big help," Deirdre said.

"I *told* you I'd talk to him for you. Send out a feeler," I interjected. Chaos looked confused.

"I thought last night she already? . . ."

"Shut up," I cut in. "Seriously, if you want me to call him."

"It'd be best if you called him yourself," Eden said. "Tell him to come out to Thebes on Sunday."

"I could do that," Deirdre said.

"I think that's a bad move," I said. "We'll all be there. Ask him out, just the two of you. Can't talk to someone when there's a bunch of people around." Deirdre shot me a look. "You need to get him alone. At least that's what a good friend told me once."

She smiled.

"What idiot said that?" Chaos asked scratching behind his ear with the dong and smelling it.

151

"I'll figure something out," she laughed. "You two morons stay out of it."

"This place is great," Chaos said. "I'm doing all my Christmas shopping right here."

XV

It wasn't two weeks after we'd started sleeping together that I was lying to Megan. I began making excuses to not see her or to not get her to stay the night, but to come for only a little while, and then go back home, so that I could continue my nightly adventures with Chaos undisturbed and unencumbered, and even more importantly, to continue my pursuit of Eden. Mine were stupid lies, some which required more creativity than others and some which even required more elaborate planning and timing. Like one where I had to tell Chaos to call me at precisely 10:05 p.m. and relay a prearranged sob story about a recent break up, so I could shuffle Megan out on the pretext that I just *had* to go be with my closest and dearest friend in his time of great need and ensure he didn't drink himself into oblivion, while still leaving myself enough time to shower, dress, and get downtown in time for the 11:00 show at The Florida Room and all the joys of another night with Eden.

It also wasn't but two weeks into my doomed, pseudo-relationship with Megan that Chaos' pervertedly accurate vision of jealousy and intrigue began taking effect and Eden started to take notice of the new lady in my life, dropping random questions at seemingly random moments at work, just like fishing.

"What's she like?" she'd ask, nonchalant, curious, aloof, trying to hide concern.

"Who?" I'd pretend, knowing damn well who, and what and what's more, why.

"You know. Your new girl toy."

"She is not."

"You're new girl *friend* then."

"She's not that either."

"Then what are you two?"

"I don't know," I said. "Right now we're just nothing. We're just having a little fun." This I knew to be a lie to myself more than anything. Megan was already showing signs that she was taking our *relationship* very seriously.

"Oh? And exactly what kind of fun is that Stone?" More direct. A crack in the armor?

"Stuff. Fun. I don't know. Went to the movies the other day. I took her to the art museum on campus last week."

"Sounds like you've got yourself a real party girl there."

"She doesn't like the night life," I said trying to defend Megan. Why was I doing that?

"*She doesn't like to boogie,*" Chaos sung in, making an entrance in his classic style, unannounced. He played his part to perfection. "But you're fuckin' her right?"

"Jesus," Eden rolled her eyes. "Is it always just sex with you two?"

"Well what else is there?" he asked feigning confusion.

"It isn't always sex," I said.

"No? What then?" Eden asked.

"Sometimes there's food," Chaos said. I tried to bring it back to a more serious level.

"I often ponder the greater meaning of life. Just the other day in my Human Species class we were learning about the nine existential questions. It was . . ."

"Boring," she yawned.

"I was going to say insightful, but I suppose it might be a little drab to some."

"OK then. Sex and the meaning of life. Wow. What else?"

"Did I already say food?" Chaos blurted in again.

"I think a lot about the future. What I'm going to do after school is done."

"And how does non-girl toy figure into it?" she asked.

"I dunno. Haven't thought about that. I'm still in the planning and figuring stage."

"It's getting a little late, isn't it? Don't you graduate in a few months?" she asked.

"Admittedly, I may be cutting it a bit close, but these things shouldn't be taken lightly. You of all people know that. I remember not all that long ago . . ."

"Have you figured *anything* out yet?" she interrupted.

"Not really. I know I want to travel somehow, but you already know that. And write. Definitely do something with my writing. Maybe work for National Geographic or something like that. Go to exotic places, meet interesting people. And get paid for it."

"Big dreams Stone."

"What other kinds are there? Besides, it's just a thought. Sometimes I want to be a professional writer, and then other times I think I should forget it all and be a fireman."

"What?" she laughed, quite surprised. "Where does *that* come from?"

"I dunno. Just something different. What, you don't think I could pull it off?"

"When I was a kid I wanted to be a rodeo clown," Chaos said. "Chicks dig danger."

"And now?" I asked.

"I kinda wanna be Spiderman."

"The lack of actual superhuman abilities must be a hindrance," I said.

"Surprisingly not. Check it out."

Eden and I watched as Chaos clambered up the closet doorframe, climbing feet in like the old palm climbers in the tropics used to do to get their precious coconuts. Monkey climbing. At the top he gripped with just his fingertips and hung himself upside down for a second before flipping over and landing right back on his feet. He struck the web slinging pose (wrists out and middle and ring fingers curled in to a perfection of angle practiced no doubt for endless hours before the mirror in his bedroom) and bounded off between the shelves.

"See, it's not all sex all the time," I said. "Though I have to admit it does take up most of it. I'd be remiss if I didn't say that wasn't fun. And I wouldn't say 'fuckin' either. I'm not as crass as that. I'd like to think I hold myself to a higher standard."

"What would you call it then?"

"I prefer the term make love."

"Then you're in love with her?" Eden asked, suddenly surprised that the word had been floated. The crack widened. Chaos bounded back.

"No. What I mean is sex is always one of the two, fucking or making love. Fucking implies force, randomness, uncaring. Not really me. But making love, that's different. That's more, I don't know, civilized. Less violent, more tender, as it should be. And there are the two types of men who do each. Me, I'm a love maker. And Chaos here,"

"I'm a fucker. I'm a dirty little fucker," he flashed a devilish, guilty grin. "Fuckers have more fun. We get the best positions."

"And what positions are those?" she asked.

"Anything that involves me sticking it in her. Preferably from the back. That way if things aren't going well you at least get a round of rodeo sex in."

"What's rodeo sex?" she asked.

"You don't want to know," I said.

"And you agree with him on this?"

"Well maybe not all of it. But I can't necessarily disagree with his preference."

"You're a pig," Eden laughed at Chaos, and then pointed at me. "And a bad influence on him."

"How so?" I objected.

"Look at you. Using some random girl for sex? That's not the Dave I thought I knew."

"I didn't think it'd bother you so much."

"It doesn't," she countered quickly, maybe too quickly. I could tell it was getting to her, eating at her just a little bit. But sometimes that's how walls fall, with hammers and chisels.

"And it's not just sex," I said, throwing more wood on the fire. "Maybe something more will come of it. Who knows? Megan's a nice girl."

"And she seems to really like you," Chaos chimed in, almost as if on cue, our brains connected by invisible waves, sending messages back and forth like distant satellites beaming out signals, racing to and fro, analyzing, evaluating, acting, reacting, and all in accord with the mission, the common goal of combining our forces to break Eden down. It was symmetry at its best. I thought for a second I could see just the faintest falling in her eyes, like she'd been beaten back, lost her chance. I dropped the bomb.

"She invited me to spend the week with her in Palm Beach. Her parents are going to the islands and we could have the house to ourselves."

"You gonna go?" Chaos asked shooting off again.

"I don't know."

"Maybe you could warm her up with some of your nine existence questions," Eden said, a hint of disappointment in her voice. "Oh, and then have more empty, meaningless sex with her."

"Hey. That's not fair."

"You two are a pair of real intellectuals. I can totally see he's having a positive influence on your way of thinking Stone."

"I resent that. And I think Chaos would too if he clearly wasn't busy saving the store and everyone in it from imminent peril right now."

"Imminent peril?" she smiled.

"It's perilously imminent in fact."

"Right. So I'm gonna go now," she started.

"Wait that's not fair either. You can't just say all that and then just leave. I mean what it is with *you* all the time?"

"What do you mean?"

"Sure, it's sex and cars and wine and silliness with us. We're men; it's what we're programmed to do. And it's not meaningless. I admit I'm not exactly sure what all is going on with this girl, but I don't think sex is ever meaningless. But what about you? What is it with *you* then? You've never been in my position? Never just fallen in with someone without thinking?"

"I don't know."

"You have to. You talk a big game, but you think about these things just as much as the rest of us. So tell me. Come on dear, what are your darkest thoughts? What's churning around in that head of yours Eden? Tell me everything."

"I don't think so."

"Now who's scared?"

"I didn't say that."

"Then what is it? It's not fair that you should be able to read me so easily, as you so seem to think you can, yet I can't know about you."

"Well what do you want to know?"

"I told you. Everything. What do you want from life, really want? Are you content or are you searching for something more? Are you happy with where you are and what you do, and more importantly, who you do it with? Let's hear it all. What's *your* favorite position?"

"Wow, look at the time!" she said employing Chaos' tactic of extrication and looking at her nonexistent watch. "That's some tough luck. And just when I was about to tell you everything. Too bad Stone. See you tomorrow."

"Run if you want, my pretty, but I'll get it out of you one way or another. In the end you'll tell me what I want to know."

Chaos swooped in as I watched her leave.

"Brick wall again?"

"Yeah, but I have to say, it's tons of fun trying to get over it. There is something unmistakably sexy about her shyness. I tell you man, I've got to get closer to her. It's not even want to anymore. It's need to."

XVI

She came to me again a few days later on a slow, sunny morning before opening, looking like she had something on her mind. It was just the two of us, me manning the counter, counting the till, and she coming over after stashing her bag under the register.

"You look troubled," I said as she quietly took a seat by my side, no good morning. She picked at a little thread at the cuff of her sleeve, lost in her thoughts.

"What?" she said as if coming out of a trance. "No, I'm fine."

I nodded and turned back to counting the money.

"It's just that," she started suddenly. "Let me ask you a question. You're a smart guy."

"I like to think so," I said.

"You want to do something with your life, right? I mean you're going to college and everything. You have goals."

"I suppose so. A vague plan at least."

"You want to travel too, right? You were telling me once about that thing at your school where they'd send you to Japan for a year."

"I was looking into it. It sounded pretty cool. A sort of work/study trade off type thing. They hook you up with an apartment and stuff and you teach English at an elementary school for a year. Decent money too. J.A.C or J.E.C, something like that. I'm still thinking of maybe putting my name in for it."

"So it's not crazy to want to move someplace far away like that, right?" she asked. I could see she was trying to justify something to herself.

"I wouldn't try it if I didn't think so."

"But if I said I wanted to do something like join the Peace Corps or something, or Greenpeace, that's not a stupid idea?"

"For you, I would say not. You've said you want to move someplace new. You like animals and helping people. You're environmentally conscious. Got a bit of the hippie in you. It'd probably be a good fit for you."

"I don't think it's stupid," she said quietly.

"I didn't say that. Who said it was stupid?" I already knew the answer, but wanted to hear her say it anyway.

"Jamie. I asked him and he was all like 'what would you want to do that for? You hate camping.' And he laughed. I said we could do it together and he just said it was a dumb idea and he didn't want to go live in some jungle or desert and be poor and sleep in some dirt floor hut."

"I always thought that kind of thing would be fun," I said. "Maybe not a dirt hut, but I don't know. I could probably grow to like it."

Nothing.

"It'd take some doing," I continued. "I looked into the Peace Corps last year. It's weird. If you sign up now, you don't go anywhere for a year. And you don't get paid. That was the kicker for me not to. You just get a little money, like two thousand when you're finished. I suppose that's why you have to wait a year to go."

"I don't care about the money."

"Just want the experience?"

She nodded. I could see the disappointment in her eyes. A dream put down by a no good lover. She looked so small and sad. An opportunity presenting itself, and before I knew it I was saying it.

"Well if you do decide to do it, and he doesn't want to go, you can count me in," I said. "Can't say I ever lived in a dirt hut before."

"I don't know. Just a thought." Resignation as she tugged at the thread on her cuff.

"Let's make it more than that. Let's go somewhere, me and you. How about Japan?"

"Japan?"

"Sure," I was getting excited now. "I'll sign up for that program and you could come with me. Or we could go be teachers. I've been reading about it online at school. There're lots of jobs. They give you a place to live. Some of them even buy you a plane ticket to go. There are places all over the world, like every country. I was going to apply to one in South Korea I saw. We could apply together."

"I looked at that stuff a couple of months ago," she said dejectedly. "You have to have college degree."

"So? I'll get a job and you can tag along. I'll be out of school in a few months. We could go in the spring. Think about it. No work, foreign country, tons to do and see."

"Sure Dave," she said, her words biting with sarcasm. She wasn't seeing any of it seriously, just random fantasy. "You get right on that."

"We could do it," I said in all seriousness turning back to the business of counting the money.

And I knew we could. The mission was set. A door was opened before me. I was going to find a way to make it happen, to make her happy.

After my shift I drove straight to the university, taking the stairs of the fine arts hall two at a time and found the office where the exchange program was based. They were closed for the day, but outside the doors flyers were tacked haphazardly to a large corkboard. There were advertisements for trips to Rome, semesters abroad in Spain, a flyer for a club of international students, and hanging from the bottom of the board a sheet for the work/ study program in Japan, with big bold letters "Live, Work, and Study in Fukuoka!" and at the very bottom in smaller text "Open to registered full time students only."

The door was closed. I was going to have to find another way. And time was running out.

XVII

The next week I was in Palm Beach with Megan. Sun, surf, and complete boredom. More vanilla sex, this time on an uncomfortable fold-out futon in her parent's stuffy guest bedroom. She was thinking our time alone was romantic and all I was thinking about was getting back. By Sunday night I was feigning illness in order to facilitate leaving at the break of dawn Monday.

Interesting developments had taken place in my short absence. Chaos had been accused of skimming from the nightly till and was subsequently fired from the Shaft in lieu of the authorities being called. It was a total white wash, we all knew. It was the modus operandi for eliminating unwanted employees. Accuse and remove. In the last few months a rotating door of employees had been accused of the same thing and were canned under the same abrupt circumstance. It just happened to be Chaos' turn this time. Not that he cared much though. He had a friend managing a store selling sunglasses just across the hall, so he walked over and got a job doing that. He didn't actually even have time to fall before landing right back on his feet. Maybe he really was Spiderman? When I got back into town he told me all about it.

"She'll get you too eventually," he said, speaking of Jen, the owner's daughter. "She got Tim last year, and then it was Rob, then Chad, now me. Soon it'll be Eden or Deirdre. Your days are numbered."

"This blows," I said. "Did you even, like, fight? I mean, you're not a thief. You could sue for slander or something."

"Why bother?" he said nonchalantly. "Who cares what that cunt says about me? I don't. It's just a job. See, I already got another one."

"Well I don't want to be fired. And I'm not a thief. And I don't want to be called one either. This is wrong. We should do something."

"Like what?"

"I don't know. Protest. Call the cops. Complain to the city."

"Won't do any good," he said. "Besides, Ken pays me more here anyway. It's cool. I'm the only one here most of the time. I want an hour for lunch? All I have to do is put up the sign and walk away. And I get a discount on new shades. Check these out."

He slipped on a pair of $180 Ray Bans and started waving his head like Stevie Wonder, a big grin on his face, and broke out into an obnoxiously bad rendition of *Superstition*, playing the glass display counter like a piano and doing guitar out the side of his mouth. A passing mother pushing stroller walked on quickly but across the way a cute Hispanic chick manning a wig cart smiled with her almond eyes.

"Well I'm glad it worked out for you," I said. "But I still think it sucks you got screwed like that. It's wrong. I mean, I don't even want to go back in there now."

"So don't. Come work over here with me."

"I'm not really the salesman type."

"Then go get another job. There're plenty of them."

"Take those things off. I can't take you seriously like that."

"How about with these?" he said and switched the Ray Bans with a pair of little pink kiddy glasses. The Latina giggled and Chaos started playing to her, switching out pair after pair, her giving nods of approval or shakes of dis, all with a pearly smile and full red lips.

"I think she likes me," he said, donning a huge set of ladies' shades that said either I'm an obnoxious Jewish grandma or an abused housewife hiding a shiner. "I think her name is Estelle. Or Edie."

"Nice names."

"Nice ass."

"Pretty lips."

"And you know what they say about a woman's lips," he said and I reflected briefly on Eden's, but then shook it off and thought back to the matter at hand.

"What do you think I should do?" I asked.

"If it were me? Knowing that at some point they're going to try to nail me for stealing or some bullshit, I'd just tell them to go fuck and walk out."

"Yeah but man I need a job though."

"I'm telling you, I can hook you up here. All I have to tell Ken is that you're cool and you're in. Just say the word." I thought it over but knew it wouldn't be the right thing to do.

"That's all right. I appreciate the offer, but I think I'll be able to find something on my own. It's just that I've never done anything like this before. Just walked off a job."

"It's incredibly freeing," he said. "Especially on a day like this, when the sun is shining, no clouds in the sky. You get to drive home with the windows down and the music cranked up. Like you just escaped from prison or something." He made it sound so nice.

"What about Eden?" I asked.

"What about her?"

"I won't get to see her as often if I go."

"All the more reason for her to want to see you though. She'll miss you. That'll make the chances you do get together that much better. With that, and Megan, you're golden. By the way, how was Palm Beach?"

"Do I really need to answer that?" I said cynically.

"That bad? I think it's had the desired effect though. You gonna end it?"

"I think I already did."

"What did you tell her?"

"Nothing. I think I'm going to take a page from your book and just not call her anymore."

"It's better that way," he said switching out pairs again, still making eyes with the Latina. "Makes it easier all around. Make a clean break of it. Take more time to focus on what's most important."

His logic, dispensed rapid fire from behind little round John Lennon frames with aqua lenses, was flawless. Absence does make the heart grow fonder. I was killing two birds with one stone, making a political statement about my best friend getting fucked and making myself more valuable in Eden's eyes. It was win-win. The completely illogical logic of love. So what if it made me unemployed? Wasn't it more important to stick to your convictions and stand up for friends, king and country?

"You're right," I said. "Fuck 'em."

"That's the spirit!" Chaos said triumphantly, a giant pair of gag glasses covering his face. "I get off at ten. Come back and we'll go out and drink to new opportunities."

"Right!" I said and turned about, a mission and purpose swelling in my chest. I went back into the store, got my pack out of the closet and slung it over my shoulder and marched right up to Jen, who was busy talking on the phone and told her I quit. I wanted to say more, to stand there and draw a scene, tell everyone who would listen how they mistreated innocent people. But she couldn't be bothered. All she did was put her hand over the receiver and say they'd send my last check in the mail.

I left with neither pomp nor circumstance. It was a completely meaningless, quiet retreat. But Eden heard and stopped me in the hall on my way out. I explained the reasoning of my little coup, and she saw merit in it, even if it was foolish to just quit without anything else lined up. But she was excited and saddened nonetheless.

"Well this place is going to suck now," she said. "You're gone, Chaos is gone. It's going to be boring as hell around here."

"Deirdre is still around," I pointed out. "And Chaos is just across the hall."

"But you're part of, I don't know, the group. Without you it isn't a group anymore."

"We still get together all the time. How's this any different?"

"I don't know," she hesitated. "It just won't be the same."

"Maybe it'll be better. I know I feel better already."

"That's just because you're not stuck here anymore."

"So? You don't have to be. Quit with me."

"Can't. Need the money."

"So do I, but there are plenty of other gigs."

"Sorry Stone. You're stronger than me."

"Don't worry," I said, suddenly turning sappy and dramatic, affecting my best Bogart to date. "I'll get something new, then I'll come back for you and take you away from all of this."

"Really?" she played, the Bergman to my Bogie. "Do you promise? Say it will be so."

"It will be my dear. Goodbye for now. But soon, look for me to the East. Where you see the sunrise, that's where I'll be."

"You're a freak you know that?" she laughed. "I have to get back."

"Saturday?" I asked. "The Florida Room?"

"Don't we always?"

XVIII

I met up with Chaos downtown later that night for our regular Tuesday outing of dinner, drinks, and general merry making, and when the elevator doors parted and I stepped out onto the street from the parking deck he was there, excited and proud, looking like the cat that just ate the canary, guilty and bursting to shout out his crime for all to hear. As it turned out, there was indeed more going on in my absence than just changing jobs. He'd met someone new, and wanted me to meet her, to get my impressions (not that they really mattered anyway).

"She's a dancer at Velvet," he explained as we sat down to beers and a basket of chicken wings; local place, usual Tuesday pre-club meeting spot. Cheap beer, good wings, lots of memories. And down on the street (the joint was on the second floor overlooking the avenue, big plate glass wall where you could look down on all the heads) a parade of clubbers drifting by, all shiny and groomed, jeans and pressed shirts, sharp open collars and gelled hair, all wide eyed, full of life, sex on the brain, on their way to their own back-alley destinies. Guys in groups, sometimes four or five, moving in a pack, on the hunt for tail. And the girls, also in huddles of two and three, playing it cool, but eyes darting and giggles reverberating down the streets, up the faces of the buildings, around corners. Perfume and cologne dampening the air like a fog, an invisible nebula drifting about, folding over and splaying out like you're walking through clouds a thousand feet off the ground. You pass a girl, the scent of peach, or maybe lily, you turn and look, but then BAM! another girl passes and then it's suddenly rose, or maybe vanilla. You turn again, but bump shoulders with a Keanu or

Brad or Denzel, and then it's "hey man", or "watch the shoes asshole" and some overzealous, overtestosteroned, overcologned, underachieving douche bag out for a fuck but who'd settle for a fight is suddenly in your face while his friends cover their mouths and point and laugh and you realize all people really are monkeys and it's fight or flight (flight most of the time) and you're lucky if you get away with just a shove, but you shrug it off (he'll get his someday) and it's all ok because here comes another girl and everything is fine again.

But for now that's all down below, and Chaos is leaning eagerly over the table telling me more about his new dancer.

"Her name is Kari, and man can she move! Red hair, red ass too. I mean so tanned it's almost red, you know the kind? Like Indian red. The feathers in the hair kind, not the dot in the forehead kind. You know sometimes I just wanna peel that thing off, look underneath and be like 'Hey! I'm a winner!' Ha! I think she's got some Italian in her. I mean more than what I already put in there!"

He'd seen her every day for the last week (all outside of work), a new record for him, and by all measures the start of an actual relationship of sorts. From what he'd described of her it was perfect for him; she was good looking, a great fuck, worked most nights, and had her own money to spend. He even proceeded to expound on her *other* talents, and spared no expense relaying the details of their first night together, from what I gathered from his frantic, pun laden description a wild romp of sweat, spit and torn clothes that ranged all over the apartment, culminating in a wet heap on the kitchen floor.

"She's a squirter!" He could barely contain himself, he was so red, shaking with giggles and eyes bulging out like they were trying to escape. He popped like a Jack in the Box. "I thought she pissed on my nuts!"

"But she's not Nikki," I pointed out. "That reminds me. I gotta tell you a real funny story . . ."

"No, she's not," he interrupted. "But fuck that and all anyway. I'm over all that. Done. Oh, and dig it, she's totally into Spiderman."

"Oh?"

"I stood him in the corner so he could watch us! I put her panties on his head!"

"Did she call you her dirty little web slinger?"

"Well I was slingin' something. Like my sticky all over her face!"

Just before ten we finished our beers and took to the streets feeling fine, a light buzz humming in my head and a silent joy at being back in town, the weight of knowing it was over with Megan off my shoulders. And in Chaos' step, an extra spring; though I knew he'd never admit it, he was glad I was back. Not that his life was boring or empty without me, but for a week he had no one to level his exploits to or to lay down his maniac ways on. But we were together again and now everything was cool and all right with the universe. Then suddenly, Chaos was off in a sprint.

I was confused. He'd shouted something, I didn't hear what, but he was at a flat out run now, a blur of blue and black vinyl shooting up the street. I started to run, I don't know what I was running toward, but I knew I had to follow him. Up ahead, at least ten paces, Chaos was already barreling toward his target, a slight Asian man, maybe thirty, in a black-on-black suit, and his girlfriend (or wife maybe?), younger, mid-twenties maybe, with long straight hair and in high heels, so she was taller than him. But that didn't stop him from smacking her repeatedly in the face: hard, open-palmed slaps across the cheeks and lips as she turned away and cowered, but he just kept swatting at the back of her head shouting an incomprehensible gibberish that echoed up the street. I knew Chaos was out for blood.

His mother was battered, as a child and as a wife, and in the dawn years of his life so was Chaos. Abuse was nothing he tolerated. Sexual violence, or rather the violence of his sex, though the stuff of constant amusement and regaled in late night tales over bottomless bottles of booze and filthy ash trays, never crossed into the realm of pain or force. No meant no, period. He accepted the abuse only until he was old enough to fight back, then his father backed off. Later he repented his crimes against his family and all was reconciled, though scars run deep and emotional ones never fully heal. It was undoubtedly the source of Chaos' misogynistic, deprecating ways, and ultimately the cause of his use of women. But violent against them? Never. It was too close to home.

So when Chaos saw a helpless woman being barraged by a drunken ingrate husband, he sprung into action like the superhero he imagined himself to be and the one I believed he really was. Like a cat he pounced and he would have landed the first solid right across the villain's face and shattered his jaw if the bouncer hadn't beaten him to the punch (no pun there, only a bone-shattering fact).

The guy seemingly came out of nowhere, but really from the door he was guarding only a few feet away. He'd seen the first blow and was already on the move when Chaos sprinted away from me. A brute of a man, arms like oak branches and a black tee that gripped his tremendous chest like a wet suit, he crashed on the husband like a meteor falling from space. In one move he grabbed a handful of hair and slammed his head flat against the hard marble face of the doorway.

"You like to hit women?" he yelled into the man's face, now white with surprise and terror. "Piece of shit!"

Chaos swept in and gave him a fierce blow to the gut while the bouncer held him fast against the wall. Hubby crumbled to his knees and curled into a ball, playing possum. The girl stood by sobbing uncontrollably. A quick flurry of blows and kicks thumping out as they descended upon the helpless, weak lump of a man collapsed on the pavement. A small crowd gathered, peering over shoulders, whispering, gasping. It was all over in a matter of seconds.

The bouncer retreated into the safety and anonymity of the throng in the club and one of the others took his place, checking IDs, nonchalant, as if nothing at all had happened.

"We've got to go," I said tugging at Chaos' sleeve, the fire still burning in his eyes. We fled up the block and around the corner, leaving the witnesses behind, but his mind was overloaded. He couldn't think, drunk on rage, wanting to go back for more, spouting curses, thirsty for blood, but I knew the cops would be coming any minute and we had to become scarce. I led us at a quick step up the next street, around another corner, taking us farther away from the scene. We ducked into a bar off the main drag and stood near the back and I got us some beers to help calm things down. Soon the adrenaline high wore off and things cooled down putting us in better spirits. After ten minutes we went back out onto the street, trying to avoid the cops on the corners, but laughing about how the guy'd cried like a little girl when they were pummeling him, and made our way to Copper. Across the street from the club I saw the couple again, he leading the way, yelling at an angry stomp and she, still sobbing, bringing up the rear. He was about to get into his car, maybe even leave her behind, when I tapped a bike cop on the shoulder.

"Hey that guy over there was beating the piss out of his wife over on Church Street. He's totally hammered. You gotta stop him." The cop beat it up the street and the last thing I saw before disappearing into the bar was him standing between the two of them, hubby bruised and bleeding looking as scared as hell, and I felt relieved that I had done my good deed for the day.

Inside, I was surprised to find Chaos at the bar with Deirdre. She was alone. Sage was at home.

"So how's all that going?" I asked. "You two a thing now?"

"I don't know," she said curiously. "I haven't seen him in a few days. He hasn't called."

"Are you two still?"

"No. I guess it was just that one time. I mean I hope it isn't."

"He's a hard guy to read," I said. "He's still feeling for Rebecca I'm sure. Maybe he just needs a little more time. You should keep after it though. If he's not calling you, you should call him."

"I thought he was coming tonight," she said. "Last time I heard from him he said they were going to show some of his stuff here again."

"A regular Pie-casso the boy is," Chaos interjected.

"Where's it at?" I asked.

Two of Sage's paintings hung on the brick wall in the back. Beside each was a little white card with his name and the title in italics. One was called *Push* and the other *Pull*. They were both new works. He was painting again.

"You should go over there tonight," I told Deirdre.

"I know," she said.

Kari arrived and she was a vixen of a girl, short and lean, curvy in all the right places and tight in the other right places too. Her skin was olive and freckled from too much time in the sun, with just a hint of a flush, just like Chaos had described, hair dyed auburn and ice blue eyes all made up and wrapped in a black skirt and heels.

They were all over each other right from the start, greeting with a kiss but quickly groping and inter angling and it wasn't long before they were dancing back to chest, ass to crotch, grinding and swaying in the crowd and acting like they were the only two people in the room and Deirdre and I were left alone.

"It's good that he's finally found a girl that he can build a real relationship with," she said, her voice laden with sarcasm and disappointment. "You know, one not just based on meaningless sex. She's not like any of the other whores he usually goes with. It's a nice change for him."

"It's just his way," I said. "You can't hold it against him. He's got a gift."

"I give it a week."

Out on the dance floor Kari was grinding her ass against Chaos' crotch, and he was saluting us with a raised beer and a wagging tongue, nodding his head in obscene glory and smug superiority. He knew we were jealous. He knew he was the king sitting in his rightful place on a throne made of women. We knew it wouldn't last, that they'd be separated by the end of the week, some meaningless scuffle. We both smiled back and gave him the finger. It wasn't magic that Deirdre's predictions actually came true the very next day.

XIX

It took two weeks to find a new job, mostly from a complete lack of trying on my part. I'd found my new unemployment quite freeing, leaving me much more time to write and engage in extracurricular activities. But all good things must come to an end. So clean-cut college kid, drug free, white, responsible looking in pressed shirt and tie that I was, I got up one Sunday morning, walked into the mall and started filling out applications. At the third store I went in, a luggage and travel shop, the manager took my application right away and interviewed me in the back store room. His name was Neal, and he was a little runt of a man, defective at birth I guessed and it made him abnormally short and nearly deaf. As gay as the day is long, I was almost certain I had seen him in The Florida Room on more than one Saturday night, and was also reasonably sure he'd seen me there too, which may have ultimately gotten me the job. Either way, after a few minutes of small talk and legal formalities he offered me a sales job and told me to start first thing the next day.

I showed up promptly at eight o'clock the next morning, an hour before opening, and waited outside the locked store gate in the hall of the deserted mall. I waited nearly forty five minutes, watching silently a sporadic parade of elderly couples in track suits and pristine white sneakers shuffle by taking their morning constitutional, until a Cuban kid, probably my age, in purple shirt and black tie, unpressed slacks, slicked back jet hair and heavy silver watch hanging from a hairy wrist, strolled up to open the doors.

"You the guy Neal hired?"

"Dave," I said, extending my hand.

"Angel," he said practically crushing my hand in a handshake brimming with Cuban machismo. "You seen Luis?"

"Luis? I don't think so. I'm afraid I don't know what he looks like."

"You go out last night?" he shouted over my shoulder. I turned to find a chubby young blonde in blue skirt and pink blouse opening the gate in front of a Claire's Accessories across the way. She couldn't have been more than eighteen, cute and round, with long straight hair and ample breasts. "Why didn't you call?"

"I lost your number," she called back. "You have to give it to me again."

"Whatever," he joked. "I see how it is."

"No," she shrilled. Her voice was piercing valley girl and echoed up to the glass atrium above. "Really, I was going to call."

"All right. Sure." Then whispering to me. "I can't wait to get in that big ass."

"What did he say?" the blonde called playfully. "Is he, like, talking about me?"

I shrugged and played dumb, motioning that I didn't hear anything and followed Angel inside. He pulled the gate down behind us and brought me into the back room, a little maze of metal racks filled with beaten boxes marked Samsonite and Tumi and Delsy stacked floor to ceiling. An open door in the corner reveled a closet toilet and sink that doubled as the broom and mop storage.

"OK, so first day on the job, this is the back room, you can eat lunch back here as long as the door is closed. There's a mini-fridge next to the bathroom. Neal says we're not supposed to eat back here at all, but he's a little fag and we don't listen to him anyway. So, here's the stock, everything's supposed to be grouped by manufacturer, but there ain't no room so we just throw shit wherever it'll fit. UPS delivers at ten, just sign for it if I'm not here. Neal give you a nametag?"

"No," I said. "I just got hired yesterday. I don't have anything."

"There's a label maker next to the embossing machine," he said pointing to a large metal contraption bolted to a work table. "Make a label with your name and I'll get a tag. If you want I'll show you how to use the embosser. It's pretty cool. Can burn your name into your wallet. Here, check this out; I put Bad Motherfucker on mine, just like in Pulp

Fiction. Check it." And sure enough there it was burned into the side of his brown billfold in heavy serif letters.

Angel took me around, showed me the rest of the store, where everything was kept, how it was arranged, gave me a crash course on using the computer register, and that was it. Periodically he would look across the way for his blonde friend.

"So what's up with that?" I asked.

"Man, I've been tryin' to hit that for like three weeks. She keeps stallin', sayin' dumb shit like she lost my number. You believe that?"

"I've heard worse."

"She's cute, right?"

"She's not ugly," I admitted. "Not my type, but certainly not bad. A little young isn't she?"

"What, you like 'em thin? Like pencil chicks?"

"No, I'm just not that crazy about blondes."

"I am," he said. "And the bigger the better. I mean not too big, not like Jabba the Hutt big, but a girl's gotta have a little *carne en los huesos*. Know what I mean?"

"Really?"

"Oh yeah, big chick's where it's at man," he said making a sucking sound through his clenched teeth. "Big juicy ass, grab right on here and here, ride it all the way home. And big chicks work for it too. They don't fuck around cuz they don't get it much. Dirty. Real dirty. Just like that one over there. Little freak with all that baby fat. She's seventeen you know. Even told me she doesn't have a gag reflex."

"You don't say?" I said, indulging him. "That's certainly a selling point I imagine."

"Just cram it right down her throat, those big titties slappin' against your legs."

"Angel you're a man of unique tastes. You know, I have a friend you should meet."

"I'm serious man; you should give big girls a try. You'll thank me."

"I'm open to just about anything, but right now I gotta say I got my eyes on a particular girl, and that's taking up most of my time."

"I got it, I got it. That's cool man, that's cool. Go get what you can get. But if you want, I know this one, works down at Lane Bryant. Big titties. I mean, *grande* man! Cute little mouth. You're a little guy, so you'd have to be on top or she'll fuck you up, crush your nuts man! I was gonna move

174

on her but then Christine started workin' over there. Assistant manager, so you know, get her to come in through the delivery door, bend her over the counter and slap that big ass '*So you wanna buy a Tumi huh?*"

"Speaking of which," I interrupted. "If we could just get back to business for a second? Are you going to show me how to sell this stuff? I've never done this before."

"Ah it's simple man. Customer comes in, just pick one up, show it to 'em, move the zippers around, you know, show 'em the wheels. If you don't know something, bam, just read it off the tag on the back. And just remember these two words: ballistic nylon. People love that shit."

"So that's it?"

"That's it."

"So what time do we open?"

"Nine."

"And when do people usually start coming in?"

"Saturday."

"Saturday?"

"Yep."

"So in the mean time what? We just stand here?"

"Pretty much," he said. "We got a TV in the back, and that little one over there got a VCR in it. Last week we watched New Jack City. And Luis got a radio around here somewhere. Go in the bathroom and read a book. I like to stand out front and watch the parade of all the little high school *chicas* playin' hooky."

"I think I'm going to like working here."

"It's not so bad," he agreed.

Two days later I had Bad Motherfucker burned into the side of my wallet.

XX

Chaos and Kari were on again. His patterns were as predictable as the path of the stars across the sky.

We'd gone back to Velvet a few days before and she was there. At first he just smiled and she just nodded from the bar where she chatted up some corpulent car salesman type sipping a gin and tonic. We took a table across the room and ordered beers, but at the next song she danced for the salesman and at every chance she turned her back to him and would catch Chaos' eye, trying to tease him, drive him to jealousy, which wasn't that difficult, as he'd mostly been watching since we'd gotten in there anyway and I knew my friend wanted her again. That's the way it is I guess. There was something about her he needed to see again. I knew it wasn't substantial, just a passing feeling, he'd had lots of them. The list of names was endless: Sarah, Jana, Becky, Jessica, and on and on. Now it was Kari. I knew it would be over again in another week, maybe two, but for now this is what he wanted. She finished up with the sweaty suit and spent the rest of the night dancing at our table. Reconciliation set to a wailing guitar riff.

Now it was the evening of my 22nd birthday, mid-March, and Chaos said he wanted to go to Copper for our regular Tuesday night venture, and Kari was coming and what's more she was bringing her new roommate Shay.

"She's a massage therapist," he said greedily over the phone. "I told them we were going out for your birthday."

"A masseuse?" I said. "Happy ending?"

"That's what I'm thinking bro. Holy shiatsu!"

"I've got a mass she can asage."

"You know the holes on those tables you put your face in look like a toilet from underneath?" he said. "I saw it once on TV. You look like you're a turd comin' out a horse's patoot!"

Copper was in full swing when we rolled up to the club and after a quick tour we saw we'd arrive first, so Chaos quickly ran to the bar to buy me my first birthday round and it was a pair of strange green martinis the bartender called antifreeze we drank down. A special of the night, he quickly ordered two more and we killed them.

The bar was hopping, packed in shoulder to shoulder as usual, and caustic, trippy acid jazz flowing like water over our heads, the drinks already taking effect, and I commented on this and Chaos just agreed with that grin.

"There's Kari," he said suddenly and was off to the door. "Man look at her friend."

"Hey, you already got one. Let another guy get a chance."

"No worries dude. I'm fine with Kari. But I bet if we play our cards right we could get both of them."

"Very drunk if we keep these flowing," I said.

"And switch off. Man Kari is a freak in bed. It's the dancer in her, or maybe the me in her. Ha! They just know how to move."

"A foursome?" I said. I could see the gears turning behind his eyes as he watched Shay approaching.

"Why not? I could go *for some* tonight, what about you?"

"I'm not partial to orgies. Switching is all right if you want, if you think they won't mind. I'll leave that to you. But separate rooms. I'm not taking my dick out in front of you. I mean we're close and all, but I gotta draw a line there."

"I don't care if it's in front of me," he said. "Just not behind me!"

"Well, it's a celebration anyway, right?"

"Happy birthday my friend."

With the girls finally arrived Chaos and Kari moved to the bar again to fetch more drinks for us and I was left alone with Shay. She was indeed pretty, older in fact than probably any of us, with shoulder length wavy blonde hair, fair blue eyes and a healthy pair of perky tits tucked beneath a thin green tee that showed just the tiniest beginnings of a belly. Bubbly would be a good word to sum her up. Her skin was tanned from an all day excursion to the beach, which I proceeded to ask about as an impetus for conversation. All in all she was quite attractive, no Eden of course, and a bit on the dumb side, but that didn't stop me from envisioning making her back at her apartment.

"So you're a massage therapist," I said.

"Not yet," she said.

"Oh. I thought Chaos said . . ."

"I'm just taking classes right now. It's really hard. Harder than I thought it would be anyway."

"I imagine so. How much longer have you got?"

"About six months. Then I can get a license."

'Do you like it? I mean I assume you'd really have to like being close to other people. What made you get into it?"

"I don't know," she said. "I just like helping people. I wanted to get into physical therapy at first, you know, like sports therapy. I love sports. Do you?"

"They're all right. I used to play baseball, but that was a long time ago." The conversation was going nowhere fast.

"I *love* soccer. And basketball too. Anyway, I wanted to get into training, but that didn't work out. Then I tried to get into sports therapy, but I didn't have the grades to get into a college. So then I had a friend who was into massage therapy and said I should try."

"Well it's a similar field anyway," I said. "I gotta say you're a better person than me. I don't think I could do it, touching a stranger like that I mean. Rubbing all over some weird guy's legs and chest and stuff. Not for me."

"I do girls too."

"Then again I suppose every job has its perks . . ."

Much later in the evening and the four of us are rolling high on green martinis and I'm feeling pretty good and getting all kinds of signals from Shay that she's into me. We spent most of the night a tightly packed little clique around a table crowded with our empty glasses and dusted with flakes of gray cigarette ash but now suddenly she wants to dance and drunk as I am I say why not and she leads me out onto the floor below and we wriggle our way out and find a little space just for us.

She was beautiful, there was no doubt about that and she looked at me through syrupy, lidded, come fuck me eyes, but with serious determined lips and slightly furrowed brow, like she was debating whether or not she really wanted to be there right then with me or maybe somewhere else, anywhere else, with anyone else. But she was there with me and there was nowhere to go. We were pushed up nearly chest to chest on the cramped dance floor and stuck in the unending confused loop in my mind of "what do I say, what do I say", I tried to come up with something amusing to make her smile, but wit was absent, probably cast out by the scruff of its neck by the five antifreezes coursing through my veins.

"We might have to leave soon," I shouted over the din of the DJ spinning thick trip hop over our heads and through our chests and ears like a hurricane. "I hear the sardines want their dance floor back."

"What?" she shouted, sticking a finger in her ear and leaning in close to my mouth.

"Nothing," I yelled back.

I looked around and spotted Chaos and Kari at the bar. His broad grin suggesting something inviting and she responded in kind. I watched them abandon their drinks as she led him by the hand toward the booths in the back.

"So it's your birthday huh?" Shay said suddenly.

I nodded.

"How old are you?"

"Twenty-two today."

"Oh my God," she said with surprise, her eyes widening temporarily to the sobriety. Then she giggled coyly and her breasts jiggled like a pair of happy bunnies, "You're just a baby."

"Oh?"

"I'm thirty-three. Almost old enough to be your mother."

I shook my head and beckoned her to lean in close. "Nonsense," I said. "You're way too beautiful to be anyone's mother."

"That's sweet," she said, then putting one hand around the back of my head, gripping my hair and drawing my ear right up to her mouth, "You know I could teach a young thing like you a thing or two," and I felt the tip of her warm, moist tongue trace a swirl around its edge and the gentle pull of her teeth on my earring.

Score.

It's really late now, the club starting to wind down, and the last few hours blurry, slurry and a confusion of dancing, drink and hot breath in ears and wet kisses on necks, close talking and bedroom eyes.

I'm in the can taking the sixth piss of the night, having left Shay at the table mid sentence and her giggling at the quirky way I excuse myself, quickly, like Groucho Marx, a flurry of rolling eyes and flying shirt tails. I'm high as a kite because we've been making out for the last ten minutes and I'm feeling good and can still taste her on my lips and it's all going great. The light over the stall blinding as I'm standing, head back, eyes twitching, cock in hand not caring anymore about my aim (was all the way up until my fourth trip but after that fuck it all, just as long as it's not on my shoes). She's thinking I'm cute and funny and all I can think about is taking her home and fucking her and screw Eden and all this useless chasing about and throwing myself against big brick walls and conventions of love, and the booze is like fire in my head and man I need a fuck.

Out of the stall a black guy in white shirt and black pants, uneven bowtie, sitting on a stool near the sink turns on the faucet for me (for the sixth time tonight) and I'm looking at the fiver I put in his glass tip jar three pisses ago lamenting my drunken stupidity for not paying closer attention to what I was doing, so no sir, no more tips for you, no matter how many paper towels you hand me, and no mints (Christ who eats a mint from a public bathroom?), but do you have any cigars left?

"How's it going out there," James asks. I got his name on my third visit to the head. We've been keeping a running conversation about my chances of bagging Shay most of the night and I've been giving the play by play.

"I do believe we are a go for launch Houston," I say popping another dollar into the jar because James *is* a nice, hardworking guy after all and damn it I like him. He chuckles when I crash into the door with my shoulder and stumble back out. "T-minus ten minutes and counting."

Chaos is standing at the table when I get back. Kari and Shay are nowhere to be seen, but he doesn't seem fazed and is just bopping to the beat.

"Bathroom," he says of the ladies.

"So is this thing happening or what?" I ask.

"Oh it's happening. We're outta here when they get back."

I'm suddenly thankful for his ability to better hold his liquor than I can and keep control of the lady situation, eyes always on the prize on these nights when it's just the two of us against the world. He understands his role perfectly. He's the wrangler, I'm the voice of reason, but not this night even though it's not like me to get completely fall down drunk as I am now, but I take exception on my birthday.

"Good, because I could use a good massage and a fuck. And about that whole switching thing . . ."

"Forget about it," he cuts in. "I've been watching you two all night. Shay's all yours. She totally wants you."

"You could have her too if you want," I say like I'm bartering a commodity that's not even mine.

"No thanks. I'm fine with Kari."

He's much more sober than I am and I'm thinking it's a damn good thing he drove when Kari and Shay come back from the bathroom and we decide to go. Then we're walking back to the garage, Kari and Chaos in front and Shay and I trailing behind and I'm watching the seams in the sidewalk trying to hold the line and so is Shay (she's had at least seven and is high as a kite) and man I just know the sex is going to be incredible if I can just keep from puking.

In the car we're both giddy with anticipation and the music is blaring again and it's all cackles and belly laughs and he's telling me how Kari practically gave him a hand job in the back booth as we follow the girls north to their new pad in Winter Park.

"So we start making out and all the sudden she starts saying how much she misses me and she's clawing at my dick through my pants with both hands, and I'm like 'Jesus babe, you trying to churn butter or what!'"

"Would you like some pepper on your salad sir?" I ask making like I'm twisting a mill and we howl with laughter with the windows down and Chaos nearly runs us off the road he's so teary eyed and wild.

We cruised on and finally reached the apartments and the girls lead us upstairs to their third floor rooms overlooking the pool and all I want to do is figure out which bedroom is Shay's but Chaos is looking out the balcony doors and asking if we want to go for a swim and I'm thinking fine, you two go for a dip and leave me and Shay alone. But Kari says she isn't feeling it and Shay asks if we want beers and we follow her into the kitchen. She cracks a few for us and we toast my birthday yet again (fourth or fifth time) and we go back into the living room where we find Kari on the couch packing weed into the business end of a little glass pipe and instantly I know it's all gone to shit.

"You want some?" Kari offers, but Chaos stoically refuses. This is something new for her, I sense, otherwise we would never have come here. Shay's turned her on to it. She asks me and when I pass she gives it an 'oh well' shrug and lights up anyway. I'm crestfallen when Shay takes a deep toke and it signals the death knell on any desire I had for her.

Neither Chaos nor I wanted anything to do with drugs of any kind. You could be a drinker, a smoker, hell you could even be a cutter. But drugs? No. Absolutely not. Chaos had watched other friends spiral into crime and failure because of them, and I knew too many people from former years who'd thrown their lives away for the same reasons. Drugs were where we drew the line. It was an unspoken rule between friends. Discouraged, we let them pass the pipe between themselves several times before finishing our beers. When they excused themselves, Kari to the bathroom and Shay to her room to get more of her stash, we made a quiet, hasty exit.

XXI

The days following the debacle that was my birthday flowed by with neither merit nor notice. Sage was still mostly incognito, though Deirdre had been making some headway managing to spend more time with him. It wasn't much though, just a few afternoons, but she'd been working at him, getting him to lay off the drink. I stayed back, refrained from calling, and let things take their course. If this was the beginnings of a burgeoning new relationship I didn't want to get in the way of anyone.

Chaos was, well, Chaos. We spent the day after Copper first lamenting, then laughing about the whole thing. He was over it in five minutes, though I wish I could say the same about the missed opportunity with Shay. I know the sex would have been incredible, a bout for the ages, but principle prevailed over pussy yet again, and ever forward as they say. I chocked the whole affair up to yet another test of the flesh on the road to Eden that I passed with flying colors.

Speaking of Eden, she had also become scarce. The week passed with neither word from nor sight of her. I returned to the monotony of work and study, finding relief only in the daily comedy of Angel the letch. He'd finally "hit dat" with Christine, providing all the gratuitous details of their rippley midnight encounter where he'd immersed himself in the heaving folds of her pleasure and got lost in between the crevices therein.

Saturday found me lounging at home when, for the first time ever, Eden actually called. She sounded at once glad that I was around, and at once distant and slightly down.

"What are you doing later?" she asked.

"It's Saturday," I said. "I assumed The Florida Room."

"Can I ask a favor?"

"Sure. Anything."

"You want to maybe do something else?"

"Like what?"

"I don't know."

"Are you all right?" I asked. "You don't sound so hot."

"I'm fine," she said unconvincingly. "It's nothing. I just don't feel like going out with everyone tonight, but I don't want to go home either. I don't know what to do."

"What about Nikki?"

"She's going to some new bar in Sanford but I really don't want to go. I just . . ." she stopped.

"How about dinner?" I asked. "We could meet somewhere."

"My car died this morning. I got a ride in from my dad today. Could you come pick me up at the Shaft?"

"Sure."

"You sure it's not too much trouble. I mean it's a long drive down here." She was suddenly sounding hesitant.

"Come on. You think it's trouble for a friend? And what's more," I added. "Dinner's on me."

I told her I'd be there when she got off and rushed to change into nicer clothes, me having lain around all afternoon in knock-around, beat-up jeans and stretched-out crew neck, an outfit in no way fit for presentation to the girl whom I loved more than life itself.

A quick shower was in order and a shave too. Luck was on my side as I had just given my car a thorough cleaning inside and out the day before, so the mental checklist complete (shower, shave, teeth, clothes, cologne, car, matches, condom), except for grabbing some cash along the way, I was out the door with plenty of time to spare.

The sun was moving west across the late afternoon sky and after stopping by an ATM and withdrawing a hundred dollars, way too much for me to spare and probably an unwise move, but this was Eden and we were going out just me and her and there was no way come hell or high water I was coming up short for anything, I headed into the city.

As I cruised into town, windows down, early spring in the air, I was running a cycle of thoughts through the wringer trying to come up with a way to parlay what was sure to be an early dinner into a longer evening when luck struck a second time (What was this all about? Was someone trying to send me a message? Was everything falling into perfect place because this was to be the night of nights, the one I'd been waiting for all this time? And what price would I have to pay for this momentary planet-aligning perfection?) and the DJ came on reminding everyone that Duran Duran would be performing later that night at Disney's Pleasure Island and wouldn't everyone head on down to see them? Tickets only twenty dollars at the gate.

So some mental math then and I realized that despite the hundred in my pocket I would probably come up short, figuring forty for the tickets and drinks with that so really closer to sixty, leaving only forty for dinner which might not cut it so I made up my mind to charge dinner (and make it a nice expensive one) and use cash for the rest so I could sleep soundly that night and worry about how I was going to get through the rest of the week another time. You cannot, absolutely must not, put a price on love. What's me starving for a few days compared to the infinite warmth and joy of being around Eden and showing her a good time? I raced on.

She was standing curbside when I picked her up and immediately I sensed she was in a foul mood. I asked if everything was all right but her answers were sharp and curt. She apologized for making me come out to get her and for the mood she was in and asked if I would just take her home.

"It's no problem," I said. "I wasn't doing anything at home anyway. Needed to get out of the house. Cabin fever and all. You've got something on your mind? Do you want to talk about anything?"

"No."

"Because if you want to be alone that's cool, but if you'd rather vent or something feel free to bounce it off me."

"It's," she stopped. "It's nothing."

"Come on, what's up?"

"I just feel like punching something I'm so angry right now," she said, her fingers clenched nearly into fists.

"Here," I said offering my shoulder. "Give it a good whack."

"What? No."

"Come on," I pressed slapping my arm and flexing strongman style. "I can take it."

She shot me a level stare.

"What? You think I can't take a punch from a woman. You think I'm a weakling?"

Nothing.

"I'll have you know I have the strength of ten men and one small boy."

More nothing.

"It's true. And not just any boy either. A real fat one. A Samoan man-child in fact."

Finally a lopsided smile and gentle snigger.

"You are so weird sometimes Stone."

"So tell me, what's bothering you?"

"I don't really want to talk about it."

"That's fine," I said. "So let's do something to take your mind off it instead."

"Like what?"

I let her know about the concert later that night and suggested we still grab something to eat and then head down and see the show. I told her to pick the place since she was the one in need of cheering up, money no object, and she decided on her favorite Chinese place that had excellent vegetarian dishes. It was her comfort food place.

When I'd first learned that Eden was a vegan, the first thing I did was run out to the find the best, most expensive vegetarian cookbook I could find. I had it in my mind to surprise her by asking her to join me for dinner, then just bowling her over with the best damn vegetarian meal she'd ever eaten. It would get me in her good graces, and give me a chance to demonstrate my cooking prowess. It was the perfect plan. It couldn't fail.

So after my shift ended one bright sunny Tuesday evening I got right in my car and raced to the nearest bookstore, took the stairs two at a time to get to the cooking section and immediately began rifling through every text I could see. So many. There were all sorts of ridiculous titles like *Great Greens!* and *Vegan for Dummies*. There was even one with a caricature of Hamlet holding a brick of something bland, drippy and white in his hand like Yorich's skull that read *Tofu or Not Tofu*.

Most of the recipes offered turned my stomach. They all included things I hated most and never ate, ever. One dish called for a puree of kidney beans over a bed of Brussels sprouts and topped with some sort of boiled onion and green bean combination. And fish, lots and lots of fish.

Fish was the enemy in my house growing up back in New Jersey. It wasn't food. It was the opposite of meat, it was the anti-meat, and my father wasn't having any of it. Once, before I was born, my mother cooked a salmon for him. Once. She spent a good two hours preparing dinner and when she served it, just the two of them at an old hand me down table in their post-collegiate second floor duplex kitchen, he took one forkful, chewed thoughtfully, then quietly rose from the table with his plate, walked over to the trash bin, and dumped the whole thing in, plate and all. That was the last time fish was ever served in our house. From there on in it's been nothing but steak, chicken, and pork. The closest we ever got to a vegetarian meal in my house was a plain cheese pizza.

So I spent the next hour sitting there in the cookbook aisle going through every one of them. When I had finally narrowed it down to just two, I was crestfallen to discover that the only ones that had even remotely edible recipes in them were both over $50. That was a lot of money for me. I still had to support myself for the next week and a half on the hundred I had. Figure in gas, groceries and booze, there was just no way I could justify the expense, no matter how disappointing it was. Besides, thinking about it more on the way home, I rationalized that for the same money, I could just as easily take Eden out to a nice dinner and still have money left over for some other activity like taking her to a movie or buying her drinks. I mean, how much could it really cost?

We had a delicious meal of steamed tofu and vegetables for her and braised beef with noodles for me, with hot tea that we sipped from little white cups and had the place nearly all to ourselves. I told her a little about the incident on the street with the abusive husband and how I wasn't seeing Megan anymore. She told me a few funny stories about the stuff I was missing at the Shaft, and before long she was in better spirits and whatever had upset her seemed far from her mind. We talked music and books and I told her all about my favorite author Henry Miller and how I aspired to be like him, leaving it all behind and just picking up and moving somewhere far away and writing novels and being all Bohemian and mystical. When she asked what I would write about I said I didn't know, but then told her an idea for a story I'd had about two spirits that keep getting reincarnated and pursuing each other through time.

"So in the beginning this guy kills a villain but is killed too, and they're both instantly reborn as two infants, like on opposite sides of the world. Different bodies but the same person, get it? So then as they get older the villain tries to do something horrible like take over a country or blow it up or something, and the other guy, the hero, has to stop him. And neither of them knows the other or who they are or why they're doing it. But then at the end it would be revealed that they've been living this same cycle for thousands of years. Like the bad guy was Hitler before, and Attila the Hun before that, and Genghis Khan before that and before that and so at the very end you find out that they were both angels fighting each other in Heaven before the fall, and even though they die at the end of my story, they're reborn again and it all goes on. One trying to do ultimate evil, the other always trying to stop him, forever and ever."

"Wow," she said, wide-eyed through the whole thing, enthralled by the intricacy. "That's pretty complex."

"Well it's just an idea. Oh, and the good guy would be helped by his own daughter at one point. I mean the daughter he had from the life he had before he died at the beginning of the story, you know? Only they don't know each other from before and he's like in his thirties but she'd be in her fifties."

"That's great!" she said.

I said I didn't know; that I had lots of ideas churning around but just couldn't seem to get any one of them to materialize into a coherent story. She said it didn't matter and that I shouldn't give up, even promising to buy every book that I write. I held my pinky out and told her to swear on it.

"No, I'm not going to do that."

"It's a New Jersey thing," I demanded. "You have to."

"A New Joisey thing," she mocked.

"Swear by the finger woman!" I yelled, drawing a great blushing giggle from Eden and a raised eyebrow form the patient waiter clearing our dishes. She swore. It was dark when we got outside, we'd stayed and talked so long. Dinner was a roaring success.

I drove us down to the concert but the show was in full swing when we got there and we could hear them cranking out *Hungry Like The Wolf* while we stood in line getting our tickets, but it was great anyway. We hurried toward the open air stage at the end of the street and snaked our way in between the standing onlookers until we got only a few feet back from the stage and could get no closer. The early spring afternoon air had turned into a late winter evening chill and Eden was cold in only tee shirt and jeans so like a true gentleman I offered my coat.

The show was all lights and glitter, a glam fest from a bygone decade, and even though many of the songs were new, they played some oldies too and Simon Le Bon was all over the stage and crowd, looking cool in high collar and velvet coat, frilly cuffs at his wrists. They'd played half an hour when we left the show temporarily and ducked over to a nearby bar for beers before going back for more. The doors were open and we could hear the mix of music from inside and out and Eden was having a good time and I was secretly patting myself on the back for this little stroke of genius, coming to the concert, and knew that for at least a little while, I helped her forget whatever it was she'd been so bothered by and just brought her a little joy.

They closed with *Rio* and a flurry of twirling lights and jumping and the crowd loved it. When it was over we went back to the bar for more drinks and talked more and laughed more, me telling stupid self-deprecating jokes to keep her mood high, and she giggling and giving me sly side eyes more than once and I knew things were going great and that she was digging me.

After an hour she said she had to open the store in the morning and should be getting home. Outside the street was still crowded with partygoers and on the inside my nerves were frayed and I was shivering with a cold fear gripping my guts. I knew that if I were ever going to have a shot with Eden that the time would never be better than this.

On the ride back I got quiet and tried to think of the right words to say but kept coming up short.

"I had a lot of fun tonight," she said, seeing maybe that my thoughts were racing and that I was intimidated by the silence, antsy in my seat, clearing my scratchy throat more than once.

I looked over and saw her face looking back at me, shifting from black to yellow then back again as we passed underneath the streetlights. At that moment she looked very small to me, helpless, almost childlike and lost.

"Glad I could help. You looked like you needed it."

"You didn't have to."

"Have had nothing to do with it. I wanted to." Then somewhat quieter, tentative, a trembling thought reaching out through the darkness, unsure of itself, but coming out anyway. "I'd like to do it more often."

She turned to look out the window and the passing blur and said almost in a whisper that she knew.

"I'm sorry," I said. "I shouldn't have said that."

"It's ok."

"No, it isn't. It's . . . I can't." I started to cold sweat. "Jesus you'd think after all this time," I chuckled, trying to hide my fear. "It's a crush. It's a . . . I don't know. You'd think I'd have come up with something better. This is such high school bullshit. Maybe I should have just passed you a note in study hall."

I looked at her looking at me in the passing lights.

"But you do that to me," I continued. "I don't know what it is. You look at me, just like you're doing now, and I just fall apart. I get all nervous and everything gets all twisted up in my head and I come off sounding like a complete idiot."

"No you don't."

"But see, I've proved you right. You always call me an idiot, and here it is."

Silence. I wanted her to say something, anything. She could have recited the Gettysburg Address just then and it would have been fine with me.

"I'm not with Jamie anymore," she said. It was a sudden reprieve for me and my heart filled with a temporary delight. "I'm not sure I really ever was."

She told me he'd left. Gone to California over a week ago, and she'd been keeping it from everyone. Moved in with a friend. Left her in the wake. He'd called that morning and it'd left her furious. That's why she'd called me.

"I thought he didn't want to leave?" I said.

"So did I. Turns out he didn't want to leave with me."

"I'm sorry."

"No you're not. I'm not either."

"No?" I questioned.

"We both knew it was over anyway I guess. I just didn't think it'd happen like this."

"You thought *you'd* be the one to leave?"

She nodded silently.

"How long were you guys together?"

"A little over a year."

"That's tough."

"He wasn't right for me. I wasn't right for him. We tried to keep it together. That trip to the beach was supposed to be . . . but it wasn't. I guess I thought I didn't love him anymore, you know? That I was staying with him because I was afraid or something."

"Do you still love him?"

"I don't think I ever really did. Maybe in the beginning."

Silence again.

"I don't know what I want," she said finally, from a distance.

"There's nothing wrong with that."

"I feel lost almost, you know?" She sniffled. I could see her eyes wetting in the passing lights.

"I do," I said. "But you're not alone. You've got friends here. People who care about you."

More silence while the words floated in the tiny space between us and I tried to concentrate on the road and this conversation and fight back a wave of tears building up behind my own eyes. "I care about you."

"I know," she said.

We rode the rest of the way back to her house in silence, the only sound the hum of the road beneath the tires. It was in silence that we rolled up to her driveway and she turned to say good night.

"I don't know what to say," she said almost laughing. A nervous laugh, hiding moist eyes.

"There's nothing to say," I said trying to sound confident but coming across more like a father than a friend. "You've got all the time in the world to figure out what you want from life. Wherever it leads you, if you follow your heart it'll be to the right place. I hope it's here. But if it isn't, then go where you need to and I'll be happy for you."

That was it and she choked back a small sob. I knew I was going to lose it but then she leaned in and quickly kissed me on the cheek and said a quiet goodnight.

I watched her get out and sat there a minute longer to see she got in before I drove off. I managed to make it all the way home before I cried.

∞

The Sage killed himself on a Tuesday. They found him in the bathroom kneeling on the floor against the inside of the door, a belt looped around his neck and tied off around the door knob. A prison hanging. He was in a T-shirt and boxer shorts, no socks. An open pack of Marlboro Reds lay next to him and one butt had been snubbed out on the tile and cast aside. There was no note.

XXII

The funeral was small, private, and far away. His parents came back to Orlando to claim his body, and then they took it back to Missouri, to his hometown, to be buried in a plot next to where they themselves had arranged to be placed when the time eventually came. None of us made the journey to see him laid to rest. We weren't welcome.

People say parents aren't supposed to outlive their children. But what if their child was as old a soul as my friend was? Is it still the same, if his mind had been wandering a thousand years before any of us even met him? Should we mourn him the same, knowing he'd lived more of a life in twenty-three years than any of us had or will in our whole lives?

I knew I'd miss everything that we were: the fights, the wine, the poetical musings at two a.m. when were high on life and all was fine. But most of all I'd miss our talks of meaning and love, the love of meaning and the meaning of love. The holes in our hearts we'd been emptying into for over a year with our endless discourse (I of Eden and he of the ethereal concepts of devotion and promise) would ultimately remain unfilled.

We knew he'd not want us to forgo or forfeit because of his demise. He'd want for Chaos to continue the mayhem, and for Deirdre to find the right man, someone better than himself. He'd expect nothing less of me than to continue the pursuit he'd accompanied me on this far. And he'd want Eden to surrender. We mourned him the only way we knew how, the way anyone else would. We simply went on.

It was several days before I saw Eden again. When we did finally meet again (caught each other passing in the hall when I'd come by to visit Chaos at his work) it was awkward, and the silence passed between us like a great ship trolling though a dense fog. Heavy. It creaked and groaned in ages of pain, neither of us daring to approach it. I had bridged the gap and finally reached out to her, and she was taken by surprise, recoiled, and uncertain. We'd both returned to our respective lives, the daily tedium and rote responsibilities of civilization. Work, eat, sleep, work. In the interim, most everything seemed to lose its meaning. I existed, but it was hollow. All day I was a shell, going through the robotic motions required to get me through the day, but inside I was questioning everything, doubting. I wondered where she had been the last few days. What had she thought about all that I said? Did she hate me for what I had done? Had I ruined everything by finally taking that leap?

I tried to put together everything that had gone through my mind that night: scattered thoughts, things unsaid, random words that floated in the aether of my brain, fading, bolding, pronouncing themselves like a roll of thunder that shook my ears and then died off to mere whispers. I replayed the car ride over and over again, recounting it verbatim to first myself, then Chaos, who listened intently, his eyes narrowed to the task as he assessed the situation. In the end he was as lost as I was.

Then she came to me unexpectedly. I was caught off guard, completely unprepared for the ever awkward post-confession conversation.

"Hi."

"Hi."

"So."

"What's new?"

"Not much. You?"

"Nothing. Working. Sleeping. The usual."

"Break any new bones recently?" she said trying to make light, though I could see something weighing heavily on her mind.

"No," I said. "I've managed to stay pretty much fracture free."

"That's good."

"I suppose. It's better from a financial standpoint. Less medical bills, more money for other stuff." Silence as our conversation turned down. She was working something out and I gave her the time. I was trying to come up with something to say, too, but did poorly to cover the panic of being dumbstruck by her presence yet again. I wanted to tell her more. There was so much I hadn't said that night, and what I did say was abortive, ill-placed and wholly unremarkable. I knew the words, I'd rehearsed them a thousand times over, recited them before dark mirrors, scribbled them down in endless lines of pathetic early morning poetry. All I needed was a second chance to make it right, to say what I needed to, but the moment had to be the right one. Was this it?

"So," she hesitated. "I'm leaving."

"Oh, ok," I said stupidly. "Yeah, you probably need to get back to work. We can catch up another time."

"No," she said. "You don't understand Dave. I'm leaving."

There it was. I felt something stab me through the back, shiving in between my ribs and passing straight through my heart. Everything ran cold and a ringing struck my ears, deafening me. My spirit jumped out of me and stood beside the scene. I was no longer participating, I was just watching it all unfold from afar.

"Wait? Really? Like *leaving*, leaving?" Something like panic, but more like dread raced through my veins.

"In two weeks," she said, averting her eyes from the horror in mine. She shifted her weight and fidgeted. It was obvious she was uncomfortable.

"Where are you going?" I asked.

"I talked to my sister. She said I could stay with her."

"Chicago?"

"Yes. She thinks she can help me get a job. Not at her place, but she has some friends. One of them said they'd be able to hook me up. It won't be much, but it'll be a start."

"Wow. Well, congratulations," I heard myself say. I just needed to get out of there. "I really don't know what else to say."

"You don't have to say anything."

"Yeah, but I feel like I should. I know you've wanted to get on for a while, I just didn't think it'd be so soon."

"I think it might be time. I mean if I don't do it now, I might never."

Silence. I tried to say something but there was little point, and I didn't even know then what it should be. We both knew.

"I should get back," she said. "But Tuesday? Copper? Nikki wants to send me off early. I'm kinda scared."

"You know I'll be there," I said, even though I knew I wouldn't.

At home, my mind racing and in pain, throbbing in my chest, bending my ribs, a roar of sadness beating at my insides to get out. I swallowed hard and held it all down, but couldn't hold back any tears. The sobs came in waves, uncontrollably at first, more cold, icy veined convulsions than anything; abortive heaves crushing in on my heart. It was racing as fast as my brain. But in the end I couldn't keep it inside. I just lay on the floor in my room, my face to the heavens, weeping quietly. Hours passed.

Later, Chaos called me and invited me over.

"I've got beer and an ear my friend," he said over the phone to my one-word replies. I dropped the phone and carried myself over. I have no memory of the drive.

"What are you going to do now?" he asked, bringing a fresh beer to me; me who was sunk in the corner of his couch, despondent, looking like the defeated mess that I was, hat pulled down over my eyes trying to hide the dampness, wrinkled shirt, unshaven face, shame.

"This isn't the end," I said, not believing it myself. "Not by a long shot. It can't be."

"I don't know," he said.

"It can't be," I spat through my teeth, rage supplanting my sadness. Then I apologized. I knew he was trying to help. But this was not his arena. I needed Sage but it was far too late for that.

"None needed," he assured, waving it off.

"I don't know where I went wrong?" I said more to myself than him. It wasn't a fluke. I might have been contemplating, I can't remember. "Everything is so fucked up I can't even see straight let alone think straight. I'm totally lost. I can't believe this. What did I do wrong? It's like a fucking punishment."

"Come on," he said, putting on his shoes. "We're going out."

"What? No. Not tonight man. I can't handle it."

"No choice my friend. You need more liquor to clear your head, and I need more to make mine blurry. I don't want to sit here and watch my best friend eat himself. I'll drive. Let's go."

196

XXIII

Now it's Thebes and the place is jamming as usual, packed three deep at the bar and patches of cliques crowded around here and there: groups of black clad Goths hunkering in the darkened corners out of reach of the roving spot lights, scissor-legged co-eds in glittering miniskirts and halter tops, tanned and smooth, chisel-chinned guys in broad collars, bulging necks and biceps, tribal tattoos, leering, looming. All of them drunk on life, content, oblivious to the drama playing out in their midst. It's her last night in town.

The last two weeks had been a blur of drink, hangovers, more drink, strippers, sleeping in my clothes, waking up on the floor, more strippers. If this was indeed the end, Chaos planned to send us off with a bang. A great big pukey bang. We'd covered nearly every club in town, sometimes two a night, and burned through who knows how many thousands of dollars. He was buying dances, booze, food, everything. We hardly slept. I hadn't seen Deirdre for days. We lived on stale pizza for breakfast and dinner (no lunches; afternoons were impromptu nap times before the next nightly debauch), and Chaos was mostly existing on a steady diet of beer and some little brown pills called Ab Fuel, a muscle building supplement he'd recently become addicted to. There were a couple of regular meals in there somewhere too, mostly at my behest for the sake of prolonging my life just a little bit longer. Somewhere in the middle of it all I graduated.

And there had been plans too. Maniacal, booze-fueled plans to abandon my job, sell all of my worldly possessions, follow her to Chicago, prove to her how much I was willing to give up just to be with her. We hatched them out in the middle of the night, sweat, spit, fire, and laughter. Crazy. It would be perfect. I was to surprise her, show up unexpectedly a few weeks after she'd left. Chaos was going to front me the cash for a one-way ticket. Just when she'd start to miss me most, there I would be, crossing the continent for her. It couldn't fail. But it was all a dream. Pointless ravings of deranged, drunken hopeless minds.

I'd stopped going to work. Initially I made up a lie, at first thought of sickness (which wasn't far from the truth, my liver had been turning somersaults for days) but then told Neal the day after Eden said she was leaving that there was a family emergency and I needed a week to go home and help out. He'd been very understanding. Told me he and Angel could cover my lost hours, to call and let him know when I would be back. I thanked him. I never called. I never went back. I sat at home during the day trying to busy myself with tedium to make the time pass quietly. At night Chaos reigned. Eden and I had spoken little, just quick hellos in passing when Chaos and I were running out into the darkness. I wanted to say something. It was all just postponing the inevitable.

Now it was Sunday and we were standing beside the bar, Eden, Chaos, Deirdre, and me, the elephant in the room. We didn't speak much. There wasn't much to say. She could sense what it was doing to me inside and she hadn't really wanted to come, it would be too hard, but Deirdre had pressed her for one last night. She tried to keep the mood light, requesting songs she thought I'd like to hear, something to get us all dancing and to forget what was speeding toward us. A good and true friend to the end.

Chaos had bought us all a round, and though the music was thumping, a fitting interlude by Souxie and the Banshees (my city was indeed lying in dust), I was caught in a trance watching Eden absently stir her drink. It was the delicate nature of her fingers. I was wanting, hollowed, knowing I was never going to know the feeling of seeing those fingers open a Valentine's card that I'd given her, or caress the soft petals of a rose I'd presented to her "just because." I felt it, the gloom, creeping up behind me.

"I'm going to miss this," Deirdre said.

"What?" Eden said.

"This. Us. Sundays. It won't be the same."

Bronski Beat came on. *Smalltown Boy*. A tale of a runaway. It was all turning too dark, like someone somewhere was punishing me for something horrible I'd done. I needed another drink.

Without a word I left the group, pushed my way through the sea of black bodies and combat boots, bumping shoulders hard with a short chubby Trent Reznor wannabe who shot me an evil sidelong glance and a twisted word of hate, but I didn't even hear it over the roar of the music and the tornado ripping through my brain. I knew they were watching behind me, her especially. I was being totally unfair, childlike even, and I knew it. This was supposed to be a celebration of new opportunities, a proper send-off of a good friend, but all I could do was stew in my own grief.

"This can't be the end," I found myself saying to my mirrored reflection in the bathroom. Under the cutting white of the fluorescent lights I saw the toll the last two weeks had taken on me. My face was drawn and my eyes were reddened from lack of proper sleep. I'd stressed (or drank) off nearly ten pounds. My left arm ached from a bruise the size of Nebraska Chaos had given me three days earlier; vacant lot behind a middle school somewhere on the west side of town, can't remember where. I splashed the cool water of the tap on my face and went out. Deirdre was waiting for me in the hall. I looked at my watch. It was coming up on one thirty. The night was already coming to an end.

"You all right?" she asked gently, a tender hand on my shoulder. I couldn't look her in the eye.

"It's all falling apart," I said, barely able to keep it inside. Two whole weeks, and I was still crumbling. "I can't." I stopped. It was killing me. "I have to," I didn't know. "Do something."

I saw the pain in her eyes. It was the same anguish she'd shown the Sage sitting on Chaos' couch those thousand years ago. I needed him now more than ever, and she knew that. She needed him too. I went back inside to find Eden.

At the bar Chaos was alone, Eden nowhere to be seen. He told me she'd slipped out when I'd gone to the bathroom, thought it was the best way to leave it. I slumped against the bar, head in my chest, eyes welling up, completely, utterly and absolutely defeated. It was just then he took a sip of his drink and over the rim of the glass I saw him staring at me, eyebrows lifted in anticipation and expectant of me, because he knew it all. In that moment he saw in me the whole struggle and the awfulness of my crumbling heart; the nights we stayed up drunk and conversing only about her, the wild poems I'd written to her beauty but never had the courage to read, all of them stacked in a drawer in my glum room, the rage I felt against her detractors and anyone who'd dare harm her, the fear of losing everything to her, for her. All of it summed up in a single glance between friends who'd been through too much. And now it was slipping away.

"Well," he said, Peter Murphy blasting out *Cuts You Up* over our heads, practically commanding me. "Are you going to go or what?"

Even then I still hesitated. I didn't want to show her my tears.

"This is it my friend. Now or never."

"Now."

I ran.

Out on the street. The music still ringing in my ears and club goers milling about. Two bike cops stopping mid-conversation to notice me looking left and right, frantically deranged. I couldn't see her anywhere.

"Which way?" I cursed to myself. I looked to the cops imploringly. "Which way?"

"What are you looking for?" one of them asked.

"Love," I said. "Tall, black dress, glasses, short brown hair and eyes like amber."

They just laughed and said they couldn't help me and I felt like leaping at them and grinding their faces into the pavement, but a girl standing next to the bouncer said she saw someone like that going right, toward the lake. She wished me luck as I thanked her and darted around the corner.

At the end of the block I came to the parking lot and a deserted intersection, the park quiet across the street and a few shadows walking the loop around the lake, but no sign of Eden or her car. A cold panic gripped my stomach and the drink was churning from the running and I didn't know which one was going to make me throw up first as I tried to catch my breath. Then I saw her solitary figure walking away down the deserted sidewalk under the trees. I ran after her, knowing that whatever was looking out for me, whatever had seen me through the agony I lived just trying to be close to her wouldn't let it all end this way.

I called out her name from a full run and she stopped and waited for me, my feet slapping loudly against the pavement as I came up and doubled over to catch my breath.

"What's wrong?" she said as I tried to speak, but could only gasp. The burning in my chest worsening. I felt, and looked, the fool.

"Wait," I said.

"OK. Take your time. Breathe."

"No," I said. "Not for me."

"What? I don't know what you're saying?"

"Don't."

"Don't what?"

"Don't go."

Silence.

"Stay here. Stay here with me."

More silence. I righted myself and looked her in those unbelievable brown eyes that I could already see starting to water. She knew it was coming.

"I love you," I said.

And there it was. Three little words that had been waiting so long to be said, that should have been said the moment I met her, because I knew from that point I would forever be in love with this girl. She said nothing. Her bottom lip was trembling and she fidgeted her fingers around her handbag.

"I love you Eden. I've loved you since the day I saw you."

"But why?" she asked, her voice quavering.

"Because you're perfect. You're everything I've ever known I wanted."

"No I'm not." She was fighting it back, averting her eyes.

"Yes you are. You're the most perfect, beautiful, smart, funny woman I've ever met, and I've fallen completely in love with you. Ask Chaos or Deirdre, I've been talking about you forever. Even Sage. Christ I talked his ear off. They must hate hearing me go on about you by now. He's probably up there right now looking down on me and rolling his eyes in shame. He knew more than all of them."

This made her laugh between a sob. She knew all of this anyway; I know they must have told her when I wasn't around. There were never any secrets among any of us.

"You're like sunshine," I went on. There was no stopping it anymore, and I couldn't even if I'd wanted to. "You're like the air. I need you. I don't know why, but I know I do. You've made me so crazy I had to write it all down. I've written poems for you, about you, tons of them. I'll read each one to you if you'll let me. A different one each day, each morning you wake up there'll be another one. I've wanted to for so long."

"Why didn't you?"

"I don't know. I was scared I guess. I didn't know what you'd say, what you'd think. I was afraid I would screw it all up and drive you away, I loved you so much. But I'm not scared anymore. I'll tell you everything. I'll tell you I love you every single day from now on. I want to be with you Eden. Don't go."

She bit her lip and looked away, up into the trees, looking for words that she knew were right there in front of her.

"I have to."

It was then that I knew I had lost her. That there was nothing I could say that would make her stay. I'd poured my heart out, laid it all on the table, and she had to look away.

"But why?"

"I don't know," she admitted. "I just know I have to. Haven't you ever felt like that? Like you were looking for something and you didn't know where it was, but you knew it wasn't where you were? That somehow everything you were doing was wrong? Wrong place, wrong time, wrong person?"

I looked to my feet, beaten, and nodded. I knew exactly what she was talking about.

"Then you know why I have to go. You of all people should understand why."

"Let me come with you," I said desperately. I felt it all falling apart and running through my fingers like dust.

"You can't. You know that's not what you want to do." We were both tearing now.

"You don't have to love me," I said. "I understand if you don't."

"It's not that I don't love you," she said. "I don't know that I don't. You're the first person in a long time that's made me feel like what I want, who I am, is worth something. No one else sees me like you do. Not even me. And I love you for that, but there's more. I don't know what it is, and maybe I'm making a mistake, but I have to try. You're a wonderful guy David."

"And you're an incredible woman," I said. "I just couldn't let you leave without knowing just how much you are. I had to try. Do or die I had to try."

I knew it was over. We both lost the words and finally she reached out, took my hand and kissed me on the cheek. It was the faintest, most gentle kiss I've ever known.

"Goodbye David."

Then she turned to go.

XXIV

Two days after Eden left I was in a miserable funk. I stayed in my apartment almost the whole time, going outside only to get food and buy more liquor. I didn't shower or shave, but just sat on the couch listening to horribly depressive sad music, trying to bury myself in my sorrow. The phone rang, I didn't answer it. Chaos knew enough to stay away, to let me heal in peace. Deirdre came over to check on me, which was nice. Worried, as usual, and even more so because of what had happened to Sage. I told her everything was all right, that I just needed time, that I wouldn't kill myself, that I was stronger than my old friend, and shut the door on her. I wasn't ready to come out of my shell yet.

On the morning of the third day I got a message on my machine from the editor of a newspaper in Kissimmee. I still wasn't answering the phone. They called to ask me in for an interview. I had sent them a resume for a reporting job three weeks before and they wanted me to come in the following day. I had been sending out resumes for jobs all over the country for the past five months without so much as a single bite. This was the first offer to come across my desk, and it figured that after all that lofty talk of traveling to exotic locales and making a name for myself as a famous novelist, it would be for a position right down the fucking street. But school was over and it was time to do something with the education that had been bought and paid for by my parents. I owed it to them to go in. I called the paper back and was told to be there at ten o'clock the next morning.

Before I went away to college I had bought one suit. That was over three years ago, and it had hung in my closet unworn that whole time. I tried it on and surprisingly it still fit somewhat. The jacket was fine, but the pants were a little tight. There was no real time to do anything about that, so I just sucked it up, and in, and figured better to look good and be uncomfortable for an hour or two than to be underdressed. I'd just leave the pants unbuttoned in the car on the way over.

I showered, ran out and got a haircut, organized my portfolio and shaved with a new razor the next morning so that when I arrived ten minutes early for the interview I didn't look the least like a man whose entire life had crumbled around him only forty-eight hours before.

The editor, a heavy set bearded guy named Jim with graying hair and in denim button down shirt, who looked more like a car salesman than a newsman, saw me in to his small office. It was a windowless room with lots of pictures hanging on the walls, many of which were framed stories from the paper. The chief copy editor was also with us. He was balding, small and nerdy, but thin and wearing a shirt that was clearly a size too large for his rickety frame, sleeves way off the shoulders, and I thought *I* was supposed to be the one worried about being underdressed?

They took turns asking me all sorts of questions about school, ethics, and building relationships with sources. It was all terribly boring and for a few minutes I was horrified by the thought that I might end up like these two, stuck in a dead end town in a tiny windowless office, going to town meetings where the hot topic of discussion would be whether or not to install a new swing set on the playground or paint new lines on a cross walk at a lonely intersection on some nowhere corner.

But I persevered and the interview ended with a couple of handshakes and a promise to call by the end of the week with a final decision. I was confident that I had gotten the job, and it made me terribly sick. I stripped off my tie and undid the button on my pants in the car and drove home more miserable than when I had woken up that morning, cursing, wanting only to lock myself away again. I thought about what I had said to Sage, about how if Eden left there'd be nothing left and I would probably leave, and now here I was about to get a job that would keep me there for years with the memory of her. I bled inside.

That night as I lay awake staring at my ceiling in the dark for what was the fourth night in a row, waiting for the two or three hours of sleep that my brain was tricking me into having so I wouldn't simply die right there in bed, the phone suddenly rang. I looked at the clock and it was almost midnight. I let it ring several more times and reflected. Sage was the only one who'd ever called me this late. What it his ghost calling? I was tempted to let the machine pick it up, but something in me resigned to start the long hard journey back to the real world and I answered.

"Hello?"

Silence.

"Hello?" louder now and slightly more annoyed.

There was a click, then another click. Then a woman's voice asked to speak to David Stone.

"You got him."

"David, hi, this is Patty Clark calling from TBL Language Center."

I said the name didn't ring a bell.

"You sent us a resume for a teaching position with our school. I'm calling from Seoul."

That got my attention. I sat up and turned on the light.

"I'm sorry, I didn't wake you did I? It's what, 11:50 there?"

"Fifty-five actually. And no, I wasn't sleeping. How can I help you?"

"I wanted to talk to you about the resume you sent and maybe have a chance to interview you for the position. If now isn't a good time . . ."

"Now's fine," I said jumping out of bed and rushing to the desk trying to find the paper with the job on it. I had no memory of sending them a resume. It had to have been weeks ago. She could hear me shuffling papers.

"If now's not convenient I can call back?"

"No, now is good. Now is perfect. You just caught me a little by surprise."

"Sorry about that," she laughed. "It's the time change."

We spoke for over an hour, first about me and my background, then about school. I told her I'd just gotten my degree (finished early thank you very much) and when I told her I was only twenty-two she said they didn't have anyone that young working there and that I'd be the youngest. Then we talked about the job, teaching English to Korean men and women, businesspeople mostly, but some homebodies, and even children. I shuddered at the thought of working with little kids, I was practically one myself, but just said I could do all of that. I told her I didn't speak a lick of Korean and she said that was fine. We talked about what life in

Seoul was like, what to expect if I were to come over. They'd give me the job and set me up in a company paid apartment so all I'd need would be clothes and a little starting money for food and basic expenses until I got my first paychecks. She said a thousand dollars would be sufficient and I told her I didn't have it but I could sell some things and certainly get it. I tried my best to lay on the charm, make her laugh, and in the end she said she liked everything I had to say and that if I wanted the job I could have it and could I possibly be in South Korea in three weeks to start teaching? Simple as that.

I couldn't believe it! A job on the other side of the planet, the chance to travel, to see the world. It was what I'd been wanting and waiting for since before I'd left home. I told her I'd be there with bells on and that I'd be easy to spot because I'd be the guy getting off the plane with the great big bells strapped to his head. She congratulated me and said she'd send me the necessary paperwork.

I got off the phone with Patty and immediately called my parents to tell them the news, not noticing that it was almost two a.m. They thought I was in some kind of trouble calling so late. Was I hurt? Was I in jail? But when I told them about the job and how I was going to move to South Korea they knew it was much worse than that. They nearly shit the bed. I was ecstatic. I hung up with them and called Deirdre, then Chaos, right then in the middle of the night. Chaos was blown away. He said it would be awesome and that he'd come visit me and we made all kinds of fantastic plans to go to Hong Kong and find Jackie Chan and eat real sushi in a real Tokyo sushi bar. It was all coming back together again. For the rest of the night I sat up dancing around my little apartment and getting all excited and making mad plans to walk the Great Wall and maybe even visit Australia, and then India. It was all going to be great. Life was starting again.

I didn't even think about Eden for the rest of the night.

The next two weeks were a whirlwind of activity. In the morning I got a call from the editor of the paper offering me a job as a local reporter, but I told him sorry, I accepted another position and laughed hysterically when I hung up the phone. Local reporter? Ha! I was a world traveler now pal, so you can keep your nowhere office at your nowhere paper in your nowhere town. I was like George Jefferson movin' on up to the east side (of the world that is). I had a grand "throw out" and trashed most of my things. Couldn't take it with me. I put up signs near the mailboxes offering to sell my couch, microwave, and TV for $150. A kid came over and offered me $75 and I said it was too low. He said he'd just wait for me to put it out in the dumpster and then he'd get it for free, but when he left I said fuck you and called Chaos over and we smashed everything with hammers and gutted the couch with a sword. Last laughs motherfucker!

The paperwork from Seoul came special delivery and then the last thing to do was to go to the Korean embassy in New York City to get my passport stamped with the official visa I'd need to get in the country. I was all packed and ready to head back to Jersey for a brief visit with my family before catching the flight to my future. It was almost time to leave Orlando forever.

XXV

Chaos wanted one last night out, just the two of us, before I left Orlando, to celebrate my new job and toast to new horizons, so he arranged for the two of us to go to Velvet and get some special treatment. He was sleeping with another one of the dancers there, this time a feisty raven-haired Latina chick named Lisa, and she told him that if we came early she'd get another girl, a friend of hers, to give me *extra* attention.

It was Friday and we got to the door promptly at nine and I don't really know what I was expecting. My enthusiasm for my impending departure and the initial joy at the prospect of leaving had begun to wane, as I knew I would sorely miss these times with Chaos. At the same time, I was still mucking through a deep depression about the loss of Eden, and most ordinary things had lost meaning for me. Even the possibility of bedding a stripper, a possibility that was not entirely out of the realm of possibility, the way Chaos was setting it up, was not all that much to get excited about.

With her physical departure had also gone the feeling of that ethereal connection I believed we had shared, whether real or just a figment of my imagination. Time and distance were taking their toll, and just as Sage had predicted, (though he never came right out and said it, his suicide stood as visceral proof positive to what I knew he too had been thinking all along but could never give life to in words) life without the one I had loved so deeply had lost much of its luster. The rising towers of the city, once gateways to mystery and joy, now just stood as giant tombstones to old memories. Drink no longer brought relief or quelled the thoughts of her swirling round my mind, and even the stars, which always shone so brightly in the high clear skies of Florida, seemed dimmer without her.

"Cheer up," Chaos said as he came back from the bar bearing beers. "There's more than enough ass to go around. Lisa and Carmen will be here in a minute and then you'll forget all about it. Drink up buddy."

"It's not that I'm not grateful," I said.

"I know."

"It's just that I still miss Eden. I'd made plans to go overseas because I always held onto the ludicrous thought that we'd be going together. And now here I am going out there alone."

"Forget about her dude. Ask yourself was it worth it all, really worth all of it? I mean you tortured yourself, I was there. I've never seen anyone as committed to it as you were. You poured your heart out to her and what did she do? She shit on it."

"No she didn't," I objected.

"Look, you loved her. But love is just a feeling, and you'll have it again. It's not a onetime thing. Trust me, there're plenty of other ones out there. There are other Edens. And in a few days you'll be in Korea and surrounded by more Asian tail than you can possibly imagine. I tell you dude, I envy the fuck out of you."

"But you'll come out and visit," I said hopefully. "You'll get your share."

"Bet your ass I will. You're going to be busy with a new job, meeting all new people, travelling. Trust me, you'll forget all about Eden once the yellow fever sets in."

I was annoyed with Chaos' flippant attitude about it and wanted to say something more, but just then Lisa strolled out of the back room with her friend in tow. They were both in glittery flowing slit dresses, Lisa in red and Carmen in gray, both with high heels, long black hair, golden skin and sultry eyes. They could have been sisters.

The DJ spun a new tune, some completely out of place country song, and up on the stage a black girl named Dominique was spinning on the pole to the delight of a lecherous looking old man with a ten spot in his fingers and Lisa started dancing for Chaos.

"Joo wanta dance?" Carmen asked and I suddenly remembered Chaos' cologne and giggled to myself and absently said yes. She slinked her hands around the back of her dress and undid the zipper at her midback and the whole number just fell to the floor at our feet revealing her taut bronze body, largish breasts and an ample ass, and for a few minutes the problems of the world just slipped away as she wriggled and gyrated and swayed and pumped to the music. At one point she turned away from me and arched her back, looking back with one onyx eye, the fisheye Chaos always called it, and with her ass right over my crotch began bouncing up and down, just her ass, as one riding a horse would, the glistening flesh on her hips and thighs rippling like water as they slapped against my lap. It was new and sexy and damn I liked it something fierce. Chaos smiled approvingly and then across the room I saw several men looking on in envy, probably wondering when they were going to get their turn with this one and all I could do was smile and say proudly to myself 'sorry boys, this one is mine.' I was suddenly feeling good again and I had to lean over and apologize to Chaos for being a downer before. He just shrugged it off "Bros before hoes" he said, gave me a wink, and turned his attention back to Lisa, whose head and moist red lips were perched precariously over his lap, one lock of her raven hair spilling down over her eye. I laughed at my own idiocy, reflecting on the fickle nature of love and how quickly the tides could turn.

The song ended and Carmen didn't bother to put her dress back on. She just sat down next to me, took a cigarette from the pack on the table, lit up and took a long drag. We sat silently side by side while Chaos and Lisa chatted away across the table. After a few seconds she broke the silence.

"Jou're friends with him?" gesturing at Chaos with a smoky finger.

"Yep. He's my best friend in fact."

"What joo guys do?"

"Not much. We work together downtown. Well worked is more appropriate. He got fired and I quit."

"Why?"

"It's not important. What about you?"

"What about me?"

"What do you do when you're not doing this?" I motioned to the rest of the room.

"Nothing especial," she said and blew through her cheeks. "I'm here most nights now, and when I'm not I'm usually just at home."

"What do you do for fun?"

"I like to dance," she said and we laughed. "Obviously." She spoke with a peasant's drawl, accenting the "o" with particular roundness.

"What else?"

"I like go to the beach. And movies." Then she lean in close. "And sex."

And that's when the music stopped, at least in my head.

"Joo want another dance?" she asked, gazing straight into my eyes and all I could do was nod dumbly. She started it all up again, working at it even harder than before. Prince blaring from a dozen speakers certainly helped.

"Lisa said jou're moving away?" she said suddenly leaning over and shaking her soft, glittery breasts in my face.

"Next week actually," I said.

"Where joo going?"

"To South Korea. I got a job there."

"Is it far away?" her lips next to my ear.

"Pretty far," I said, my eyes fixed on her thighs and not much else.

"Are joo scared?"

"A little. But this is certainly helping."

"I don't think I could go someplace like Korea. I wouldn't like it much."

"Why not?" I asked.

"I don't like European men."

You know that look children get on their faces on Christmas morning when they're handed a huge, beautifully wrapped box and their minds are full of wonder and magic about what's inside and then they open it and it's a sweater? That was the look I was wearing when Chaos and I caught eyes.

"So joo want to go back to the VIP room?" she whispered in my ear. "Jour friend asked me to give you a especial dance as a going away present."

"Oh, I don't know about that."

"Come on. Don't joo want jour especial dance?" she said, poising her breast right before my mouth.

"OK, maybe for just one dance."

She took my hand and I looked back at Chaos, who just raised his bottle and nodded knowingly with that damned smile as she led me out of the room around a corner and up three little steps. At the top sat a heavy bouncer with clipboard who told me to sign my name and note the time, but she told him it was already paid for and he let us pass.

"Four honey," he said as she led us down a dimly lit hall to a small room at the end that was lined with mirrors and had three white leather couches arranged in a horseshoe shape around a golden pole rising in the center.

"Sit down," she said and closed the door with a click and I took a seat in the middle couch. The music from around the way was still pounding from the main room, but it was quieter in there, muffled, the only real sound being the creaking of the leather as I fidgeted in my seat and she walked slowly back toward me, sloe eyes and a smirk on her face.

Carmen immediately straddled me, shoving her breasts in my face, burying it really in the valley of her chest. She slapped them gently against my cheeks with her hands and I could feel the charm of her silver necklace bouncing off my forehead. Her skin was warm, but powdery and smelled faintly of strawberry.

"So what do joo want?" she said, her voice low and sultry and I knew she meant business.

"I don't know," I said stupidly.

"Jour friend said joo could have whatever joo want. His treat." She ran the flat of her palm over my crotch. "Do joo want to fuck me? Joo can if joo want. I'll suck jour dick first. Joo can even fuck my ass."

"So you really weren't kidding about liking sex," I said nervously and she laughed and suddenly felt like Jerry Lewis. Hey lady!

"Jour cute. I like joo," she said and started to unbutton my pants. "I want joo." Her hands were in and she grabbed me and sighed and smiled when she saw my eyes flash. Then she took me out and rubbed her crotch against me through her little silver G-string and I felt like I was about to slip inside her, but she backed off and started to unwrap a condom.

"Wait," I said.

"It's ok," she said. "If joo brought jour own?"

"No, it's not that."

"What then? Joo don't like me?"

"No, it's not that either," I put my dick back in my pants and zipped up. "I like you plenty. You're beautiful."

"So what's the problem?" she said, playfully trying to open my fly again, the round rolling "o" making its presence known again. "Joo want to do it a different way? Joo want me from behind?"

"You don't even know me, but you want to have sex with me."

"Yes."

"But why?'

"I told joo, I like sex. Lisa and jour friend said joo were cool. And if jou're as good as he is, then . . ."

"Wait," I interrupted. "You had sex with Chaos?"

"Jess. What's wrong with that?"

"When?"

"A couple of weeks ago. I got drunk at his apartment and we wound up in bed."

"But he's with Lisa. Well, I mean he's been *seeing* Lisa lately. Aren't you two friends?"

"Sure we are. But she was there. It was cool."

"So wait, the three of you?" He'd done it after all, the son of a bitch.

"Jess. Does that make you hot? Thinking of me with a woman?"

She slid off the couch and put me in her mouth, and I closed my eyes, but all I off a sudden I felt Eden's presence in my mind again. She was watching. I couldn't get her out of my head. I told Carmen I was sorry but that it all a big mistake. She didn't seem to mind one way or the other. She'd already been paid.

"Joo don't know what jou're missing," she said, pulling her dress back on and zipping it up, taking a seat on the couch and lighting up again. For her this would just be a clandestine ten minute break.

"I probably don't," I admitted sadly. "And I'm sure I'm going to regret this later." It was all ruined for me anyway. There was no way I could break free of the hold Eden had on me. I knew it was all pointless to try to deny my sadness and force it out with cheap sex with cheap sluts and Chaos' sloppy seconds at that. I wasn't ready for any of it. I wasn't ready to let go of her yet.

XXVI

The world had finally gone quiet, and the moon, bright and full, hung overhead, enveloped in a haze of purple and gray clouds drifting idly by in a peaceful astral lullaby. I lay in bed awake, my apartment mostly a hollow shell of its former self. All of the furniture was gone, the kitchen cleaned and the fridge empty save for a single sandwich and can of Coke I'd bought for the trip home. My two suitcases were piled in the corner, next to three cardboard boxes sealed up and holding all my worldly possessions.

Chaos and Deirdre'd seen me off earlier at Copper, our last night together. Music and drink, solemn companions that had seen us all through thick and thin, now witnessing another leaving the fold. Deirdre'd cried at the end, and seeing her made me shed a few tears too. Chaos was stronger though. He flashed that Cheshire grin and nodded wisely, knowing in a few months, after I settled in, he'd come to visit me in the great Far East. He wasn't fazed in the least with my departure. He just gave me a handshake and bid me farewell, for now, and we left it up to fate to reunite us at another time, the same way it had over a year before. Just two lost souls travelling through time . . .

I couldn't sleep. The ringing was still fresh in my ears and my head spun from the drink. Even had it not been this way, I still wasn't able to sleep soundly through the night because of her.

It'd been almost three weeks since Eden had left for Chicago, and the last time I'd heard from her. After that night on the street outside Thebes and the passing of time I knew I had failed, that she wasn't coming back, that she would never be mine, that all my efforts and engineering, my self-recriminations and bastardizations of the reality that was always staring me right in the face were just wasted energy. I loved her, and maybe, in some way, she loved me, but it was simply something that was never meant to be. And now I was alone again.

The phone rang. Somehow I knew it was her and I fought back the urge to answer it on the first ring. I've experienced that feeling before, that strange, almost psychic phenomenon where you're thinking about someone and then suddenly you see them, or they call and you're like "hey I was just thinking about you!" Like you willed it to be so or some such bullshit. I rolled on my side, the sheets twisting around my damp legs, and stared at the phone. It rang and rang. I was preparing myself, finally picking up the receiver. It was quiet on the other end. Three o'clock Chicago time. Was she lying awake in the darkness too?

"Hello David." Her voice, even through the grittiness of the phone and across the vast central plains of America, was like a warm hand placed over my heart. "I didn't wake you did I?"

"No, I was just laying here. Too hot to sleep. How are you?"

"I was thinking about you today, so I thought I'd call. Don't know why I thought to do it so late. It was kind of stupid, but I couldn't sleep."

"No worries," I said.

"I was thinking . . . I don't know. I just wanted to . . ." She was faltering. I closed my eyes and fought back a tear, then shook it off and knew I couldn't let it go like this, awkward and halting and sorry.

"Oh? See some handsome young buck on the street did you?" I joked, trying to sound cavalier. "Remind you of me? The rippling chest and rakish good looks?"

"That exactly what happened," she laughed, relieved. It warmed me again.

"So how is it up there?"

"It's all right," she said, and my heart broke. Secretly I was hoping she'd be miserable, broke, and desperate to come back. She told me all about her first few weeks. How she was sleeping on the couch, and how her sister's friend who managed a clothing store in the mall gave her a job. I asked if she liked the work and she said no, but it was a job and something to get started with. She'd gone with next to nothing and was anxious to start saving money to get her own place. I told her about Korea and how I was leaving for home in the morning, then I was heading out the next week. She said she'd heard all about it from Deirdre and was jealous as hell, but she knew she'd get to travel someday too. That's when I realized she'd been speaking to Deirdre and that they'd been keeping it from me. I knew why, and it was all right. Then she told me about Mina.

Mina was a girl she'd met at a local hotspot. First they were drinking, then they were talking, as it always is. They'd taken an immediate liking to each other. Mina was a free spirit of sorts, interested in art, a part-time musician, and intellectual too, and she listened with intent to Eden's story of sacrifice and search. Since then they'd seen each other almost every day, talking and laughing, swapping stories, and it was the beginning. She said she felt more comfortable with this girl in the last two weeks than she'd ever felt with Jamie, or even me. The only other time she'd felt something like it was when she was with Nikki; they'd recently discovered themselves in the same boat of confusion and denial. But with Mina it was different somehow. It was more mature; she was surer it was right. I swallowed hard. It was killing me inside.

"I think," she started haltingly, almost relieved she was saying it out loud. "I think I'm done with men."

"That's a bold move. A bit drastic, isn't it?"

"I'm serious," she said.

"So am I."

She went on to tell me all the reasons she was swearing off men. I listened attentively. Men were priggish, piggish and judgmental. They lied and were deceitful. She wasn't angry about it, and this was nothing new, rather she seemed to be affirming feelings she'd been harboring all along but gave no focus or credence to until recently. It wasn't hate or spite that drove her, far from it. But things were surfacing, logic was falling into place, attractions and emotions made themselves known and she'd grown tired of trying to deceive herself and the world of facts she knew in her heart to be true.

"And women aren't those things?" I said, suddenly shouldered with the unenviable burden of defending the whole of the male race. "I'd say women can be ten times as bad as men. And they're a whole lot more vindictive to boot. Besides I take offense to that. I'm neither priggish nor piggish." I had no idea what priggish meant, but it sounded bad and I knew whatever it was I didn't want to be it. "And unlike some other men might have in the past, I for one have never lied to you."

"That's not what I meant. I didn't mean you. Not all men. You're different," she flustered. "This is all coming out wrong."

I told her to stop then and think for a second and then tell me what it was she was feeling. She started again with more direction and clarity.

"In the past, I just always felt, I don't know, like I was supposed to live up to some sort of idea of what a girl is supposed to be, like I have a roll to fill, you know?"

I knew exactly what she meant.

"You're always in constant competition with another woman, or an image, or a concept of some utopian perfection sought after by all men. They want a woman as an object to be conquered and displayed for everyone to see. I mean look at Chaos."

"I'd say he's an exception though," I said defending my partisan. "He makes no bones about what he wants, and the types of women he pulls in are the ones who go in expecting nothing more than what he has to offer on the surface. They know perfectly well what they're getting into with him."

"All right, maybe he's a bad example," she admitted.

"On the contrary, I'd say he's a perfect example. I just don't think I should be lumped in with him. I mean he's my best friend, and we have tons in common, but we're worlds apart when it comes to sex."

"I know that. I'm just . . . This is hard to explain."

"You don't have to. I'm not trying to push."

"I know," she said and then fell silent.

"Is this how you've always felt?"

"I think it is. But recently it's been different."

"It's been right," I said.

More silence filled the void between us. It was the silence of realization, of knowing and of discovery. She was awakening to the person who she always was but had been deceiving herself into believing she wasn't.

"When you talk about this, you sound happier," I said.

"I am."

"Then I'm happy for you."

"Liar," she said quickly.

"I've never lied to you Eden. I'm not about to start now."

"Now I know you're lying."

It was my turn to be silent.

"I know I hurt you," she said. Her voice fell.

"Listen. I've made no secret how I feel about you. But that's something you don't want. This is what you want. And if that's the case, you just need to go for it."

"But I don't want to hurt your feelings."

"My feelings are irrelevant. You have to do what your heart tells you, even if it means hurting someone else."

"See, that's what I mean. That's what I'm talking about. That's why I know you're not like Chaos. He'd never say something like that."

"It's always been out of love," I said. "Just like everything else I've ever said to you."

It was quiet again. All that was said was said and there was no more. An eternity passed between us.

"Right," I said suddenly quickening, trying to sound upbeat, to draw what had been an agony to a close. "So, do you want to be with this girl Mina?"

"I think so?" she said, less of a question, but still looking for validation.

"Does she make you happy?"

"Yes."

"Then that's all there is. If you're happy with her, and it's something you want, then I want you to have it, be happy and love. She might not be the right one for you. Maybe there is another. But you've got all the time in the world to find her. If this is what you want then I say have it."

"Really? No lie?"

I told her again how I've never lied to her and this seemed to comfort her.

"She just makes me feel . . . I can't explain it."

"There's no need to kid. I know how that is."

She tried anyway. She still felt the need to justify her feelings, to find and label the words that her heart tried to speak and seek some sort of approval from me. I told her not to ponder it any further; that if she was truly happy with this new love, then I was happy for her.

I was lying.

Infinite Truth

She walked out of my life on a Sunday. She said she was chasing something. When I asked what that something was, she couldn't reply. We both knew there was no need to. We were young and stupid and we were all chasing something then. And now, some dozen years later, some of us still are.

Her journey would take her west to California, a continent away, and then in the years to come to even farther shores. It was a trip she had to take alone, and now, looking back on it all, I know that it had to be that way. She was exploring the first fertile green fields of her newfound sexual freedom in a land where the unknown was the only place to find the answers she was unable to find at home, amongst friends and all that was familiar and close.

Home is warm and soft. The world is cold and hard. That's the way it is for most of us. The final record spun for the night, the lights come on and everyone files off the dance floor and out into the streets deaf, bleary and lost. The end of another dream beneath looming towers of a downtown night out. Tomorrow it will all start up again. The music will go on, and so would I in the end. While she was disappearing over the western horizon, never to be mine, and never to return to my life again, I was packing a bag and marching into my own future in the east. Korea beckoned, and with it all the same uncertainty and loneliness that surely awaited Eden on those far shores of her burgeoning self.

Eden Cole, the girl of my dreams, was gone.

CPSIA information can be obtained at www.ICGtesting.com
Printed in the USA
BVOW050238031011

272668BV00001B/34/P